PERIL BY PONYTAIL

This Large Print Book carries the
Seal of Approval of N.A.V.H.

A BAD HAIR DAY MYSTERY

PERIL BY PONYTAIL

NANCY J. COHEN

WHEELER PUBLISHING
A part of Gale, Cengage Learning

GALE
CENGAGE Learning·

Farmington Hills, Mich • San Francisco • New York • Waterville, Maine
Meriden, Conn • Mason, Ohio • Chicago

Pub 27-

GALE
CENGAGE Learning®

Wheeler Publishing Large Print Cozy Mystery.
The text of this Large Print edition is unabridged.
Other aspects of the book may vary from the original edition.
Set in 16 pt. Plantin.

LIBRARY OF CONGRESS CATALOGING-IN-PUBLICATION DATA

Cohen, Nancy J., 1948–
    Peril by ponytail : a bad hair day mystery / by Nancy J. Cohen. — Large
print edition.
        pages cm. — (Wheeler Publishing large print cozy mystery)
    ISBN 978-1-4104-8489-5 (softcover) — ISBN 1-4104-8489-0 (softcover)
    1. Shore, Marla (Fictitious character)—Fiction. 2. Women detectives—
Florida—Fiction. 3. Murder—Investigation—Fiction. 4. Beauty operators—
Fiction. 5. Family secrets—Fiction. 6. Large type books. I. Title.
PS3553.O4258P45 2016
813'.54—dc23   2015032998

Published in 2016 by arrangement with The Evan Marshall Agency

Printed in the United States of America
1 2 3 4 5 6 7 19 20 18 17 16

I dedicate this book with gratitude and love to my cousin, Janice Sklar, a resident of Arizona and my source of inspiration and knowledge for this story. Many thanks for your personal tour of the region and for your gracious hospitality. This book is a direct result of your encouragement, suggestions, and advice.

ACKNOWLEDGMENTS

To the staff at Tanque Verde Ranch (http://tanqueverderanch.com), many thanks for taking the time from your busy schedules to answer my numerous questions: Jim Bankson, General Manager; Andrew Fine, Manager; Jonathan Johnson, Wrangler; Lisa the Bartender; Rick the Naturalist; and Troy from Maintenance. This book wouldn't have been possible without your input and generous information.

Another book in the Bad Hair Day series can't go by without thanking Five Star's dedicated staff — Senior Editor Deni Dietz for her expert guidance and insights, publicist extraordinaire Tiffany Schofield for her enthusiastic support, my creative cover designer, and the rest of the Five Star personnel who work so hard to deliver our books to readers.

CAST OF CHARACTERS

Alberto Gomez — Construction supervisor at the Craggy Peak ghost town project.

Annie Campbell — Wayne's younger sister and a registered dietitian.

Carol Campbell — Wayne's wife and the ranch's financial manager.

Christine Reardon — Annie's teenage client and Tate's daughter.

Dalton Vail — Marla's husband and a homicide detective from Palm Haven, Florida.

Eleanor Reardon — Tate Reardon's wife.

Eduardo Rivera — Missing ghost town worker.

Garrett Long — A forest ranger.

Hugh Donovan — Owner of Dead Gulch Ranch and a widower. His sons are Ben and Jake.

Jesse Parker — A wrangler on Last Trail Dude Ranch.

Juanita Martinez — A housekeeper on Last Trail Dude Ranch.

Kevin Franks — A wrangler on Last Trail Dude Ranch.

Luke Beresby — Sheriff.

Marla Vail — Dalton's wife is a hairstylist and salon owner in Palm Haven, Florida.

Matthew Brigham — An environmental engineer and inspector.

Otto Lovelace — Owner of Arizona Mountain High bottled water company.

Raymond Campbell — Owner of the Last Trail Ranch and Craggy Peak ghost town.

Sherry Long — Garrett's wife.

Tate Reardon — Manager for the water bottling plant.

Wayne Campbell — Dalton's cousin and general manager of Last Trail Dude Ranch.

CHAPTER ONE

"How can everyone be dead?" Marla Vail asked from the rear seat of the car. Weary after a four and a half-hour flight from Fort Lauderdale to Phoenix, she leaned against her husband Dalton's broad shoulder. Except for the driver, they were the only passengers in the battered Jeep Cherokee.

"I'm just kidding. Craggy Peak is a ghost town," Carol Campbell explained, her hands on the steering wheel as she navigated through airport traffic. "Most of the people who lived there in the heyday of the copper mine are long gone. Wayne's dad plans to turn the place into a tourist attraction. I'd hate to see him fail when he's pouring so much money into it."

Wayne was Dalton's cousin who'd invited them to stay on his dude ranch for their belated honeymoon. Although she'd met her husband's family at their wedding, Marla didn't remember much about them.

She had recalled Carol was a lithe blonde with a perennial tan, and Wayne had a ruggedly handsome face as befit a born and bred rancher.

"So Uncle Ray is renovating this former mining camp?" Dalton asked.

"That's right. We can use the revenue to supplement our income from the ranch. The resort is open year-round, but it gets quiet in the summer. With the heat, people head for cooler climates. An additional influx of tourist dollars would raise our bottom line. In case you're wondering, I work as the ranch's financial manager."

Half listening, Marla tickled her way up Dalton's arm. He smiled at her in that special way he had just for her. She hoped they'd have enough privacy at the ranch.

When Dalton's cousin had offered them a suite at his resort, her husband had leapt at the chance. He'd accepted before informing her. Not wishing to rock the boat after ten months of marriage, she'd bitten her tongue and feigned joy at the prospect. But if he had bothered to ask her first, she would have chosen to spend their romantic getaway in the tropics. Paradise to her meant a lounge chair on the beach and a tall rum drink.

Her brows lifted in surprise as she glanced

out the window. The desert had more vegetation than she'd thought. Although the reddish-brown dirt lacked grass, plenty of shrubs and low-lying trees dotted the landscape, along with a variety of cacti. Arizona had another good thing going for it. The highway was in top condition — smooth paving with artistic designs embedded into the walls and bridges. Those creative displays alone impressed her at how well the state maintained its property.

"Who owns the ghost town?"

Dalton's question jolted her attention back to the conversation. She tilted her head to listen more carefully.

"Raymond owns title to the land and the buildings, same as he does for our resort. He's lucky most of the structures are still standing." Carol glanced at them in the rearview mirror. "I love his idea, but he may have taken on more than he can handle. The site is having problems lately, and I can't help wondering if they're related to the incidents on our ranch."

"What do you mean?" Marla asked, curious to learn more about her relatives by marriage. This being a second time around for both her and Dalton, Marla had vowed to get more involved in his family. Taking on the job of stepmother to his teenaged

13

daughter, Brianna, had been the first step. Already she missed the girl, who had stayed home under the care of Marla's in-laws.

"Bad things have been happening lately. We've had a fire in the kitchen. Someone opened the corral gate and let the horses out. Car tires have been slashed. Then this morning, a water heater sprang a leak and flooded the dining room. That's why Wayne couldn't come to the airport. He's supervising the cleanup."

Marla elbowed her husband. "Did you know about these problems?"

His sheepish grin gave her the answer. "Wayne mentioned them when we spoke on the phone."

"I see." She gritted her teeth, suddenly aware of why they were taking a honeymoon in the desert. Not only had Dalton's cousin offered them a free stay, but likely he'd asked for her detective husband's help in catching the culprit. Maybe someone with a grudge was at the root of their problems. "Has Raymond owned the Last Trail Dude Ranch for a long time?"

Carol waited to reply until she'd changed course on the highway. They had a substantial ride to reach the resort, nestled in the mountains a distance away.

"Raymond inherited the property from his

14

father. The original purchase dates back to 1870, when a Mexican landowner purchased the site. After he died, an Easterner took it over and invited his friends to stay on the ranch. This guy extended the business into a resort. Raymond's dad purchased the property from him in the fifties and expanded the facilities. When he died in '99, Raymond assumed the reins."

"How many staff members do you have?" Marla had looked up their site online. The place appeared to be large enough to require a map to navigate.

"We've a hundred and twenty employees. Wayne will introduce you around. You'll have plenty to do if you want to participate in the activities, or you can simply hang out and relax."

Dalton took Marla's hand and gave it a squeeze. The look in his eyes told her what he planned to do in their spare time. Her heart fluttered. Even though this might not be her ideal vacation spot, being with her husband was what mattered.

She'd have a discussion with him later about his presumptive decision making.

Settling back in her seat, she watched the desert landscape zoom past. Most noteworthy were the tall, branched stalks stretching toward the sky.

"What are those cacti called?" she asked, still unused to the dry earth and lack of grass.

"Those are our saguaro." Carol pronounced it *sa-wa-ro.* "They grow as a single stalk for up to seventy-five years before branching out. The plant can reach sixty feet in height and may live as long as two hundred years. It's native to our Sonoran desert, and its white blossom is our state flower. They only thrive up to thirty-five hundred feet in elevation, though. Our ranch sits at twenty-eight hundred, so you'll see plenty of them."

Marla's ears popped, telling her they were climbing. While Dalton conversed with Carol, she sagged against the seat cushion. She must have dozed off, because when she opened her eyes, they were navigating the hills. Magnificent vistas opened before them as the road dipped and curved, the pink mountainsides dotted with greenery. Boulders piled by the roadside.

Marla eyed the towering rocks with trepidation. She hoped they didn't have landslides here. This terrain was so foreign compared to flat Florida.

At the base of another hill, they finally turned down a dusty road toward the ranch, passing several horse corrals and a flower farm along the way.

"Look, there's two deer!" She nearly jumped out of her seat in excitement.

"Actually, those might have been elk," Carol said as they sped past. "We spot more of them than deer around here."

A sign for the Last Trail Dude Ranch came into view. Carol entered a private driveway that led to the main lobby. This building stood apart from the others. Single-story pink adobe structures dotted the property. Flowering plants and attractive shrubbery provided splashes of color against paved walkways.

Carol pulled into an empty space and shut off the ignition. "What's the sheriff doing here? It's Sunday. He should be home relaxing." She shoved her door open and exited.

Marla had noted the labeled black SUV parked in the main lot. So had Dalton, judging from his springy step as he emerged from the rear seat. He reminded her of a hound who'd just picked up a scent, especially when she sniffed a distinctive aroma in the air.

Outside, her gaze zeroed in on the animals milling inside a fenced corral. "Look, horses!"

"We *are* at a dude ranch," Dalton said with a grin.

"Yes, but I didn't realize they'd be so many different colors."

"They're beautiful creatures. I would have liked to visit here when I was younger, but Mom rarely spoke about Uncle Ray. I knew little about him and his family until we researched them for our wedding." He lowered his voice so Carol wouldn't overhear his last remarks.

Carol popped the trunk, and Dalton lifted out their luggage. He set their bags on the pavement until they got their room assignment.

"I'd better see what's going on." Carol cast a worried glance at the sheriff's car.

"Maybe Wayne is reporting the latest incident to him," Dalton suggested. "Is there evidence the leak was anything other than wear and tear on the water heater?"

"I have no idea. Either way, Wayne hasn't told any of our problems to Sheriff Beresby before now. He likes to keep things in the family."

"That's why he invited *you*, isn't it?" Marla said, poking her husband.

"He invited *us* to stay here and enjoy the facilities. Let's see what this is all about."

They followed Carol up the front steps and into the building. A fragrant floral scent pervaded the spacious lobby. It came from a bouquet of fresh flowers set on a central round table. Marla observed the western décor with a sense of pleasure she hadn't expected. Dark brown leather couches in an L-shape faced a huge stone fireplace, while carved wood tables and accent pieces enhanced the space. Indian art, metal sculptures of cowboys and horses, and other knickknacks added to the theme. The tied-back drapes had a bright southwestern design that matched the colors in a large area rug.

An attractive redhead at the front desk glanced up at their approach. "Carol, I see you've brought our guests. How was the drive?"

"Not bad. Marla and Dalton Vail, meet Janice Sklar. Jan is Director of Reservations."

Janice flashed them a smile. "I expect you'll want your room keys. You have Hacienda Number Seventy-Five. Here's a map." She circled a few buildings and offered a quick review of their room location and other highlights. "Do you need help with your luggage?"

"I'll get it, thanks." Dalton stepped up to the counter to complete the formalities. That included the key to a loaner car from Wayne.

"What's happening, Jan? Why is the sheriff here?" Carol asked.

The fortyish lady thumbed her finger at an inner door. "Ask your husband, hon."

"This way," Carol told her guests. She led them through a door marked Private.

They entered a long corridor with offices on either side. Marla spied a conference room, sales department, catering office, and a collection of computer equipment.

"Here's where I work." Carol indicated an office marked Accounting. "And next door is Wayne's place." She led them to a corner suite from where male voices emanated.

Two men stood as they entered. Marla recognized the tall man behind the desk. While Dalton's ebony hair was peppered with silver, Wayne's dark brown head hadn't changed. She couldn't recall how many years younger Wayne was from Dalton's forty-five. He was even more imposing than she remembered with his square jaw and massive shoulders. Seeing him in the context of the ranch, she knew how he'd gotten his name.

Move over, John Wayne. Your replacement is here.

"Dalton, it's great to see you. Marla, what a pleasure."

Wayne circled his desk to greet them

personally. They exchanged embraces before Wayne formally introduced Sheriff Beresby.

"Luke, this is my cousin, Dalton Vail, and his wife, Marla. Dalton, I'd like you to meet Sheriff Luke Beresby. I've been telling him how you're a topnotch homicide detective back home."

The men shook hands. The sheriff's somber face was lined with ridges like a dry riverbed. He had a thatch of gray hair and a droopy mustache. From his paunch and general features, Marla estimated his age to be in the mid-fifties.

"Wayne has high praise for you." The sheriff's keen gaze scrutinized Dalton.

"He's been known to exaggerate," Dalton said with a grin.

Marla stood by, feeling as though she'd suddenly entered a men's club. The leather furnishings, bookshelves full of bound hardcovers, and paintings of Indian battle scenes on the walls added to the ambiance.

"What's going on?" Carol asked, glancing between her husband and the sheriff.

Wayne clapped a hand on her shoulder. "Luke came to tell us that Garrett Long is dead."

Carol gasped and jerked away. "What? How?"

"He was found by a couple of hikers on

the Snakehead Trail," Beresby replied. "Looks like he took a tumble off a hillside, although I've yet to determine what he was doing out on that ledge by himself. Garrett Long was a ranger with the national forest service," he explained to Marla and Dalton.

Marla heard the doubt in his tone. Did he suspect this accident was more than it seemed? What did forest rangers do besides enforcing rules and chasing off squatters?

"Why come to us with this news?" Carol said, her face pale. "I mean, I'd want to know, but shouldn't you be talking to his co-workers?"

The sheriff's lips compressed. "Long had a note in his pocket, ma'am. Maybe you know something about it. The note was a reminder for him to call Raymond, your father-in-law."

Wayne's forehead creased. "Dad and Garrett were riding buddies and often made dates together. Did you talk to Dad?"

"Not yet. I suppose I'll find him over at the ghost town?"

"Yep. He'll be upset to hear about Garrett. It's a shock to us all."

The sheriff eyed Wayne. "Did your daddy ever locate that worker who vanished?"

"Not yet. I've urged him to file a formal report, but he's thinking the guy ran off for

22

some reason. Dad has enough trouble keeping the other laborers in line. They're saying Eduardo saw an apparition on the hill, and it may have been the goddess of death summoning him to his doom. They're a superstitious lot. The men were ready to walk away from the job, but the foreman convinced them to remain. We're having problems on the ranch, too. I'm beginning to wonder if these incidents are related."

"Oh? What kind of problems?" Sheriff Beresby said.

Wayne swept his hand toward the door. "Just minor stuff so far. I don't want to keep you. If you see Dad, please tell him to come home in time for dinner. His nephew has arrived."

"So, are you the sole investigator in town?" Dalton asked, accompanying the sheriff down the hallway while the others trailed after them.

Uh-oh. Dalton's fascinated expression didn't bode well for their vacation.

"Pretty much," the sheriff replied. "Our office covers the unincorporated territory in these parts, so we're stretched thin. The larger towns have their own police departments."

"Maybe I can buy you a drink sometime, and we can swap stories. I'd enjoy hearing about your experiences."

"I'll bet you have some good ones, too."

"Florida has its share of wackos."

Marla nudged him. "Dalton, I'm sure the sheriff has enough to keep him busy. And we're here for our honeymoon, remember?"

Carol rallied to her defense. "That's right. Wayne, we need to settle our guests in their room and then give them a tour of the resort. Or would you two like to rest? There's a three-hour time difference from back east. You must be exhausted."

Marla glanced at her watch. "It's four o'clock here and seven back home. We should switch to your schedule and stay awake until later. A tour sounds great."

"Wayne, if you wouldn't mind taking over, I need to talk to the chef about those cooking classes starting next week. I'll see you guys at dinner."

"No problem, you run along. Thanks for doing airport duty." Wayne gave his wife a kiss before she dashed off. "Come on, we'll get your luggage, and then I'll show you the grounds. Did Jan give you a resort map?"

"I believe so." Dalton still carried the papers given him by the receptionist. He rustled through them, retrieving a printed diagram.

"Is our room far from here?" Marla asked.

The various buildings were located along winding paths and partially hidden by shrubbery.

"You're up this hill." Wayne pointed on the map. "Your loaner car is parked there, too. We can walk, but it's a haul for your bags. I'll drive you in the golf cart."

He and Dalton loaded their luggage, and then they climbed into the vehicle. As they rumbled to a start, Wayne pointed left toward another road. "Down that way is the lake. It's where we hold our weekly barbecues. You'll want to sign up for that event. And a hiking trail heads off from there. We do nature walks several times a week." He glanced at Marla's sandals. "I hope you brought sturdier shoes or riding boots."

Oh, yeah, like you're going to get me on a horse. The only thing I want to ride is my husband. Horsepower to her meant a car engine. As for rodeos, she'd rather watch the polish chip off her fingernails. She'd seen the shows listed on the weekly activity list.

Then again, a rodeo might be a good place to meet other guests and sound them out about the staff. And maybe she'd learn a thing or two about ropes that could come in handy.

"What is it?" Dalton asked in a solicitous

tone. "Are you tired? We can rest if you're feeling jet-lagged."

"No, I'm fine. I'm just thinking about what we can do in our room later once we have some privacy."

"Ah." His hand gripped hers, and he gave her a sexy grin.

They drove up a curving road and past a series of one-story adobe structures that Wayne said housed ordinary hotel rooms. The view of the distant mountains took her breath away. She could see how their colors might change with time of day. Now they appeared hazy and bluish in the afternoon sun.

Further along the road were individual buildings with lanais. They were the casitas. Apparently the higher the elevation, the more expensive the accommodations.

Suddenly, the foothills were right at their doorstep. A mound rose on the right with tall brown grasses amid shrubbery, cacti, and boulders. The rocks graduated into a mountainside.

"Here's your hacienda. Go check it out." Wayne helped unload their luggage curbside at a separate unit with stone chimneys.

Two lounge chairs and a large potted cactus decorated a covered front porch. What a wonderful view they'd have while relaxing there or on the rear patio. Marla waited as Dalton swiped his key card. Before entering, he handed her a duplicate key.

Inside, she surveyed an upholstered sofa facing one of the fireplaces. Its zigzag design matched the avocado, brick red, and tan colors from the carpet. Plush armchairs added to the cozy ambiance. A kitchenette occupied one alcove with a small fridge, microwave, and coffeemaker. Good, that meant they wouldn't have to rush out in the mornings. They could drink their own brew at that table with four wicker chairs.

Glad to settle in, Marla strode ahead through an interior door to the adjacent bedroom. A king-sized bed dominated the space, while spacious drape-lined windows provided an awesome mountain view. One entire wall consisted of built-in wooden drawers and cabinets. Two nightstands, a chair, lamps, and a desk completed the furnishings. Another fireplace took up one corner.

"Where's the TV?" Dalton halted inside the space after wheeling in his suitcase.

"We don't have them in our guest rooms," Wayne hollered from the front door. "The ranch offers enough to keep you busy. You'll be worn out by the evening."

Not too worn out to enjoy our privacy, I hope.
Marla put down her purse and went to
examine the bathroom. She shrieked upon
noticing a dark brown spider streaking
across the marble-tiled shower.

Wayne rushed inside. "Oh, that's a wolf
spider. I'll get it." He grabbed a wad of tis-
sues as Marla stepped out of his way and
let him take charge.

At least the bathroom had modern amenities, with a granite countertop, double sinks,
and generous counter space. Nonetheless,
she might want to leave a light on here at
night to avoid further insect encounters.
Scorpions and rattlesnakes inhabited the
desert, too, didn't they? She'd better look
under the sheets before getting into bed.

*Scratch the rustic atmosphere. I'll take a
luxury hotel any day.*

After refreshing herself, she joined the
guys outside for the rest of their tour. She'd
hung up a few of her garments and would
unpack the remainder later.

Trying for a more positive outlook, she
imagined herself relaxing in a lounge chair
and admiring the mountains. In fact, lying
around reading magazines, sitting by the
pool, or visiting the spa sounded ideal.
Dalton could engage in all the sports he
wanted while she chilled out. The best part

of this stay was not having to cook. Plus the dry air provided a welcome change from Florida's humidity and made being outdoors a pleasure.

Wayne led them on a winding path with abundant landscaping and shady trees. Some of the plants were labeled, like that prickly pear cactus. It had a purplish tint and Mickey Mouse shaped ears. She particularly liked the spreading mesquite tree with its fern-like leaves, and the beautiful palo verde tree with its bright green trunk and leafy canopy. Never mind the nature walk. She could learn about the native plants by exploring the resort. Despite its lack of grass, the grounds had their own beauty.

Wayne introduced them to other guests they passed along the way. Like a good host, he knew everyone's name. From the friendly greetings, she surmised that he was well-liked.

"This is the main building," he said as they approached a large adobe structure in a central location. "It holds our restaurant, card room, lecture hall, library, and a lounge with a television. The gift shop is located here, too."

Under the covered patio were wood benches with wagon wheels at either end for support. She halted on the brick flooring while Wayne pointed out a bulletin board listing the day's activities. Signs for the Laundry and Bike Shop pointed down an alleyway.

Marla noted the limited dining hours. "Is this where we'll come for meals?"

"You can eat either here or in the staff cafeteria since you're family. You're welcome to join me and Carol at home in the evenings. I'll give you directions. We're expecting you for dinner tonight at least since our kids are eager to meet you. We don't get relatives out this way very often."

He ended on a slightly bitter note, making Marla wonder at the sentiment behind his words. Dalton's mother rarely spoke about this side of the family. How had Kate become estranged from her brother, Raymond?

"Did you get your water heater fixed?" Dalton asked, shading his face against the sun.

Wayne's lips thinned. "Yes, but we had a mess in there. The plumber said a valve had been opened. We have the air-conditioning going full blast to help dry things out."

"A valve wouldn't turn by itself, unless it had failed because the unit was old."

"I know. These troublesome incidents have been happening more often lately. I can't prove anyone is behind them, but they worry me."

A guy sauntered past in a plaid shirt, cowboy hat, and boots. He waved to Wayne on his way. From his lean body and lined face, Marla surmised he was one of the staff.

"That's Nick, a wrangler," Wayne said, confirming her theory. "Let me show you the horses. You'll want to make reservations for your rides. You have ridden before, right? If not, the boys give lessons but you have to sign up early."

Marla smelled the animals the closer they got to the corral. It appeared emptier than when they'd first arrived. As they descended a slope toward the riding station, she noted far to the left a place where the horses appeared to be led for the night. There wasn't just one fenced corral. It was a series leading out almost to the hills.

"Here's our nature center." Wayne pointed out a structure with a flight of stairs. "Stop by and talk to our naturalist when you have a chance. He'll explain the exhibits. That building beyond has a ballroom for conferences or large social affairs."

Marla noted a tennis court, children's playground, and arena with bleachers down a path to the side of the last building. It would be fun to explore the resort's nooks

31

and crannies. Then again, if Dalton went riding in the mornings, she would have time on her own to laze around. Her shoulders sagged. Relaxing would feel good right about now. Either the jet lag was catching up to her, or she was hungry. This would be three hours later back home.

Dalton nudged her. "We'll have to sign up for the breakfast ride. They make blueberry pancakes with bacon and scrambled eggs."

Oh, joy. "Sure," she said, not wishing to disavow him of the notion that she'd be joining him. Maybe she should give it a try. She'd taken a lesson or two in her youth. It couldn't be so difficult to catch on again. And the thought of eating breakfast in the great outdoors had its appeal, minus the bees and flies.

She swatted away a fly, realizing they were much more in abundance here than in South Florida. No mosquitoes, though. The dry air took care of those pests.

"Hey, Jesse," Wayne hollered to a wrangler with a trim black beard and dark eyes to match. He was busy putting away some equipment. "I'd like you to meet my cousins."

"One minute. I'll come out through the tack room." He disappeared behind the building in front of them.

Marla's sandals crunched on gravel as the paved walkway ended. She needed better shoes. Not only was this terrain hillier than she'd expected, but being near horses brought to mind unforeseen hazards. She didn't care to step in something unpleasant.

Several closed doors faced them on the beige structure ahead. Signs indicated the Wrangler's Roost, Riders Entrance, Game Room, and Staff Only. The last door burst open, and the man named Jesse strode toward them. Marla's gaze zeroed in on his tar-black hair, mustache, and beard.

Her eyes narrowed. That tint was suspiciously uniform. Did he dye his hair?

Wayne introduced them. "Jesse Parker is the man I'd recommend if you need lessons, although any of our wranglers would suit. Jesse has a broad-based knowledge and can answer any questions you might have about the horses or the ranch."

"Nice to meet you," Jesse said with a polite expression. He didn't offer his hand, likely because he'd been out in the field.

He looked fairly young, maybe in his late twenties, but his eyes held years of experience and a hint of inner pain. What drew men to become wranglers? Did they like horses more than people? They still had to work with guests at the resort. Maybe it was in their blood, like dog lovers.

A pang hit her for her own pets. She hoped Lucky and Spooks were doing well in their absence. Thankfully, the dogs were fine after being sedated by a killer who'd used them to lure Marla into a trap. After she'd escaped, Dalton had rescued their precious pets.

"You take good care of these people, you hear?" Wayne advised Jesse. "This is their first visit to Arizona."

"Is that right? Where do you guys live?" Jesse hooked his thumbs into his belt. He wore a dark brown cowboy hat, plaid shirt, and jeans tucked into a pair of high boots with spurs. His belt carried a cell phone, radio unit, and big knife in a leather sheath.

"We're from Florida," Dalton replied, giving him a onceover.

"Dalton is a police detective back home," Wayne remarked. "We had a problem earlier today with the water heater near the dining room. A valve opened, and the floor got flooded. I'm troubled by the incidents we've been having lately and am hoping Dalton might shed some light on them."

"No kidding? Is that why I saw the sheriff's car here earlier?"

"Uh-uh. He came to tell us Garrett Long is dead. His body was found out on the

Snakehead Trail by a couple of hikers."

"What? That's impossible." Jesse's tan faded under his sudden pallor.

"I know. It's hard to believe Garrett would be so careless as to fall off a ledge. Hopefully, the sheriff's office will investigate and determine what happened."

"You don't understand. He must have gotten too close. I've gotta go." Jesse spun and dashed back into the tack room, slamming the door while they stared after him.

CHAPTER TWO

"What did Jesse mean by saying Garrett must have gotten too close?" Marla asked her husband's cousin. "Too close to what?"

Wayne scratched his head. "Damned if I know, but I'll leave it up to you two to find out." His cell phone trilled. He took it out and read a text message. "I have to run. We'll see you at dinner, right?"

Dalton nodded and his cousin took off.

Marla hooked her arm into Dalton's. "Let's go back to our room and rest for a while. We can deal with these problems later." They weren't her personal issues, but she knew Dalton would want to help his relatives. And until they talked to Jesse again or learned more about him from another employee, they'd have no clue what his mysterious words meant.

After washing up and changing into fresh clothes, they headed over to Wayne's house.

When they arrived, an older guy opened

the door. "Dalton, it's good to finally meet you in person."

"You must be Uncle Ray. This is my wife, Marla." They all shook hands.

Raymond's lean build and deeply lined face hinted at years of outdoor living. He had short, cropped white hair, sharp brown eyes behind wire-rimmed glasses, and ruddy cheekbones. Having expected a grizzled old coot, Marla was surprised by his clean-shaven appearance. He wore the typical rancher outfit of a plaid shirt, blue jeans, and boots.

"Come on inside. The gals are in the kitchen, and the children are watching TV. We can chat until the meal is ready."

"Can I help?" Marla offered, wishing they'd been able to stop off somewhere and buy a bottle of wine. She didn't know where people did their food shopping around town.

"Nope, Carol has everything under control. Wayne is late getting home. He should be here shortly."

The Campbells lived off-site from the ranch in the small town of Rustler Ridge. A cozy community, it could almost be missed if you travelled by on the highway. Marla still couldn't get over the wide, open spaces between most big cities in Arizona. South

Florida held one town after another, suburban congestion flowing nonstop from the cities toward the Everglades.

The sloped yard in front of the Campbell's Mediterranean-style home was attractively landscaped with various cacti and palo verde trees amid a ground cover of red rocks. A metal statue of a donkey stood next to a miniature wooden cart. Huge polished wood doors led inside.

As she followed the men into the interior, Marla noted mixed Mexican and southwestern influences in the furniture and décor. They passed a formal living and dining area on their way to the kitchen, where she sniffed garlic and rosemary. She spied a stone fireplace and imagined cold winters in the desert. Mornings were cool enough by her standards, down into the sixties. She'd brought a wrap for her skirt ensemble in case the evening temperature dropped.

Raymond led them toward a combined open kitchen, casual dining nook, and family room with an entertainment center. Greetings rang out as Marla and Dalton met Brian, age nine, and Ariel, age six. They were adorable kids, albeit a bit boisterous.

A kid's show blasted on the television. To the right of the TV unit was a bar complete with a granite counter and glassware.

Mounted on the wall was an oval mirror. Its colorful frame, decorated with jungle parrots, matched the carved barstools and coffee table in front of a U-shaped sofa. Another fireplace sat to the left of the entertainment console.

Carol dried her hands on a dishtowel and strode over to welcome them. "This is Wayne's sister, Annie," she said, signaling for a slender brunette to approach. "Annie is a dietitian. She runs a nutrition clinic downtown."

"Really? That's great." Marla pumped the younger woman's hand, liking her warm smile and independent attitude. "How can you be out of college? You look so young."

"I'm thirty-one. There's a seven year age difference between me and Wayne. I still get carded at bars."

"Oh, I'm only a year younger than him then." She'd turned thirty-seven in February.

"I hear you're a hairdresser. Maybe you can tell me what to do with my hair. I tie it back in a ponytail because it's easy, but I should get a decent cut."

"Braids are popular today if you want to leave it one length, but I'd be happy to discuss styles with you any time."

"That sounds like fun. When you come

into town, stop by my clinic. We can have lunch together, and I'll tell you where to go shopping if you want."

"You've got a deal. I really need to buy a pair of boots."

Annie returned to the kitchen to finish tossing a salad. Marla glanced at the floor-to-ceiling window panels overlooking a free-form pool and covered patio with a view of the mountains. Flowering pink bougain-villea grew over the fencing. The patio had a large gas grill, a generous seating area, a round table and chairs, and yet another fireplace. How were those things heated? There weren't any logs piled around.

Dusk had fallen, and soon it would be dark. Marla hoped she and Dalton could find their way back to the ranch on the country road.

Meanwhile, they milled around the kitchen, snacking on appetizers Carol had put out on the counter and drinking wine. When Wayne arrived, they took their places in the formal dining room.

"Kids, mind your manners," Carol told her children. She bustled back toward the kitchen to get their first course.

Raymond sat at one end of the table with the opposite armchair reserved for Carol. Her children flanked her. Next to Ariel

40

came Annie and then Marla. Dalton sat across from her beside Wayne on one side and Raymond on the other.

After they'd eaten a hearty vegetable bean soup, Raymond addressed Wayne. "Did you get that leaky water heater fixed?"

Wayne's mouth tightened. "Yes, we did. The plumber said a valve had been loosened. Maybe it got knocked open by a broom that may have fallen over, but I think it was deliberate. At least we were able to clean the dining hall in time for the next meal."

"I told you to put more video cameras in place."

"Carol is still waiting for an estimate from the security company. Why do you look like you swallowed a lemon pit? I'll take care of it."

Raymond gripped his water glass. "I attended a town council meeting today. Hugh Donovan is stirring up trouble again."

"What did he want this time? Donovan owns the Dead Gulch Ranch on the other side of the mountain," Wayne explained in an aside to Marla and Dalton.

"His cattle aren't doing well, and he blames my renovations," Raymond said. "The guy's an idiot. We've done the proper environmental impact studies, and they were approved. There's no way our ghost town project can be contaminating his property."

"It's not the first time he's complained, and you can bet it won't be the last." Carol rose to take away their empty soup bowls.

Annie stood to assist her, while the two kids slid a dessert spoon back and forth across the table at each other. Brian made sputtering noises like a damaged motor.

"Children, keep it down," Raymond chided. "We're trying to have a conversation here."

"Why does this fellow worry you so much?" Dalton asked, voicing the thought in Marla's head.

"The man has it in for me, and don't ask why because it's nobody's business but mine. I'll need more approvals for my construction. If the council refuses to issue even one permit, it'll put us behind schedule."

"And how does that benefit Donovan?" Wayne said in a frustrated tone.

Marla figured he must have asked his father before about Hugh Donovan without satisfaction. What had happened between the two men to cause animosity?

"He hopes I'll run out of money if he delays things long enough. I've had offers to buy that property, and I suspect he's behind them. If the council doesn't heed him, he'll find other ways to shut me down."

"Any word on the missing guy from the ghost town?" Wayne asked.

"Nope. The man never returned to his bunk. You know what I'm thinking."

Dalton twirled his fork and then put it down. "Surely you don't believe this other rancher caused the man's disappearance?"

"Hugh is capable of anything in order to stop me." Raymond's brows drew together like two mating caterpillars. "His claim about the cattle being sick is hogwash, if you ask me."

"Doesn't your ranch have cattle, too, Uncle Ray?"

"You bet. We have five hundred head of cattle, mostly breeding stock. We sell the cows. Up on the mountain, we lease sixty thousand acres from the forest service."

Impressed, Marla stared at him. "How many people do you have working the cattle?"

"It takes two employees except for periodic roundups, when we need six to eight men."

"Wow, that's a big difference from the number of employees at the dude ranch. Carol said you have one hundred and

43

twenty people on the staff. What do they all do?"

Raymond's eyes crinkled as he eased into the subject. "We have our wranglers, of course. Then there's housekeeping and lodging, food and beverage, our naturalist who runs the nature center, directors for our kids' programs, fishing and hiking specialists."

"Fishing?" Dalton's brows lifted. "Where is there water?"

"We have a pond fed by a natural spring on the ranch, and there are lakes in the area."

"So Wayne is the general manager, and Carol manages the finances?" Marla sought to clarify the different positions. "Who else is in charge?" Did Raymond take an active role in the ranch's day-to-day supervision, or was his focus solely on the ghost town project?

"Besides Carol and Wayne, we have ten other managers. They're all capable of functioning in multiple roles. I'm confident they can handle things, although I am concerned about this latest rash of incidents. It's too coincidental that we're having similar problems over at Craggy Peak."

"I'm hoping Dalton can help us, Dad," Wayne said, leaning back as Carol and Annie delivered steaming platters to the table.

"How many visitors can the ranch accommodate?" Marla piped in, curious to know.

"At full capacity, we can house up to two hundred and twenty-five people." Wayne helped himself to a heap of roasted potatoes and then passed the dish. "The buildings are spread out over seven hundred acres."

"Yes, I've noticed how they're scattered around. How many guest quarters are there?"

"One hundred and eighty. Some are part of multi-unit buildings, and others are stand-alones, like the haciendas."

"Can I ask a delicate question?" Dalton interceded. "Do you still have a mortgage on the place?"

Raymond's face reddened. "No, sirree. We are completely debt-free. However, it's not always easy to make ends meet, especially during the summer months. That's why I was hoping to get the ghost town running as a tourist attraction. It would bring more people into the area, and some of them would need a place to stay."

"What about Craggy Peak? That must occupy a big piece of land."

"The town was happy to get a buyer after foreclosing on the previous owner, who'd neglected to pay his taxes. I made an out-

45

right purchase."

"Is that so?" Dalton looked as though he wanted to ask more, but he clamped his lips shut and reached for a slice of cornbread.

An awkward silence fell, while Marla wondered where Raymond had obtained the funds to buy Craggy Peak if he was barely making ends meet at the dude ranch. Not only did he have to purchase the land and deserted buildings, but then there was the construction crew to pay and permits to acquire. He might even have had to pay those back taxes.

Financing wasn't the only subject Raymond avoided. He hadn't once asked about his sister, Kate. Had Dalton noticed his uncle's reticence to speak about his mother?

"Can you explain to me how your families are related?" she said in a bright tone to get the conversation rolling again. She lifted her fork and stabbed into a stalk of asparagus.

"My mother is Uncle Ray's sister," Dalton said in a subdued tone. Clearly familial relations weren't a topic he was eager to pursue. "You knew that."

"Yes, but tell me again about your ancestry."

"Our heritage dates back to Ireland." Wayne shared a hooded glance with Dalton. "My great-grandfather, Paddy O'Hara, immigrated to New York. He married a woman named Rose Sherman and they had one daughter, Hannah."

Rose Sherman? Marla sipped her Arizona-made red wine. That sounded like a Jewish name. Could an Irish Catholic have married a Jewish bride back in 1800's New York? From Raymond's high cheekbones, she might have guessed he had Indian blood. Huh. This family might have a more interesting background than she'd surmised.

"Go on." She gave Wayne an encouraging nod.

"Hannah married Sean Campbell, and they had two children — Kate and my dad."

Raymond cleared his throat. "Let's not dredge up the past, folks. What matters now is that you're here, Dalton, with your lovely bride. Sorry I couldn't make the wedding, but at least Wayne and Carol represented the family."

"We were sorry Annie couldn't come, either." Marla offered her female cousin by marriage a friendly smile. Did Annie sense the undercurrents of tension here, too?

"You came to us, so I got to meet you after all." Annie grinned back at her.

"It's impressive that you run your own diet clinic. How come you're not working on the ranch? It appears to be the family

47

business."

"It isn't my thing. I had weight issues when I was young, despite the exercise I got riding. I wanted to counsel teens about good nutrition, especially when obesity is such an epidemic in America. Good eating habits have to start early." She aimed a meaningful glance at her sister-in-law. "It's hard to watch your diet around here when every other meal is a steak."

"Hey, the men need hearty food," Carol said. "They work it off during the day."

"Carol, we've discussed this before. You don't want them to drop from a heart attack. There are healthier choices that can be just as tasty."

"You're right. That's why I made this lemon chicken. You gave me the recipe."

"The last time I ate here, you served ribs. You know I don't eat red meat."

"You liked the corn and barley dish, though. When you cook for a family, you'll understand."

Raymond snorted. "That'll be the day. You might have to wheel me down the aisle by then."

"Don't start, Dad." Annie threw her napkin on the table.

"Annie, tell me about your nutrition clinic," Marla said to mollify her. "How did you get started? I own my salon and lease the space from our landlord. We just opened an adjacent day spa earlier this year."

They spent a pleasant few minutes chatting about business ownership.

"Promise me you'll come into town soon," Annie concluded, her eyes sparkling. "I can't wait to show you around."

"And I can't wait to work on your hair. We'll have a fun day together."

Although Carol was closer to her age, Marla felt more akin to Annie, a businesswoman like herself. But Marla wasn't single anymore, and she had a stepchild now. Her circumstances had changed, and so had her meal preparations. Cooking for three instead of one meant making modifications. She could relate to both Carol and Annie's viewpoints.

"Speaking of meals, I guess big breakfasts are a cowboy thing," she said to change the subject. "What can we look forward to having on the menu at the ranch?"

"Breakfasts and lunches are buffets, so you'll have lots of choices." Wayne's tone held relief, as though he were eager to speak on a more comfortable topic. "Our chef gets a high rating so I'm confident you'll like the food. You be sure to tell me if something doesn't set right by you, though. We're always on the lookout for improvements."

"Where do the wranglers eat? You'd mentioned a staff cafeteria?"

"That's right. I'll eat there sometimes when I'm working late. It's open for all three meals daily."

"Do the managers rotate shifts? Who's on night duty?" Dalton asked, putting his last forkful into his mouth.

"We have a security detail from ten at night to six in the morning. And one of the managers is always on duty, plus a guy from maintenance."

"I imagine the wranglers have to get in early to ready the horses for the day?"

Wayne handed his empty plate to his sister, who'd risen to help Carol clear the table. "They let the horses in from the outer corrals around seven in the morning. If you're up early, head over to watch. The staging is an impressive sight, all those beauties stampeding together in one direction."

"How many horses do you keep on the ranch?" Marla asked, curious despite her reservations about riding. It would have to be a decent number to accommodate so many guests.

"We have one hundred and eighty when we're full. In the summer, we send some of our stock to Colorado and northern California. In turn, we'll lease from other ranches during our peak season. We help each other out."

"But not you and Hugh Donovan?" Dalton asked in a casual tone that made her wonder about his purpose. If she knew him, he had an ulterior motive behind his question.

"I wouldn't ask Hugh Donovan if we were down to our last mare," Raymond roared. "That man is up to no good. I had another inquiry about buying Last Trail not that long ago. It came from a real estate agent who didn't mention her client's name, but I'll bet my boots it was him. He's after both of my properties."

Hmm, could this Donovan person be responsible for the incidents plaguing the ranch plus the ghost town? Did the rival rancher really hope to ruin Raymond financially so he'd be forced to sell his holdings? She wondered again where Dalton's uncle had gotten the cash for his purchase of the ghost town.

"We met a wrangler today named Jesse Parker. He's a young fellow," Dalton said to Raymond. "How long has he been working for you?"

"Five years. The man is competent and

well-experienced."

"He seemed unnerved by the news about that forest ranger."

Ah, now Marla understood where Dalton was steering the conversation.

Raymond rubbed his face. "Who wouldn't be? Garrett Long was a solid citizen and a dedicated forest ranger. I find it hard to believe he's gone."

"Hadn't you and he been riding buddies? The sheriff found a note to call you in the guy's pocket."

"He probably wanted to ask about his horse. The animal had been limping, and I had our vet take a look at him. It was a simple problem that was easily fixed. Garrett kept his horse at our ranch." Raymond lowered his head. "I guess his wife will own Sierra now. I need to give Sherry a call to find out about funeral arrangements."

"I'm not clear about the circumstances of his death," Dalton said, his tone persistent. "The man fell off a ledge on the mountain?"

Oh, no, Marla thought. Was her husband so bored already that he needed a murder case to solve? As far as they knew, the ranger's demise was an accident.

He was too far for her to kick him under the table. If she could get him alone, she'd give him distraction enough so he wouldn't think about work.

"We don't know the details. I feel bad for his family."

"Did he have any children?"

"Sherry had a son from a previous marriage. She and Garrett never had kids together." Raymond stretched and stood. "Excuse me a moment. Nature calls."

He strode away while Dalton stared thoughtfully after him. Marla's gaze lit on a pair of animal horns mounted over the living room's fireplace. Were those real? She shuddered at the thought of someone shooting a live elk or other creature.

Needing to be useful, she rose and strolled into the kitchen to help Carol and Annie. Carol was loading rinsed dishes into the dishwasher, while Annie scooped whipped topping onto plated slices of blueberry pie.

"How did Raymond hear about Garrett Long?" she asked Carol in a low voice.

Had the sheriff found him at the ghost town? Or had he already gone home? Actually, where did Carol's father-in-law live? Or Annie, for that matter? They couldn't all reside here with Carol and Wayne's family. True, the house seemed enormous with a whole lower level she hadn't seen, but would Carol tolerate them living there?

"Wayne called to tell Raymond the news

before the sheriff spoke to him. It's a shame. Garrett was a fine man. He truly loved the forest and was devoted to its protection."

"As a ranger, I'd think he would be familiar with the territory and its hazards."

Carol shot her a narrowed glance. "What are you implying?"

"He should have been more careful if he knew the ground was unstable."

"Marla, it's your honeymoon. Don't stray from the reason why you're here."

Was that a subtle warning, or could Marla be reading things into these discussions that weren't there? Could a person really be behind the incidents on the ranch as Wayne suspected, or had he become paranoid like his dad?

It did seem odd that the ghost town was also experiencing a jinx of sorts. She'd like to meet Hugh Donovan, the source of their suspicions, but that encounter seemed unlikely.

The children's laughter reached her ears. They'd been excused to return to the family room and were playing a video game on TV. Marla's stepdaughter, Brianna, loved the tablet computer she'd gotten from her grandparents for her birthday and often had her head bent over the device. Young people became attached to their technology so early these days.

"So tell me, where do you live, Annie?" Marla picked up a dessert plate and carried it into the dining room, while the younger woman did the same.

Annie placed her plates on the table where the men sat chatting. "I rent an apartment in town. I love having my own place, and it isn't too far from Dad's house if he needs me."

"You're welcome to move in with me and save money," Raymond's voice boomed.

"No, thanks. You should build yourself a casita on the ranch like you've been saying. That house is too big for you all by your-self."

"It is not. I manage just fine. Wayne wouldn't want me underfoot, plus I'm closer to Craggy Peak from town."

"How old is your father?" Marla asked in an undertone on their way back to the kitchen.

"Would you believe he's seventy-three? I hope I'm in as good shape when I reach his age."

"How did he get interested in renovating the ghost town?"

"The rundown buildings became an eye-sore to the area. There was talk about tear-ing them down. Garrett tried to get an historical preservation society started, but he couldn't rouse enough interest."

"Garrett Long, the forest ranger?"

"That's right. He was a history buff and loved to talk about the region's rich past."

"Really? I thought Garrett and your Dad went riding together, and that's how he was acquainted with the family."

"That, too. Anyway, Garrett convinced Dad that saving the town would be a worthwhile venture. So Dad bought the property and started the project. Carol ran the figures and said the additional income, once the attraction was up and running, would help their bottom line."

"How did your father finance the title purchase and initial construction costs?"

Annie's lips tightened. "I assume he used his savings. Anyway, the project gives him a purpose, and I have to admit I like the idea. I'll help him find merchants once the place is ready."

"What do you mean?" Marla pictured a dead town with tumbleweeds rolling through and empty saloon doors swinging in the wind. Come to think of it, she hadn't seen a single tumbleweed in the Arizona landscape.

"He wants to model it after Tombstone, the historic site of the battle at the O.K.

Corral. Besides a recreation of the gunfight, the town has quaint shops and restaurants. It attracts quite a crowd."

"Oh, I see." That wasn't her impression of a ghost town at all, but then her notion came from the handful of western movies she'd seen. The genre didn't hold much appeal for her.

"If you and Dalton find the time, you should take a ride to Tombstone. You'd want to stay overnight as it's a long drive from here. Otherwise, you'll have to come back for another visit to see the rest of the state." She grinned broadly, making Marla smile in response.

"So are there any ghosts associated with Raymond's project, or is it called a ghost town because everyone deserted it?"

"Ask Dad to tell you the stories. They're fun if nothing else." In the kitchen, she picked up another couple of dessert plates and walked them over to the children. "Here you go, kids. Don't spill anything."

Marla stood by awkwardly, wondering if she should offer to help Carol, who was scrubbing pots. But Annie returned to resume their conversation.

"I love those kids. They're like my own for now."

"Any boyfriends on the horizon?" Marla

57

asked with a glance in Carol's direction. Carol had her back turned to them, but Marla bet she was listening.

"Nuh-uh. Anyway, I hope Dad learns what happened to that worker who went missing. It's put a cog in his wheel. His work force is a superstitious bunch."

"So I've heard. They believe the man saw a ghost on the hillside and followed it?"

"He might have followed someone, but I doubt it was an apparition."

CHAPTER THREE

"Did you learn why your mother and uncle aren't speaking?" Marla asked Dalton on the drive back to the ranch. The headlights of their black Toyota RAV4 lit the winding road ahead, while stars sprinkled the sky. Accustomed to the city glow of suburbia, she marveled at the view.

"Uncle Ray didn't say anything on the subject. He's more concerned about this other rancher — Hugh Donovan — as the source of his current troubles."

"Do you think he's right?"

Dalton's jaw clenched as he focused forward. "Wayne seems inclined to agree with him."

"And what about Raymond's relationship with the dead forest ranger? I sensed something more than he let on."

"That's the sheriff's business. As far as we know, the man's death was an accident. It's a loss for Uncle Ray because they'd been friends."

"Annie would like to see her father move to the ranch. He's in his seventies and living alone in his house. He'd have his meals provided for him there."

"He gets around fine on his own. Besides, she doesn't live that far from him if he should need her." He spared Marla a glance. "You and Annie hit it off quite well."

A smile played around her mouth. "I like Annie. She's independent and business oriented, like me. I promised to stop by her clinic, and while I'm in town, I can buy a pair of boots and a few other things we need. Let's check the activities scheduled for the next few days to see when we can fit in the time."

They did so after showering and getting ready for bed. Marla sorted through the papers Dalton had dumped on the dinette table and found the agenda for the week.

"Forget horseback rides for me until I get properly outfitted, but you can go if you want. For tomorrow, different riding sessions begin at nine. Then we can choose from a nature walk, a more strenuous hike, or a tennis mixer. After lunch, the ranch offers fishing at a lake, a lecture about venom, or a demonstration on horsemanship."

"I'd rather take a ride to Craggy Peak.

Aren't you curious to see Uncle Ray's ghost town? We can relax here later in the day."

Dalton, wearing a towel wrapped around his waist and nothing more, approached in a manner that let her know what was on his mind. Her interest flared, but she tamped it down until they covered an important topic.

"I wish you'd told me your reasons for coming here before you accepted Wayne's invitation."

He halted and frowned at her. "How so?"

"You could have said he was having problems and needed your help. I would have understood your choice better."

"Does it matter?"

"It matters to me. I was hurt that you made the decision alone. It's true I agreed with your arrangements, but Arizona wouldn't have been my prime choice for a honeymoon. You know how I've always dreamed of going to Tahiti. That island might be out of our budget, but an all-inclusive resort in the Caribbean would have served the same purpose."

"You should have said something sooner." Consternation lit his features, but she held firm to her stance. They had to clear the air on this now, so it didn't happen again.

"You're right, I should have expressed how I felt," she said. "However, I knew it was important for you to be with your family."

"We could have made plans to come out here some other time. Our honeymoon should be special to both of us." He stepped forward and put his hands on her shoulders. "I'm sorry I didn't realize how you felt earlier."

"Hereafter, please ask me before making plans that affect us both. It's not the only time this has happened."

"Guilty as charged."

His look of chagrin softened her heart. "I know you want to help your cousin get to the bottom of his problems, and I'll admit that he has me curious, too. However, this *is* our honeymoon, and it's likely to be the only time off we have together for quite a while."

"Oh, don't worry. My focus is entirely on you." His hot gaze perused her body in its see-through nightie, while his muscular chest mere inches away stirred her more intimate regions.

"Stop that. We need to finish this discussion." The heat from his skin raised her temperature as he edged closer. "You're seducing me. That's not fair."

"I promise to consult you about our plans from now on. I get it. It's true I tend to take charge, but I have to remember two of us are involved now. Can you forgive me?"

Meeting his gaze, she noted the sincerity in his smoky gray eyes, and her resistance melted. He closed the distance between them and lowered his head. His kiss dissolved any remaining dregs of anger as their celebration began in earnest.

Monday morning, they arose early to partake of the breakfast buffet and to explore the grounds. Marla admired the various relics decorating the landscape. The dusty ore car, wheel contraption, and broken-down wooden cart added to the ambiance as much as the cacti.

Horses whinnied in the near distance while an earthy scent entered her nose. She paused beside a set of bleachers overlooking the arena for rodeos and other demos. "When do you want to go to Craggy Peak?" She glanced at her watch. "It's too early yet. Your uncle might not be there. We should wait until after lunch."

Dalton gazed at a densely-branched cholla plant amid a bed of reddish dirt. "In that case, do you feel up to a round of tennis, or would you rather go on the nature walk?"

"Let's take the hike if it goes into the forest. Maybe we'll find the spot where the ranger fell off the ledge. You can head to the lobby to sign us up. I'll meet you after I change into sneakers."

With a bounce in her step, Marla turned toward their hacienda located at the summit of the hill. That gave them a grand view, but it was a trek to access the public areas.

Along the way, she glanced at a sign marked Laundry and the path beyond. That alleyway might provide a shortcut. She followed the narrow path edged between two concrete walls. An employee parking lot ahead and to the right served as a storage depot, judging from the stacks of plastic crates and folding chairs piled there.

The path veered left toward an upper level. As she passed the laundry room, a crash sounded from the interior, followed by a curse in Spanish. Did someone need help? Marla wondered if these facilities were for staff or for guests.

As she stepped inside, she glimpsed a woman in a uniform bent over a collection of broken pottery shards on the floor. The employee straightened at Marla's entry and swiped her eyes. Had she been crying? She wore her raven hair in a long braid down her back.

"Are you okay? I heard a crash outside."

"Thank you, I am fine, *señora*. I am

clumsy and knocked over a bowl," the woman said in a heavy Hispanic accent.

"I can help you. Is there a broom around?" A quick sweep of the premises revealed a row of washers and dryers and ironing facilities. "I'm Marla Vail, by the way."

"I am Juanita, a housekeeper." The young woman was attractive despite her sad dark eyes. At a long counter against one wall, she retrieved a basket. Together, she and Marla recovered the pottery pieces and set them in the woven container. Packets of detergent, evidently the bowl's contents, lay scattered on the ground. They picked those up, too.

"Thank you," Juanita said when they had finished the cleanup. She gave a heavy sigh and rolled her shoulders as though her burden was too heavy to bear.

"You seem upset," Marla said. Maybe she should mention her relation to the ranch manager. If it was an employment problem, she could offer to intervene on the woman's behalf, depending on the situation.

Juanita chewed on her lower lip. "I worry about my boyfriend. He has heard some bad news about a man he knew."

"Oh, I'm sorry. That can be troubling." Maybe she should leave, but the housekeeper looked as though she wanted to talk.

65

So Marla waited with a sympathetic look on her face.

Juanita hesitated. "The person is dead."

Marla gave her a startled glance. That wasn't what she'd expected to hear. A memory surfaced of the wrangler she and Dalton had met recently. He'd been disturbed by news of the forest ranger's death.

"Is your friend's name Jesse, by any chance?"

"*Si,* it is him. Please, do not tell anyone what I say." Juanita aimed a furtive glance toward the door. "We have been seeing each other for a little over a year. I want to tell others, but Jesse says no. He is not ready."

"Some men take longer." Marla wanted to question her about Jesse's acquaintance with the dead guy but didn't dare appear too interested.

Juanita emptied a dryer of linens and took the bundle over to a folding table. "I have said too much. I should get back to work."

"And I need to go." Marla took out a business card and wrote her room number on the back. "Here, if you need a friend, please come by. I'm always willing to listen."

By the time Marla reached her lodging, Dalton had returned. She tossed her purse on the counter, eager to tell him what she'd just learned.

"Where were you? I got here ahead of you and you left before me."

"I made a detour. Did you sign us up for anything?"

"Yes, the tour leaves at ten. We'll be back by twelve-thirty in time for lunch. Afterwards, we can drive over to Craggy Peak."

"Sounds like a plan." She proceeded to change into sneakers, while Dalton donned a baseball cap and sunglasses. Since it was already heating up outside, she'd leave her sweater behind. "By the way, I was passing by the laundry room when I heard a crash inside. A housekeeper had dropped a pottery bowl that smashed on the ground. I helped her pick up the pieces since she seemed upset, and we got to chatting."

"Naturally," Dalton said in a wry tone.

"Juanita's boyfriend is the wrangler, Jesse. She said Jesse knew Garrett Long and was disturbed by his death. I wasn't able to question her further as she clammed up at that point, and I didn't want to appear too nosy."

"So that confirms what we've already suspected. Jesse and the deceased were acquainted, and it goes beyond Jesse saddling Garrett's horse when he went riding with Uncle Ray."

"I wish I could have learned more. The

tragic loss of a guest, even a friend of the owner, isn't enough reason to go stomping off the way Jesse did yesterday."

"Maybe this housekeeper will tell you more if you run into her again."

Aware they couldn't solve anything at the moment, she gestured to him. "Let's go."

By the time they finished their hike, she was starving. They ate lunch in the dining hall, the bounteous buffet making her glad they'd exercised earlier. At one o'clock, the temperature had risen into the eighties, and she felt as though she'd worked out all day. Fortunately, two cups of coffee revived her, so she got her second wind.

Dalton drove their loaner SUV up the mountain toward Craggy Peak after getting directions from Janice at the front desk. Neither one of them had run into Wayne so far that day. He must have had business elsewhere. Marla wasn't sure she wanted to spend another awkward evening in the family's company so soon after the last one, but she didn't mention it to Dalton. Dinner was later. They had enough to do to occupy themselves for now.

After a climb where her ears popped, they arrived at the construction site. Hammering and drilling noises sounded as they parked their car on a gravelly swale. At this elevation, evergreens, tall brown grasses, and yellow wildflowers provided a splash of color against the rocky landscape. Panoramic vistas with mountain views showed from every angle, while wispy clouds graced a brilliant blue sky. A breeze blew hair into her face as she stepped from the car.

Walking uphill as they headed toward the noise made her short of breath. Where she lived in South Florida, stair climbing was rare and slopes non-existent. The only exercise she got at an incline was climbing the escalator in the shopping mall.

"This must be the main street." Dalton halted to survey the road where it rose to the base of a higher mountain and veered around a bend. Wood-framed structures in various states of disrepair mixed with brick buildings along the avenue. Electric wires strung overhead brought a sense of modernity to the scene, as did the construction equipment from the work crew. Posts along the wood-planked sidewalks remained for tying horses, a remnant from the bygone era.

The sinewy laborers glanced at the new arrivals and then went back to work. Marla hoped they spoke English as she and Dalton approached one fellow applying a coat of paint to window trim. She sidestepped past a ladder on the walkway and tools on the ground.

"Where can we find Raymond Campbell?" Dalton asked, hooking a thumb into his belt. He wore a navy sport shirt tucked into jeans and ankle-high boots.

The guy muttered something in Spanish and then wagged his finger toward a two-story stone structure. A sign hanging over its entrance delineated it the Silver Bar Saloon. They headed in through a set of beautiful glass-paneled doors.

Raymond stood inside, conferring with a worker wearing a cowboy hat and a frown. Their relative's eyes brightened upon spying them.

"What a surprise! You guys, come and meet Alberto Gomez. He's my foreman. Al, this is my nephew, Dalton, and his wife, Marla."

They shook hands, the foreman bobbing his head and giving them a broad smile.

"Nice to meet you," he said in accented English.

"Look at this place. Isn't it magnificent?" Raymond swept his hand in a broad gesture.

Marla did a full turn and took in the gleaming wood bar, the huge mirrors, and the decorative hanging lamps. Painted portraits adorned the walls.

"It's lovely," she said. "You've done a great job."

"The copper mine was discovered in 1889. Back in its heyday, the town held one hundred and eight registered saloons. Many of them were lost to fires. This one is my showpiece because the original bar still stands. She's a beauty, isn't she? Once our renovations are finished, I'll lease these buildings. We'll have shops and restaurants, maybe a museum or two."

"Too bad there isn't a historical society to support your efforts."

Raymond raked his fingers through his short, white hair. "Garrett tried to raise interest, but people cited their economic problems as a deterrent, plus their lack of time to volunteer. They didn't have the foresight to see what a boon this attraction will be to the local economy. Meanwhile, we're providing jobs and paying taxes. Once we bring in merchants, the revenue will increase. Folks at Rustler Ridge are too narrow-minded to see beyond their noses."

"It's a shame they're not more encouraging. They should realize that when the attraction opens and tourists arrive, it'll bring more people into town."

"They're looking out for their own self-interest. They should have been more like

Garrett. He was proud of the region's history and recognized the value of these old buildings."

Marla shifted feet. Too bad the restored saloon didn't have any tables and chairs. "What happened to shut things down? Did the copper mine run out of ore?"

"Nope, copper prices dropped. It wasn't profitable anymore, so the owners closed the operation. There wasn't any point to the miners and their families sticking around. Come on, I'll show you more. I'm glad you decided to visit." He turned to Alberto, who'd stood by looking politely interested. "Go ahead and order those awnings. I don't care what they cost. The originals are too decrepit. And don't worry, I'm sure news of Eduardo will surface eventually."

"Is he the man who went missing?" Dalton said after the foreman left.

"Yep. I think he walked off the job, but his friends insist he saw a ghost and followed it up the hill. This is a ghost town, after all. It comes with its own share of stories, and most of these guys believe them."

"I can understand why." Marla glanced around, soaking in the atmosphere. Dust clogged her nostrils, sensitive from the dry air. "Any ghosts associated with this saloon?"

"Supposedly, three spirits haunt this establishment. We've had reports of a guy in a cowboy hat spotted by the restrooms. And a woman in a white dress with long hair appears in photos but not in person. Rumor has it they're guarding a stash of cash that they hid in the basement after a robbery. I've searched the place, and there's nothing down there except old wine barrels."

"Who's the third ghost?"

"He was a fellow who got shot while drinking whiskey at the bar. Nearly all of our buildings have stories associated with them, and not only the courthouse with the gallows out back."

"Did you search these structures for your missing workman?" Dalton asked.

"Hell, yes. He isn't anywhere to be found."

"I presume you'll hold nightly ghost tours once things are operational?" Marla took a few steps toward the door, eager to see some of the other buildings. It was gloomy in there with a heavy miasma. Or maybe the ghostly tales were affecting her.

"Of course. Once you see what's at stake, you'll agree this project is worthwhile. The town is a historic treasure to be preserved. Our construction cannot possibly be responsible for the dry conditions affecting Hugh Donovan's ranch."

"Where is his place from here?" Dalton asked when they'd emerged outside.

Raymond pointed to the top of the hill. "If you go that way, the road curves around the mountain, and then you're in his territory. He's just looking for an excuse to shut me down."

"You've been having your own problems on the project, I understand. What's been happening?"

"We've had scaffolding collapse, graffiti sprayed across newly painted walls, equipment misplaced. The workers say we've disturbed the spirits, and they're causing the incidents. Watch where you drive, because nails and broken glass have appeared on the road on more than one occasion."

He led them a few doors down, while Marla wondered who could be the saboteur. And what was his purpose? To scare the laborers off the job? To cause delays? Or maybe Raymond was jinxing himself to raise credibility for his ghost stories.

"Here's the Neville Hotel." Raymond pointed out a four-story structure. "Originally built in 1898, it burnt down in a fire and was reconstructed in brick. Upstairs were rooms for up to forty guests. And that concrete building next door is a former bank. See the apothecary shop across the street? I'd like to have a soda fountain come in there when it's finished."

Marla gawked at the sights. It was an ambitious project but definitely worth the effort to save this wondrous history. Her imagination conjured tea parlors and quaint cafés among the proposed shops, hotels, and museums.

"What about brothels?" Dalton asked with a raised eyebrow. "Prostitution was as big in those days as gambling."

"On the next street over are the pleasure palaces with their cribs," Raymond replied. "A crib is the bedroom where women entertained their guests. One of them, Maddy Terrence, did so well she bought herself a saloon and hung naked pictures of herself on the walls. Here's the old theatre. Do you want to come inside? It's pretty well preserved and is said to be haunted."

"Can I take pictures?" Marla remembered she'd brought her camera. At Raymond's nod, she fetched it from her purse and began snapping shots of the various buildings and the mountain views beyond. A few steps away, she viewed the whole valley laid out below.

She followed the men inside the ancient

theatre, which consisted of a hardwood floor, a stage at the far end, and box seats on either side at an upper level. The dingy chandelier didn't make for good lighting, but maybe an apparition would show when she put her photos online. She snapped away, more interested in the area behind the stage.

"The theatre is two stories with a basement," Raymond said, gingerly sidestepping a broken chair in their path. "It held a saloon and gambling hall as well as the stage and balcony seating. The place was popular and kept its doors open until the mine closed."

The floor creaked as they proceeded behind the scenes. Relics and odd pieces of furniture littered the open space. Marla tilted her head. Was that whispering she heard?

Downstairs, they moved on to a combination bar and gambling den. Here were dressing rooms for the performers, a bedroom, and a lavatory. Marla smelled perfume as she peered into the bedroom that retained its old furnishings. A mannequin lay on the bed, lending a note of authenticity with its period dress.

"Why is the place supposed to be

haunted?" she said. "Did someone die here?"

A movement in her peripheral vision made her shoot a second glance at the bedroom. The hairs on her nape elevated. Where before she'd seen a figure, now the bed was empty.

She swallowed with unease but had enough presence of mind to snap pictures. Her imagination must be running wild.

Raymond regarded her and stroked his jaw. "Well now, there's the tale about the two women who liked the same man, gambler Billy McLean. One evening, his girlfriend pulled a knife on the hussy chiseling in on her guy. Delilah died right here over a gaming table. Then we have the man who was shot to death in his box seat. Some folks claim they've seen his ghost still sitting there. Another guy committed suicide after losing his fortune at cards."

"What's in that crawl space underneath the stage?" Dalton indicated an opening that led off into the dark.

"Old furniture and other items were discarded there and left behind. We'll go through them eventually to see if any of it can be restored. Come, let's go back upstairs."

Marla accompanied them, eager to leave

the premises. While the history fascinated her, this place creeped her out. She still wondered about that figure on the bed.

Raymond halted in the middle of the main floor facing the stage. "I've had a hard time getting the workers to come in here. They've reported hearing footsteps, finding items moved from one spot to another, their work being undone. They'll nail a section one day, and when they return, the nails are popped out. They might believe spirits are to blame, but I know better."

"What are their beliefs about the afterlife?" Marla asked, curious. She'd heard of the Day of the Dead where Mexicans revered their ancestors, but did they believe in actual ghosts?

"In the old days, people believed they were partners of the gods, chosen to nourish them. The energy residing in their hearts and blood, the *teyolia* or soul, sustained these deities. This is why the Aztecs held human sacrifices, to feed the gods the energy they needed to survive. After death, a person's *teyolia* fled to the world of the dead, known as the sky of the sun."

"So they don't believe in heaven or hell?" Living in Florida, Marla knew more about the Cuban culture, but even then her knowledge was pitifully inadequate.

"Not in the sense that we do. Souls exist after death, waiting for the one day each year when they can return home to be with their loved ones," Raymond explained. "Then there's La Catrina, a goddess of death. She's represented in Day of the Dead figures that look like female skeletons dressed in finery. People buy them as sculptures made from native materials. I don't encourage these practices among my crew. Superstition doesn't serve any useful purpose."

"So do the workmen believe this goddess called to the man who disappeared? He saw her apparition on the hill and went for a look?"

"That's correct. They think La Catrina summoned him to glory. I took a look around there myself and came up empty. These ghost stories are good for publicity, but they're not real."

"The only thing we have to fear is other people, not spirits." Dalton's statement put them firmly back on the ground.

Marla glanced up as a shadow flickered in her peripheral vision. Was someone in the rafters?

A rattling noise sounded right before the chandelier descended from above.

CHAPTER FOUR

Dalton flung her to the ground and shielded her with his body as the chandelier crashed to the floor with a huge clang and the sound of shattering glass. Clouds of dust and slivers of crystal billowed into the air.

"Uncle Ray, are you all right?" he called once the debris had settled.

"I'm still here. Are you guys okay?"

Marla, crushed under her husband, wriggled free. "We're fine. Aren't we?" She brushed off her clothes after Dalton helped her to stand. Her body trembled. She folded her arms across her chest while her racing heart calmed.

"That was close," Dalton said, his face somber.

His gaze scanned the catwalks, as did Marla's. She didn't discern anything unusual. Had she imagined the shadow before? Or the hint of laughter in her ears now?

Historic theatres would never again hold

the same appeal for her.

Raymond's eyes blazed behind his spectacles. "This wasn't any accident. We could have been killed."

"I should go up there and take a look around." Dalton turned to Marla. "Why don't you wait outside? It's not safe in here."

"All right, but please be careful." She couldn't leave this place too soon in her opinion.

Waiting on the street, she considered who might have been following their movements. Somebody had noticed them entering the old theatre and had taken advantage of the opportunity to cause harm. Had it been a member of Raymond's crew or someone else?

"How well do you know your workers?" she asked Raymond when he and Dalton had rejoined her. Dalton's negative shake of the head indicated his mission hadn't proven fruitful.

"We're on passable terms. I wouldn't say I know each guy personally."

"Did you hire them yourself?"

"I brought in Gomez. He vetted the applicants. Don't worry, they're legal. They each had to show their documents, and I had my lawyer verify them. We wouldn't risk skirting the law."

"By *we*, you mean yourself and Gomez?"

Raymond's gaze shuttered. "That's right."

Somehow she didn't think he'd meant his foreman.

Drilling noises impacted her ears. Marla inhaled a deep breath of earth-scented mountain air to restore her equilibrium.

Raymond gestured expansively. "Let me show you the hearse before you go. We discovered it intact, and it only needed a bit of polish." He led them down the street at a fairly steep decline.

A hearse. Oh, joy. They'd nearly ended up in one.

Along the way, Marla put on her sunglasses. Curiosity propelled her thoughts away from their near-miss and back to their surroundings.

"Did people leave here gradually or in a hurry?" she asked, wondering if residents had lingered after the mining operation shut down.

"When the mine closed, there wasn't any point in other folks staying. The miners would have gone elsewhere searching for jobs. That meant fewer people were around to buy goods and services from the merchants and tradespeople, and so they left, too. These towns could be deserted rather fast."

"What about their furniture and other goods?" Possibly the buildings hid a treasure trove of antiques.

"Most of the items we've found are in disrepair and not worth restoring."

It was sad how these old settlements had died. The settings were so picturesque. Marla could imagine an art colony loving a place like this set among the hills.

"Where did the miners live?" She stepped around a wooden electric pole that looked about to teeter over.

"The company built houses and rented them to the miners and their families. Single men often shared a place together. Since they worked twelve-hour shifts, they weren't all home at the same time. The houses were shotgun style. You could see in through the front door straight back to the rear."

"And these places are abandoned now?"

"That's right." He pointed down a narrow lane, where dilapidated wood-framed structures lined the worn road. "I don't have any plans to restore them at this time. Maybe later I'll consider it, if there's interest from people wanting to move here, but we'll see how it goes."

"Where was the ore refined?" Dalton asked as they descended a steep set of stairs to a lower level. "Was there a smelter, or was it shipped by rail elsewhere?"

"The ore went to a stamping mill further up on the mountain and toward the other side. A narrow gauge railway ran from there to the main line. This train brought in supplies and transported the processed minerals to other locations. Now a water bottling company owns the property and operates a facility where the refinery used to stand."

"Is anything left of the train tracks?"

"Nah, they got sold to Mexico. I imagine the depot is long gone by now. You can drive along the old rail bed, but it's supposed to be a harrowing ride with dangerous curves and steep drops. Look, here's the horse-drawn hearse."

Marla's glance flitted over the shiny black vehicle, but then her attention shifted to a two-story house beyond. It looked fancier than other buildings with fresh white paint and red trim and a balcony with carved wood posts.

"What's that place?" she asked.

Raymond's eyes crinkled in bemusement. "That's where the better known prostitutes entertained their guests. Some of those ladies even married their regulars. I didn't show you the dance hall another street over, but it was a popular place. In the rear were rooms where dancers offered private entertainments."

"I imagine that drinking, whoring, and gambling must have been the main amusements for off-duty miners," Dalton remarked in a wry tone.

"You're probably right." Marla glanced at the greenery between the buildings. "I'm surprised by how many taller trees grow this far up the mountain."

"We have juniper, cypress, pinyon pines, and scrub oaks. It's not like down on the ranch where vegetation is more sparse," Raymond said.

Following him uphill again, Marla thought how pleasant it would be to stroll here when the restoration was complete. Her heart thumped in excitement as she glimpsed his vision for the future.

He stopped before a sturdy two-story stone house with brown dirt for a yard. "This is where the mayor lived. The tale goes that he fancied Doris McFee, who sang nightly at the Fat Hog Saloon. Doris had a beloved reputation around town because she visited the sick and brought food to the poor. When the mayor took ill, she moved into his house to care for him. One night, a man who had a grudge against the mayor attempted to shoot him. He killed Doris instead."

"That's terrible." Marla wondered how many people died from gunshot wounds in the mining camp compared to death by disease or other means.

"Where was the mine entrance?" Dalton asked.

"If you follow the road around the mountain, it's uphill from there. The main shaft has long since been sealed."

"Will you run shuttles from the dude ranch up here for visitors?"

Raymond matched his long-legged stride. "That's the plan. I'm hoping somebody will open a bed-and-breakfast place in town. I have a house in mind to renovate for that purpose. Plus we'll lease the hotel once it's restored."

"That would take business away from Last Trail. Isn't your point to raise revenue to balance out the slow season?"

"People who want the dude ranch experience can stay there. It'll be a win-win for our bottom line either way. Now if you'll excuse me, I'd better have a talk with Alberto about that falling chandelier. Feel free to stroll around. And if you get any exciting ideas about what might look good, be sure to tell me."

"Will we see you at dinner?" Marla would love to hear more stories about the region's past. She couldn't imagine life as a miner. And it wasn't one relegated to the history books, either. Dangerous mining conditions still existed around the world, whether for coal or diamonds or other materials. The role of women in the earlier century fascinated her, too. Aside from the red-light district, did women fill any other positions in town besides pioneer wife?

"I'll probably be here late, so I may grab something to eat on my way into town later. Over by the highway are a few fast food places. Listen, let me know if you guys need anything, you hear? Meanwhile, enjoy your stay on the ranch. Have you been riding yet?"

"We'll get to it." Dalton gave him a clap on the shoulder. "Good luck with this project. I'm impressed by how much you've accomplished so far."

"Thanks, son. See you later."

Marla faced her husband in the empty street after they were left alone. "So do you want to explore the hillside or head back to the ranch?"

"Let's take a look at the hill as long as we're in the area. We might see something the others missed in regards to the worker who vanished. I don't think the sheriff would have investigated since they haven't officially declared the guy as missing."

Her breath came short as she climbed the steep stairs to the main level. "Man, I need to get in shape."

"You're not used to this altitude. The air is thinner here."

"That's true." She trudged toward the hill at the far end of Harrison Street, the main road through town. Sounds of hammering mingled with the whine of drills and the steady thumping noise of heavier construction. Dust filled her nostrils and covered her sneakers.

They passed an open lot holding various relics — a stone statue of a monk, an old bathtub, rusty wagon wheels, and more. A breeze rustled leaves on nearby shade trees.

"If Eduardo saw something he interpreted as an apparition, it might have been situated up there." Dalton pointed to a summit looming over the town to their left. "We'll have to find a way across to that location."

Marla slung her purse strap diagonally over one shoulder, wishing she'd locked her bag in their car. Her walking shoes crunched on a pile of stones as she took her first steps off the road and up a slight rise. A higher stretch forced her to reach upwards and clamber onto a higher rock, her fingers gripping its cool surface. At least this slope was fairly gentle, with small rock ledges for hand and footholds.

After maneuvering across several flat-topped boulders that rose in ridges, she found an easier gravel path to follow. Dodging bushes and boulders, she gasped and huffed her way upward. Cactus didn't grow at this elevation, but other shrubs and a few scraggly trees mingled with evergreens. By her standards, they were sparsely scattered among the red dirt and rocks, and they provided little shelter from the blazing sun.

She paused to adjust her sunglasses, thinking she should add a wide-brimmed hat to her shopping list. She'd forgotten to pack one of her sun hats from Florida.

"Watch out for rattlesnakes," Dalton said with a teasing grin. He took the lead, and she followed his broad back on their make-shift trail.

"Oh, joy. I suppose scorpions can be hiding under these rocks as well." Despite the sweat breaking out on her brow and her heavy breathing, she was enjoying the exercise. "We should have brought snacks and water bottles in a backpack."

"You're right. Remember it for next time."

Her skin felt dry, and her hairs stood out from static electricity. Missing Florida's humidity, Marla breathed through her nose to minimize moisture loss.

She halted at the top of a rise. Small bushes dotted the terrain but not much else. Two hills rose on either side of them. She guessed they should stay to the left toward the town. If Eduardo, the guy who'd vanished, had seen something on the hillside, it might have been from there as Dalton had suggested.

Unfortunately, the slope on that side consisted of solid chunks of rocks. They had to climb further, helping each other over one rise after another.

"Ow," she said, banging her toe on her last attempt as she half-crawled over a boulder.

"We're almost there." Dalton surveyed the territory ahead. "This isn't getting any easier. Who knows what could be hiding up here? They have coyotes and mountain lions in these parts."

"How nice of you to share that information. Hey, pick up that dead branch. You can use it to stir the dirt and chase any snakes away."

They roamed the area, peering at the town below and the mountainous vistas surrounding them. Marla took photos, but that's all they came away with other than a few scrapes and bruises. They didn't find any clues as to where Eduardo might have gone.

As she headed back, Marla stumbled over a pile of rubble. A cold wind seemed to grab her, whistling in her ears. It smelled faintly like rust. She cast a nervous gaze around but saw nothing except rocks intermingled with various shrubs and interspersed with boulders.

Maybe a ghostly presence was making itself known. She seemed to attract them, remembering the playful spirit in the elevator at Sugar Crest Plantation Resort on Florida's west coast. Never mind the spirits in the old theatre below. She hurried away, pausing on a swath of gravel to admire the valley stretched out before them and the town nestled in its crease.

At the horizon rose another mountain range in murky tones of blue. White wildflowers sprinkled the ground where she'd stopped. Overhead, cirrus clouds drifted across the azure sky.

A sense of peace and tranquility invaded her. But all wasn't as calm as it seemed. Secrets buried in these hills might prove deadly if the forest ranger's death turned out to be more than an accident.

"Let's head back to the ranch," she said, resuming their descent to Craggy Peak. "I'd like to relax this afternoon. We can go into town tomorrow to buy supplies."

"All right. I might sign up for a morning ride. Do you want to give it a try?"

"I'll need to take a lesson first. Maybe I should ask for a pony. I'm not thrilled about getting on a big, powerful horse."

"Why not? You ride me, don't you?"

His sexy grin lifted her spirits. "Come on, I'll beat you downhill."

Marla was glad to take a breather at the ranch, but she couldn't rest for long. She'd promised Dalton to meet him in the Jail House Saloon after he signed them both up for activities tomorrow morning with the wranglers.

The lounge must have just opened, because when she peeked inside, no one else greeted her except for the bartender. A pretty girl with her hair pinned atop her head, she was busy polishing glassware behind a gleaming wood bar that took up an entire wall. Marla turned away, quietly shut the door and went to find her husband. He might be down by the corrals.

Her nose wrinkled as she got closer to the horses. The cowhands must get used to the smell, she thought with a moue of displeasure. Horses in all colors roamed the fenced enclosure to her right. She marveled at the powerful beasts before moving on to the main staging building.

Swatting away a fly, she studied its four closed doors. She doubted he'd gone into the Staff Only entry. That left the Wrangler's Roost, Riders Entrance, or Game Room. Feeling like a player in a video game picking which door held the treasure, she chose the Riders Entrance.

Inside was a tiled room with a couch facing a television console, armchairs, and a coffee table. This must be where guests waited before riding lessons. As no one was there, she tried the game room next. It held a ping pong table, billiards, and table hockey but no people at the moment. As for the Wrangler's Roost, the door was locked.

Could Dalton have entered the staff's private enclave? She peeked inside a long hallway with saddles and riding helmets hung on the walls. It was open at the far end.

Wondering if he'd be around back, she crunched along the gravel at the building's side. Horses ranged inside the corral there, and she saw a wrangler whom she hadn't met, but her husband's tall figure was nowhere in sight.

Great, now what? Maybe Dalton had

taken a different route to the Jail House Saloon. She spied a dirt path leading in that direction. It passed the tennis courts on one side and the rear of the reception hall on the other. The hum of an air-conditioning unit and an occasional horse whinny broke the stillness as she headed that way.

It was pleasant out with the temperature reaching eighty. A maintenance guy strode past, identified by his logo baseball cap and the large radio hooked on his belt. They nodded greetings to each other. Bird twitters and a trickling fountain tempted her to explore a nearby butterfly garden, but she'd spotted two figures up ahead beside a pine tree in a secluded nook. A black horse was tied nearby.

As she neared, she observed a familiar figure, but it wasn't Dalton. Their conversation reached her as she trod closer, careful to keep her presence hidden. Sure enough, the bearded man was Jesse, the wrangler.

"Raymond can't blame the Donovans for everything," the other guy said. He had a lean frame and a height over six feet. From what she could see of his face under his hat, she'd place him in his thirties. "We're not responsible. When are you going to step in and show your hand?"

"I need more information first. Did you

talk to the old man?"

"You know how he feels about things. Why don't you pay him a visit?"

"It's not a good idea."

"That's what you always say. If you keep playing this game, you'll get exposed."

"I'll take that risk. Once I have proof, I'll come out in the open."

Were they discussing Hugh Donovan? What did that other guy mean by saying, *we're not responsible?* Did he come from their ranch? What was Jesse doing talking to someone from there, anyway? And what kind of proof did he need?

She moved off before they could spot her and ducked in between two buildings toward the main path. Lost in thought, she almost collided with Dalton coming the opposite way.

"Here you are." She grasped his arm. "I was looking for you."

"The receptionist was in a chatty mood when I went to sign us up for morning activities. I got delayed. Let's head for the bar. I could use a drink, and I have news to share."

He held the saloon door open for her. "Do you want to sit inside or out on the terrace?" A covered patio held tables and chairs with a lovely view of the mountains. Other guests had already claimed seats there.

"Let's stay indoors. We can talk in that quiet corner by the fireplace."

She waited until they got seated and ordered their drinks. Meanwhile, she scanned the Indian paintings on the walls, the billiards table in another corner, the mannequin of a Mexican in a sombrero sitting in a chair, and the family with three kids who were the only other occupants. Country music played in the background.

The smell of popcorn drifted from a machine near the entrance. It was free to guests, but she'd rather wait for dinner. However, she did dip her fingers into the carafe of spicy snack mix the bartender brought along with their drinks.

She related the conversation she'd overheard between Jesse and the other guy.

"So you think he's colluding with someone from the Donovan ranch?" Dalton said, gripping his ale glass. A brooding expression crossed his face.

Marla took a sip of Chardonnay. "That's how it sounded. Clearly there's more to Jesse than meets the eye. Maybe his name is as false as his hair color."

"I'll see if I can get Wayne to tell me more about him."

"You might not have to bother." She

signaled the lady bartender. "Hi, can you answer a few questions for me? I have a lesson tomorrow with Jesse Parker. Do you know him?"

The brunette's eyes twinkled. "Sure do. He's a hunk, but don't tell him I said so."

"How long has he been working here?" she asked, even though she knew the answer.

"Five years, I believe. The guy knows his business, better than some of the older wranglers. He must have been brought up on a ranch."

"You think so? Where is he from, Patty?" Marla had read the girl's name tag.

"Dunno. He doesn't talk much about himself, but I imagine he put that info on his job application. He's qualified to teach you, if that's what you're wondering."

"Where does the fellow live?" Dalton picked out a few cashews from the carafe. "I gather most of the employees don't reside on the ranch."

"Most of us live in town." Patty sank into an empty seat at their table. "You might want to ask Juanita. He's sweet on her."

"Oh? I thought it was the other way around." Marla watched for her reaction.

"Jesse tries not to show it, but you can see how they feel about each other whenever they sneak a moment together. I notice things from the patio."

"Did you spot him out there earlier talking to a stranger?"

"Sorry, I was busy getting the bar set up for the evening."

Realizing this discussion was a dead end, Marla tried another tack. Dalton seemed content to let her take the lead. "Some people are saying this place is jinxed, like the ghost town up the mountain. Have you had any unusual incidents in the saloon?"

Her lips pursed. "Huh. I came in one morning, and a keg had emptied all over the floor. I guess you can count that as unusual. I figured I'd left the spigot open by mistake, but I always double check everything before closing each evening."

"Were the doors locked when you came to work?"

"Yes, they were. Why, do you think somebody may have broken in here and opened the keg? But then they must have used a key."

Dalton gave Marla an oblique glance. "Don't your maintenance men have master keys to use in case of emergencies?"

"Well, yes, but —"

"So if there's a saboteur around, he could get in anywhere," Marla concluded, not liking the implications. So far the incidents had been merely mischievous. What would happen if things escalated? And what was the guy's purpose — to chase guests away or to annoy the staff?

"Did you hear about the flood in the dining room? Something similar happened, only it was a water heater valve that opened seemingly by itself," Dalton informed Patty. "Do you think someone might be causing trouble on purpose?"

As more customers entered, Patty rose. "Don't ask me. I haven't got a clue."

"Thanks for talking to us," Marla called as she strode away to seat the newcomers.

"It seems as though someone is methodically going around and causing mischief," Dalton remarked, popping more nuts into his mouth.

"If you're counting the ghost town, I wouldn't call our near-miss in the theatre a minor incident. We could have been seriously hurt."

"You're right. Janice the receptionist said there hasn't been anyone new on the ranch staff in the past year. People like working here and hang onto their jobs. And everyone seems to like Wayne and Carol, so a personal grudge against one of them appears unlikely."

"Raymond owns both properties. It's

more likely he's the target. Do you think he's right in blaming the other rancher?"

"Didn't you just overhear Jesse saying the Donovans aren't at fault?"

"How would Jesse know, unless he has reason to suspect someone else? Anyway, I'm basing my theories on supposition. And how does Raymond's relationship to the dead forest ranger fit into this picture?"

"Those are all valid questions."

Then how about this one, Marla thought but didn't voice aloud. *Why hasn't your uncle once mentioned your mother, Kate? What happened between them that he wouldn't attend our wedding?*

CHAPTER FIVE

Solving crimes was easier than getting on a horse, Marla discovered early Tuesday morning at her first riding lesson. Dalton had taken off at seven-fifteen for the breakfast ride, leaving her to enjoy the buffet alone until her nine o'clock engagement. She hadn't realized so many choices in horsemanship were offered to guests. Loping, walking, and intermediate rides or lessons were available as well as grooming fundamentals and team penning.

Wearing jeans, sneakers, and a long-sleeved top for the chillier morning air, she entered the door marked Riders Entrance and took a seat until a wrangler came to get her. Inside, the air-conditioning unit hummed as she waited with several other victims who seemed to know each other and stood around in clusters. She sat wringing her hands and wishing she'd signed up for a massage instead. She'd only agreed to this activity so she could start accompanying Dalton on the gentler rides.

"Don't you have a pony for me?" she asked the wrangler who'd summoned her. She had been fabricating when she'd told the bartender her lesson was with Jesse. This guy's name was Tom Mallory. Outside, she eyed the brown creature he'd selected with trepidation, while other horses snorted and whinnied in the corral. "This horse is too spirited."

"Nah, you'll do fine. Candy is real gentle. Put on this helmet and then place your foot right here." He showed her how to get on the horse.

Marla mounted with his assistance and sat there, wondering what she should do next. Tom explained the different parts of the saddle and some basic horse lore. Then he led her around the corral while she grew accustomed to her seat. It took a while to get the hang of pressing in with her thighs as he taught her. She suspected she'd be sore after being locked into this position. Muscles that she didn't normally use were getting a workout.

By the end of the hour, she was able to trot around the fenced enclosure if not with ease, at least with more confidence. She could probably handle a walking ride but needed more lessons to feel comfortable going faster.

"How long have you been working here?" she asked Tom during one of their rounds. She patted the horse, pleased with Candy's tolerance of her mistakes. The horse nickered in response, as though approving of her awkward efforts.

"I've been here nearly seventeen years now. Hard to believe it's been that long." He stroked his grizzled jaw, squinting under his cowboy hat as he walked beside her horse, letting her handle the reins.

"Have you seen many changes in that time?" She glanced at the mountains in the distance from behind her sunglasses. Saguaro cacti dotted the landscape like aged sentinels on guard.

"Sure have, ma'am. Raymond brought us into the technical age and raised our visibility on the global networks. Guests from around the world come here now. Plus, he improved on the expansion his daddy started."

"Did you see him more often before he got involved with his ghost town project?"

"Raymond was never one to micro-manage, if you know what I mean. Wayne and Carol take a personal interest in everybody and make us feel like family. Raymond did too, but more from a distance. He was a stickler for safety rules, but that's to be expected after the tragedy their family experienced."

Her ears perked up. "What happened?"

"You don't know?" His brows lifted in surprise. "I suggest you ask your cousin for the particulars. It's not my place to say. Most of them keep mum about it, and I don't blame them. Why dredge up old hurts?"

Because it might help to explain why Kate doesn't speak to her brother, Marla thought. She wouldn't ask Carol. Marla had promised to visit Wayne's sister at her nutrition clinic. Annie might know about the events affecting her parents' generation.

Thus when she and Dalton drove into town, they split up. Marla had called ahead to verify that Annie would be free for lunch, so Dalton dropped her off and set a time to meet her later. He wanted to stop by the sheriff's office while she was occupied.

Stiff and sore from her morning exertion, Marla gave her name to the receptionist inside the tan adobe building. Did Annie own the property or lease it? The waiting area appeared to be well maintained. It held comfortable jade upholstered chairs, a filled magazine rack, a coffee table, and a water cooler. The tile floor appeared spotless.

A blonde behind a glass partition glanced up at her arrival and smiled. "Hello, can I help you? Do you have an appointment?"

"My name is Marla Vail, and I'm here to see Annie. She's my cousin by marriage. We have a lunch date."

The receptionist's expression softened. "I'll let her know you're here."

Marla took a seat until the inner door burst open, and Annie gestured for her to enter. As she crossed the threshold, a young girl was checking out at the billing desk.

"Chris, I'll see you next time," Annie said. "Call me if anything comes up before then."

Figuring this teen must be one of Annie's patients, Marla's gaze inadvertently lifted to her straight brown hair hanging down her back. The ends could use a trim, plus highlights would bring out the color in her hazel eyes.

"By the way, this is my cousin's wife. They're visiting us from back east. Marla Vail, meet Christine Reardon," Annie said.

"Nice to meet you." Marla smiled at the girl, whose stick-thin figure could use a few pounds. "We're staying at the dude ranch. I had my first horseback riding lesson this morning. So if I walk funny, you'll know why," she said with a chuckle.

"Have a good vacation. I'm sure Annie is happy you're visiting."

Annie led Marla down a corridor. She wore her hair in a ponytail and a white lab coat over her street clothes.

"This place isn't very big. I don't need treatment rooms, but I do show videos to my patients in that cubicle over there, and we have a kitchenette and laundry area. This is one of the former historic houses in town. I was allowed to convert the inside but not the exterior design."

"Do you own it or rent the premises?"

"I lease the space. I'd worked for a doctor's group before branching out on my own. I love being independent. I had built up my clientele along the way, so they followed me here. Rumor says an urgent care center is going to be built over by the drugstore at the highway exit. I might offer them my services for extra income."

In such a small town, Marla wondered how she stayed afloat at all. "What's wrong with that girl who just left? She looked healthy, albeit a bit too thin."

"Let's sit a minute, and I'll tell you. Here's my office where I interview patients and discuss treatment plans," Annie said, gesturing inside. "We can go to lunch at noon."

Annie sat behind her large mahogany desk

while Marla took a seat opposite in a cozy armchair no doubt meant to encourage confidences. She sniffed the eucalyptus aroma scenting the room and relaxed back on the cushioned seat. It felt good after the morning's exertion.

Annie folded her hands on the desktop. "Chris is suffering from bulimia. Normally I wouldn't betray a client's confidence, but I have a reason in this case. I know you've helped Dalton solve crimes, so you must be good at detective work. I need help getting to the bottom of what's ailing Chris. I'm afraid the source of her problems might relate to our family."

"How so?" Marla knew bulimia was an eating disorder that involved food bingeing followed by purging. It seemed to affect mostly women and teenaged girls. The purging segment could take the form of vomiting, extreme exercise, or using laxatives.

"You know stress can trigger the disorder?" Annie said.

"So can an obsession with being thin." Look at the actresses in movies and the models in magazines. Women's beauty was measured by their weight and their face lifts.

"Christine's mother brought her to see me because the girl was too skinny. I interviewed Eleanor first, and it appeared that

Christine had some of the characteristic symptoms."

"Like what?"

"She'll run into the bathroom right after meals. Even when she should be taking it easy, she forces herself to exercise. Plus she often complains about her figure."

"So do most women."

"Yes, but these patients might hoard food or prefer to eat alone. And they might have swollen cheeks from making themselves heave. It's dangerous to go without treatment. They can get various ailments such as osteoporosis, heart problems and kidney disease."

Marla grimaced. "How do you treat it?"

"Counseling helps, and sometimes anti-depressants are prescribed. Often these people have low self-esteem, but I don't believe that's the case for Christine. From things she's said, I've gathered she is troubled because of her father's frequent absences. According to Eleanor, operations have doubled at the water bottling plant where Tate Reardon is manager. He's been working overtime, even sleeping at the facility some nights."

"Do you think he's having an affair, and Christine senses it?"

"This might be something else entirely.

What if she's aware that something funky is going on at her father's place of work? His facility could be stealing water from the town. That would account for the dry conditions at the Donovan ranch. Mr. Reardon might either be directly involved or acting under orders from his employer. If he's conflicted about his role, he might be transmitting these feelings to Christine."

"Why don't you make an appointment to interview him? You have the perfect reason with his daughter's health at stake."

Annie's mouth compressed. "I was hoping you'd ask around about his facility. Hugh Donovan isn't right to blame my father for the problems he's having with his cattle. In the meantime, I'll make an appointment to talk to Christine's mother again but in their home environment this time. Maybe you'd like to come along for the drive up the mountain?"

"I'd love to, thanks."

As they headed to lunch, Marla inquired about Annie's work. The young woman counseled people with any kind of dietary restriction, allergies, or related disease conditions. It was admirable how she'd established her own clientele.

Marla didn't get around to broaching the subject of Raymond's relationship to his sister, Kate, until they were seated at an outdoor café. She ordered butternut squash ravioli with Portobello mushroom sauce and sat sipping an unsweetened iced tea.

A fly zeroed in on their bread basket. She swatted it away, determined to steer their conversation. Starting with a lighter topic, she shared the hair-raising adventure of her morning riding lesson. Her description made Annie chuckle.

"The soreness will go away once you're used to the saddle. You should ride every day. You'll be surprised by how quickly you catch on." Annie buttered a roll as she spoke, her posture relaxed and a half-smile on her face.

A crumb fell on her patterned shirt. Annie brushed it off, while Marla wondered if she wore a stylish skirt ensemble out of respect for her clients or from personal preference. With nearly everyone in the area wearing jeans and cowboy hats, Marla had become accustomed to the casual western garb.

"You must have started riding when very young. Ranch life would be born and bred in you. How come you didn't want to stay and help Wayne run the place when your father's interests turned elsewhere?"

Annie's brow crinkled. "I wanted to live in the city. I'd had a taste of it in college, and I loved the frenetic lifestyle. But a year in L.A. convinced me to come back home. Plus, I felt I could really help folks here. There weren't that many registered dietitians who counseled people in rural parts like this one. With obesity reaching almost epidemic proportions and diabetes on the rise, nutritional advice is badly needed."

"So you opened your own office after working with a doctor's group?"

"That's right. I had enough clients that I felt I could make it on my own."

"Did you father support your decision?"

"Of course not. He'd rather I take on a role at the ranch. Now he's trying to get me involved in his ghost town. He says with my college education and computer skills, I should design their marketing campaign." She shrugged. "I can help out in my spare time. One thing I'll say about my dad. He keeps up with technology. Dad wired up the ranch as soon as the Internet became available."

"The wrangler, Tom, started working there when your dad ran the daily operations. He gives Raymond credit for publicizing the resort overseas."

"Dad can be very focused. When he's dedicated to a project, he'll go all out and won't let anything stop him."

"Yet I got the impression from Tom that your father's management style was more casual than Wayne's."

Annie's eyes glinted. "My father hired competent people and let them do their thing. Wayne has more of a direct approach. He wants to know what's going on minute-by-minute. It's not because he's obsessive, but because he cares about our employees."

Marla didn't miss her use of the word *our*. Perhaps Annie was more attached to the ranch than she realized.

"We're very grateful that Wayne invited us to spend our honeymoon there."

Annie frowned and gripped her water glass. "Yeah, well, he has an ulterior motive. He's hoping Dalton can delve into these mysterious incidents that have been hap-pening lately."

"Do you feel they're coincidental, or might someone be deliberately causing them?"

"I'm not sure, but I wouldn't be so quick to blame Hugh Donovan. The animosity between him and Dad goes way back. It's easy for Dad to target him when things go wrong."

"Why is that?" Marla leaned back as the waitress delivered their meals. The rich smell of cooked mushrooms made her eager to eat. She picked up her fork.

"I don't know the details, but something nasty happened between them. It's a shame. From early photos I've seen, he and Hugh used to be close friends when they were young."

"I've wondered why your father and Dalton's mother don't speak. Might this have involved Kate as well?"

"It's possible. Dad doesn't talk about it. I just know there's bad blood between him and Hugh Donovan."

"Yes, but it's a shame that he and Kate are estranged."

"I haven't been successful in getting Dad to fess up. Maybe you can coax him to talk."

"Your father isn't the only one casting blame. According to Raymond, Hugh is trying to convince the town council that his renovation project is causing environmental damage. The cattle on his ranch are suffering as a result."

"I told you, look into the water bottling plant on the mountain. It might be the source of his problems."

"I'll do that, thanks." And why was it her business? Because she was part of this family now, and she wanted to see Raymond's tourist attraction succeed. Craggy Peak had a lot of history, and it would be wonderful if people could appreciate its value.

Annie swallowed a piece of her grilled veggie sandwich. "I'm still wondering how Dad was able to purchase the ghost town property without needing a mortgage," she said, voicing one of many thoughts in Marla's head.

"Since the buildings were in such bad shape, he must have gotten a terrific deal."

"You'd think so. Rustler Ridge should have been glad for someone to take that eyesore off their hands." She pointed to the hills. "Look, you can see smoke from the bottling facility. Isn't it odd how it sits there above Hugh's place, which is suffering from dry conditions?"

"Yes, that's true. Who would know about their water rights?"

Annie gestured down the street. "The engineer has an office here. He does the approvals for plant operations, so you could start with him. I'll look up his address, but first you have to buy a pair of boots." And their discussion melded into a shopping talk about which brand to get.

After lunch, Marla shopped with Annie and then phoned Dalton to find out where he'd parked the car. He wasn't ready to meet her yet, so she stashed the packages inside using the extra key he'd given her.

Annie had already returned to work. With time to spare, Marla headed over to the office of the district's environmental engineer.

Matthew Brigham's name was emblazoned on the outside of a brick building further along the main row, where the shops and restaurants gave way to a business section.

Marla stepped into a spacious office holding a desk strewn with papers, a couple of armchairs, file cabinets, and office machinery. Stacks of papers filled the windowsills and other available surfaces. A rectangular table by a wall held blueprint-type documents, but what caught her eye was the model train set occupying one corner.

"How can I help you?" said a man with white hair and a matching beard from behind the desk. He studied her with steely gray eyes under wire-rimmed glasses.

"Are you Matthew Brigham?" At his nod, she approached and held out her hand. "I'm Marla Vail. I have a few questions for a blog article I'm writing, and I wonder if you can help."

He rose and accepted her handshake. "Sure, have a seat."

She didn't give the real reason for her visit, figuring it might not be wise to reveal Annie's suspicions about someone stealing water from the town when this man was responsible for permit inspections. Better to sound him out in a more general manner to see where he stood on environmental issues. Her glance flicked to the photos mounted on the walls. Some of them showed the engineer as a member of a costumed four-man troupe.

She lifted an eyebrow. "Those look pretty recent. Are you a performer?"

"It's a hobby of mine. I sing in a barbershop quartet. We're quite popular during town events." He resumed his seat and grinned, exposing a row of even teeth.

"And I see you're a train enthusiast."

"Don't get me started, ma'am, unless you want to hear about every railroad line that existed in this territory."

"I'm sure the history is quite fascinating. My husband and I are guests at the dude ranch. It's our first visit to Arizona. We've noticed the white smoke on the horizon. Should we be concerned about forest fires?"

He looked at her as though she'd sprouted elk horns. "Certainly not, that's steam coming from the water bottling plant on the mountain. It isn't anything for you to worry about."

"I thought resources were scarce in the west. Where does the plant get its water?"

"Where are you from, Mrs. Vail?"

"South Florida. We have issues with drought in the winters but nothing like you experience."

Hunching forward, he folded his hands on the desk. "Arizona gets its supply from the Colorado River via a system of canals, pipelines, and reservoirs. Plus we have storage basins for groundwater. There's plenty to go around if we don't waste it on lawns like you do."

"This is still a desert. You might have a few lakes but not an abundance of fresh water streams and rivers. The only greenery is cacti plus scattered trees or plants."

"I beg to differ. The Sonoran grows lots of vegetation despite the drier climate. At higher elevations, you'll see evergreens and many tall trees. And we have our monsoon season. Nonetheless, we get enough flow from the Colorado River to supply our population under current conditions."

Putting her purse in her lap, she crossed her legs. "Colorado lets you share their water?"

"The Colorado River Compact of 1922 divided the resource between several states. Once the water arrives, it still has to be distributed. CAP — the Central Arizona Project Canal — uses pipelines to move the water to the far reaches of our state. That can be costly, which is why many of our cities get their water supply from underground aquifers. Groundwater is our cheapest and most available resource."

"But that won't last forever, will it?"

"Population growth is our main problem. Plus, some cities don't have the infrastructure to utilize the CAP water. They can tap into the Salt River Project that uses water from the Salt and Verde Rivers, but ranches and farms compete for those resources."

"So increased demand is causing a shortage?"

He picked up a pen and twirled it. "Yes, along with a strain on city finances."

"I can see how this issue would cause tension."

He snorted. "There's always been competition over water rights. In 1934, Arizona called militia units to the California border to protest the construction of the Parker Dam because it would divert water from the Colorado River. The dispute ended up in court."

"Don't regulations dictate who gets what amounts of water from the river?"

"They do, but California and Arizona had to resolve their differences. Arizona asked the Supreme Court for a decision. The case lasted eleven years and cost nearly five million dollars until it was settled. It set a precedent for future battles between the states over unused portions of their water allocations."

"So you're saying fights over these resources will always occur?"

"Right now there's enough water, but it isn't going to last. As I said, population growth is a problem. So are higher climactic temperatures and diminishing snowfalls in the Rockies. Consider this old refrain: 'Whiskey's for drinking, and water's for fighting.' "

"So environmental changes, in addition to increased demand from more people in the area, are contributing to a potential shortage?"

"You got it. Add in the conservation folks who sue on behalf of endangered species, the Native Americans pursuing water rights, and local communities fighting over groundwater supplies, and you have a volatile mix."

Marla ticked off the problems on her fingers. "Population growth, competition from farmers and ranchers, Native Americans demanding their share, and unfavorable ecological conditions will lead to a depletion of underground aquifers and a financial strain for cities that have to buy more water."

"That's it in a nutshell." The engineer put down his pen and steepled his fingers.

"So with all these strains on local resources, where does the bottling plant get its water?" she said, repeating her original question.

"They lease water rights from the town. The facility obtains its water at the source of a natural mountain spring."

"And who makes sure they aren't taking more than their proper allocation?"

"That's my job. The plant is within its parameters. Why is it a concern of yours, ma'am?"

"The white smoke bothers me. I thought water bottling was a clean industry?"

"I told you, the plume is merely steam. But here comes the owner, so you can ask him yourself." The door opened and a burly fellow strode inside. "Marla Vail, meet Otto Lovelace, owner of Arizona Mountain High Water Company."

The newcomer had a receding dark hairline, penetrating slate eyes, and a double chin. He wore a sleeveless vest over his shirt with a fob watch in its pocket. She stood to shake his hand.

His gaze dipped to her wedding ring. "It is a pleasure, Mrs. Vail." He spoke with an accent she couldn't place.

"You're the man of the hour, Otto. We were just talking about you," Brigham said in a casual tone.

"How so?"

"The lady is interested in water resources in the area. She's questioning your company's compliance with regulations."

Otto shot her a wary glance. "You're not one of those ecology nuts, are you? Because I run my plant properly, and I have the certifications to prove it."

"I don't need you to prove anything, Mr. Lovelace. I'm writing a blog article about my visit to Arizona, and I was curious about the emissions from your factory. I presume your plant has had environmental impact studies?"

"We follow all the legalities. In fact, the reason I'm here is to schedule our next inspection." Otto swept his arm expansively. "Most people consider us a boon to the community. We provide extra jobs and pay our taxes."

Raymond said the same thing about his ghost town.

"Yes, I suppose so."

"You're welcome to visit our facility and see things for yourself." He handed her a card. "Call me or my manager anytime for an appointment. We'd be happy to give you a tour."

"Thanks, I'll do that. I've never visited a bottling plant before, and it could be educational. Now if you'll excuse me, I must be on my way. Thank you both for answering my questions."

Brigham scraped back his chair and rose. "My office is always open in case you need more information."

"You are staying nearby?" Otto asked in a curious tone.

"My husband and I are guests at Last Trail Dude Ranch. We're on our honeymoon, but it's a great opportunity for me to conduct research while we're here. Including regional issues will give added depth to my article."

"Allow me to give you some advice. If you go riding while at the ranch, stick to the proven trails. The territory around here can be treacherous."

CHAPTER SIX

What did Otto mean by his warning? She should watch out for rattlesnakes or ditches if she rode one of the trails, or something more? Did they have flash floods in this area?

Something in his tone told her he hadn't meant environmental hazards.

Silence followed her to the door. Once outside, she peeked in the window and noted the two fellows in a heated discussion. She'd like to be a fly on the wall to hear what they were saying about her. Marla had no doubt she was the topic of their discussion.

Should she have been more subtle? Hopefully, they'd regard her as an annoying tourist. They didn't know about her connection to Raymond or his family.

Speaking of family, it nagged at her that Annie's young patient was affected by her father's job. Anything that bothered Dalton's clan had become her concern. In this case, gaining information about the water bottling company might prove useful.

As she strode down the street in the hot afternoon sun, she wondered if all bottling plants were located near a natural source like Otto's place was, or did they reside in cities and use municipal water? She'd have to research the subject later and maybe take Otto up on his offer to give her a tour. And how come he'd shown up in person to make an appointment with Brigham? He could have phoned or had his manager schedule the inspection.

Her musings fled when she spotted Dalton waiting for her at their designated meeting site. His expression brightened at her approach.

"How was your chat with the sheriff?" she said, warmed by his presence.

"Good. We had lunch together and swapped stories. Did you enjoy your visit with Annie?"

"It was lovely. I like her a lot. She's smart and independent, like me." Marla couldn't help the broad grin on her face. "Where did you eat? You could have joined us."

"Nah, we got burgers at the corner grill, and then I shopped around for a hat. Come, I'll show you the one I picked out."

She followed Dalton to the store and ended up buying a costly hat for herself, along with a western-style blouse, a leather belt, some souvenirs, and a pack of Arizona Mountain High bottled water to keep in their resort suite.

Marla's replay of her conversation in Brigham's office hovered in her throat, but she suppressed telling her husband about it until later. Instead, she addressed the shopkeeper while Dalton paid for their purchases with a credit card.

"I gather this water is bottled right there on the mountain. How awesome. What's the source, a natural spring?" She spoke in a light, breezy tone like a curious tourist.

"Yes, ma'am." The man spoke in a drawl as he gave Dalton the charge slip to sign.

"What else have you heard about the place? Have you met its owner, Otto Lovelace?"

"Oh, sure. Dude comes into town to buy supplies every now and then. He's a strange one. Doesn't say much and keeps an eye on his watch like he's in a hurry to be somewhere else."

"Is that right? Does he come alone or with his family?"

"Ain't got no family from what I heard. He lives in a fancy mansion all by himself on the hilltop yonder." He pointed out the window in the general direction of the bottling plant.

"I ran into him earlier," she said while Dalton stared daggers at her. No doubt he wondered why she hadn't mentioned this tidbit to him. "He says the white smoke is due to steam emissions from his plant. I gather Matthew Brigham, the engineer, has certified the place as clean. Is he the main person in charge of inspections around here?"

"Rightly so. At least, he's the only one who can get near Lovelace's operation." The shopkeeper leaned forward and lowered his voice. "There's some heavy artillery guarding that place. You don't want to go anywhere near it."

"What do you mean?" Dalton said in a sharp tone.

"A couple of hikers got lost on the hillside and met armed guards patrolling the perimeter."

"That seems a bit extreme for a water bottling facility," Marla commented.

"Not really, if you consider what some of those environmental nutcases out there will do. Lovelace is right to be wary of them."

"Why would he be concerned about environmentalists? Have they made a fuss around here?"

The man handed Dalton a receipt. "You can ask the sheriff, ma'am. He's dealt with them a time or two. Maybe Lovelace is afraid they'll blow up his place like those eco-terrorists did in Colorado. Those folks can be fanatical in their beliefs."

They thanked the man and then moseyed on to their SUV to stick their packages inside.

"Now what? Do you want to see the sheriff again to ask him about those armed guards?" Marla said from the sidewalk. "Maybe there's substance to this radical movement angle. Extremists could be involved in the accidents at the ghost town."

Dalton checked the time. "I hate to bother him again, but we're right here."

"By the way, I met the engineer, Matthew Brigham, who does the water plant inspections. At Annie's suggestion, I stopped by his office. We were having a nice talk when Otto Lovelace walked inside." She related their conversations.

"Let's see what Sheriff Beresby has to say on these issues. We didn't talk about Garrett's death. I thought it was best to get to know the sheriff on a personal basis."

Brushing aside Dalton's apology for taking up more of his time, the mustached lawman ushered them into his enclave and bid them take seats.

"Those activists are nothing but trouble," Beresby said from behind his desk, while Marla and Dalton sat opposite him. "Garrett Long had his hands full keeping track of their activities."

"I know you can't say much, but did you get any reports in yet?" Dalton asked.

Beresby gave him a grim nod. "I'm calling it a homicide. Garrett didn't fall off that ledge by himself. He'd know his way around the ridge with a blindfold on. My guess is that someone lured him there and then pushed him."

"Find any evidence at the scene?"

Marla glanced between the men. Why would the sheriff reveal details of an ongoing investigation to two strangers from out of town?

"I looked you up, you know," he told Dalton without answering his question. "You have a sterling reputation. Your case closure rate is unusually high."

"I do my best." Dalton patted Marla's shoulder. "And I have a very sharp-witted, albeit unofficial, sidekick."

"Actually, I've heard something that might help in your investigation," she said to the sheriff. "While we were out shopping, I noticed the white smoke coming from the mountain. I understand the plume is steam issuing from Otto Lovelace's bottling plant. One of the store cashiers told us that armed guards patrol his property. Is that usual in these parts? Are environmental groups active here and causing trouble?"

Beresby stroked his mustache. "Domestic terrorism is a major concern. Radical animal rights and environmental groups have claimed responsibility for hundreds of crimes, so it isn't uncommon for them to resort to violence. They've caused millions of dollars in damage and even target people who work for companies they believe might be causing harm. Over in Colorado, one of these groups bombed a water bottling facility. So Lovelace's precautions are reasonable. As they work in scattered terrorist cells, they're often difficult to trace."

"Has my uncle mentioned anything to you about strange goings-on at his project?" Dalton said, shooting Marla a sidelong glance.

"Besides the workman who ran off? He never made that report official."

"There have been other incidents. He'd get angry at me for telling you, but you should be aware that apparent acts of sabotage have been happening there and on the ranch. Uncle Ray says Hugh Donovan is at fault."

"Does he?" Beresby's expression shuttered.

"I'm stretching here, but Uncle Ray and Garrett Long were riding buddies. Could my uncle be in danger? I mean, what if they'd both come across something on the trail they didn't realize was dangerous? Garrett may have taken it upon himself to investigate, and he ended up dead. Could it involve one of these terrorist cells?"

The sheriff raised a hand. "I'll admit eco-terrorists are a possibility. In his job, Garrett might have made many enemies. We're consulting with the rangers on that angle. But I'm more concerned with looking closer to home. Garrett's family, friends, and colleagues, for example, aren't above suspicion."

Before either of them could respond, a loud knock sounded on the door.

A deputy burst inside. "You're needed, Sheriff. There's been an explosion at Craggy Peak."

Marla's heart lurched, and she shot to her feet. "Is anyone hurt?"

"I don't know, ma'am. The rescue team is on its way."

Dalton was halfway to the door before she

130

collected her wits. "We'll meet you there, Sheriff. Come on, Marla."

Her heart raced as they careened up the mountain in their loaner SUV. Was Raymond all right? Had any workers been injured? What had caused the explosion?

Chaos met them along the curving road when they reached the construction site. Flashing lights came from emergency vehicles blocking their path ahead. Dalton diverted onto a side street and found a parking space. The warm afternoon sun beat down on their heads as they emerged and climbed a set of steep concrete stairs to the next level.

Marla's breath came short, either from the altitude or her anxiety. What would they find among the rubble?

Dust and debris spread everywhere. Men in soiled work clothes milled around a gaping hole that had opened between two buildings. Backed up to a wall of rock, it fortunately hadn't taken along any of the adjacent structures into the crater. Rescue personnel struggled to extricate survivors while sheriff's deputies maintained crowd control.

Marla searched people's heads for Raymond's tall figure. She identified him by his cowboy hat and heaved a whoosh of relief.

A deputy stood by taking notes.

She yanked on Dalton's arm and drew him in their direction.

"Uncle Ray," she called. She gave the startled older man a quick hug. "We're glad you're okay. We were talking to Sheriff Beresby in town when he got the news."

Raymond's face pinched. "We're going to have to halt operations until we get things cleaned up and inspected again per safety regulations. I lost two men, and several others are injured."

"What happened?" Dalton asked, his expression grim.

Raymond glared at him as though he should have prevented the collapse. "Looks like we hit a cache of old dynamite left over from the mining days while we were working on this building's foundation. It's always been a possibility with all the tunnels underlying the town."

"You can't be too careful around here with our history," Beresby said, approaching with a shake of his head. "It was only a matter of time before you came upon some blasting caps or dynamite waiting to blow."

"Was it? Maybe we dug too deep and hit a mine shaft, or maybe somebody planted this stuff here and wanted us to believe so."

"We'll be able to tell if any modern materials were used to set off the explosion. Consider your site shut down for now."

Raymond stamped his booted foot. "This delay is going to cost me."

Marla was taken aback by his seeming lack of concern for the workers who'd been killed. "I hope you have insurance," she murmured, wondering what hospital the injured would be taken to in the area. During the mining camp's heyday, there had been one nearby.

"We have workmen's compensation, liability, the whole bit. Not to worry there. These boys will be well looked after until they're on their feet, and I'll take care of the families for the ones we lost. My gut tells me this wasn't an accident. We've had our heavy equipment out here and haven't hit a time bomb like this before now."

Beresby, having waved off his deputy, hooked his thumbs into his belt. "As I said, these hills can be hazardous. You never know what will turn up. Now if you'll excuse me, I'll go see how the rescue operation is coming along."

"I'm sorry for your loss," Marla said softly to Raymond after the sheriff left.

His eyes glittered in the late afternoon rays. "Thanks. I'm glad you two are here. Son, you have to get to the bottom of this," he told Dalton. "Someone's out to get me. They want me to fail so I'll have to sell my properties. That's never going to happen."

"Do you have any evidence to support your theory?" her husband inquired in the noncommittal tone he used to interview suspects.

"No, whoever is doing this is careful to cover his tracks."

Like you? What if he'd planted the explosive himself? It would throw suspicion off him, if the sheriff harbored any notions that Raymond might be involved in Garrett Long's death.

The sheriff must know more about their relationship. Did the two men only go riding together? Or were they friends who confided in each other? Had Raymond told Garrett why he felt such animosity toward Hugh Donovan?

Perhaps the reverse had happened. Garrett told Raymond about a problem he'd encountered at work. Now Garrett was dead. Perhaps the murderer had set his sights on Raymond next to eliminate the threat of exposure.

Or not. Dalton had suggested maybe his uncle and Garrett had come across something related to criminal activity on a riding trail and hadn't realized its significance.

Confused, she scrubbed a hand over her face. Clearly the attacks on Raymond's project were escalating from mischievous incidents to lethal levels. She'd like to meet Hugh Donovan in person to assess his involvement. Raymond was quick to blame the guy for reasons yet unknown.

Rescue workers lifted an injured man in a sling out of the pit. Raymond wandered off to confer with his foreman.

"You look upset," Dalton said. "We should return to the ranch."

"I could use a drink at the Jail House. Let's eat in the dining room tonight. It'll give us a chance to talk in private." *And out of earshot of your relatives.*

"That wrangler, Jesse, knows something about Garrett Long's death. While you're getting refreshed, I'll see if he's around to answer some questions," Dalton said on the drive back to the ranch. "Let's meet at the bar around five and hang out there until dinner."

Feeling she should touch base with Carol, Marla washed and changed and then headed over to the reception building. Janice, on duty at the front desk, waved her on back.

Marla knocked on Carol's half-open office door before proceeding inside. The blonde's face split into a grin at Marla's appearance.

"Hi, I don't want to bother you, but I thought I should let you know that we'll be eating dinner at the ranch again tonight. There's a venom talk we might attend afterward," she said for an excuse.

"Sure, Marla. You're always welcome at our house. I fix dinner for an army since you never know who'll drop by. Wayne's dad gets lonely sometimes, and Annie likes a home cooked meal. So I prepare for company. Please, have a seat."

Carol appeared unruffled considering how her father-in-law might have been blown up that afternoon. Maybe she didn't know? Best to ease into the topic then.

"We went into town today. I met Annie for lunch and saw her clinic. She's doing a great job there from what I can tell. Her services seem to fill a need in the community."

Carol smiled with pride. "She loves her work. It's too bad Raymond doesn't respect her choice. He won't quit nagging her to take an interest in the family business."

"It doesn't bother you that she's alone?"

"Single and unattached, yes. A successful nutritional counselor? I'm happy she's found her calling. I just worry about her being without a partner for the rest of her life."

"She's young yet. Is she interested in finding someone?"

"I think so, but there aren't many eligible prospects in a town this size."

"At least she's a safe distance from Raymond's properties, considering what happened today at the ghost town."

Carol's brow scrunched. "What do you mean?"

"A piece of construction machinery hit a cache of dynamite from back in the mining era. The explosives went off and collapsed a wall."

"No! Was anyone hurt?"

Marla laid her purse in her lap. Maybe she and Dalton should have stayed on site and offered to help? Nah, they'd have only gotten in the way.

"A couple of workers were killed and others injured. Wayne's dad is okay, although shaken."

"Thank goodness. I'll bet he's more upset about this roadblock in his master plan than anything else."

How well you know your father-in-law. "Raymond doesn't believe it was an accident."

"Don't tell me. He blames Hugh Donovan." Carol stood and paced. "Hugh is a handy scapegoat for Wayne's dad and vice versa. Whenever something goes wrong, the other one is at fault. I wish they'd clear the air already."

"What happened to make them hate each other so much?"

"Raymond won't talk about it. I'm not sure how far it dates back, either. I'd rather not pry, but the past can lead to tension when things are left unresolved."

Amen to that. Marla had experienced her own share of past haunts. She could only move on once she'd shed the guilt.

"I'm glad you and Wayne came to our wedding. It meant a lot to Dalton."

"And we're glad you guys reached out to us. Wayne always felt bad he'd never had the chance to know his aunt. Since Raymond doesn't talk about her, the only way he learned anything was from Doc Harrigan."

"Who's that?" Marla's glance rose to study a colorful figurine of Kokopelli, the fertility deity revered by Native Americans. She'd seen similar ones in the gift shops in town. Kokopelli was depicted hunched over and playing a flute. Rather a bizarre figure in her opinion, he had feathers or protrusions coming from his head. Besides enhancing fertility, he was associated with changing winter into spring and bringing rain to the land. She should pick up a statue to bring home as a memento of their trip.

"Doctor Harrigan is our vet. Or rather, he's semi-retired, and his son has taken over the practice. Doc senior knows Raymond longer than anybody."

"Have you ever asked him what went down so many years ago?"

"I didn't want to stir a hornets' nest. Wayne should be the one to ask, but I think he's afraid to unravel his father's dark secrets. He'd get Doc senior to talk about Kate, though. Said there was a sad light in the vet's eyes whenever he mentioned her."

"Does he have an office in town?" Marla put this visit on her priority list.

"Yes, but you can catch him in the morning at the ranch. He comes by with his son twice a week to check our horses and deal with any non-emergency problems. He'll be over by the corrals around eight tomorrow. If you're up earlier and are comfortable on a horse, maybe you'd like to join me on my morning ride. I saddle up every morning at seven."

"I'll wait until I take a few more lessons, thanks. Would you mind if I spoke to the vet? Dalton and I would like to understand these tangled family relationships."

"It's fine with me. Maybe I should have

prompted Wayne to dig deeper, but I didn't want to upset him. You might have better luck."

Marla's curiosity intensified about what skeletons hid in Raymond's proverbial closet. So she made it her business to meet the veterinarian the next morning after breakfast. Dalton accompanied her, hoping to interview Jesse Parker. The wrangler hadn't been available when Dalton sought him out the evening before.

As they approached the main corral, Marla scanned the fenced enclosure. The horses available for riding that day stood around while wranglers scurried back and forth tending to their chores. Jesse's tall figure wasn't among them. Birds twittered while she wondered where to find the animal doctor. An occasional horse snorted, and the wranglers bantered with each other as they went about their daily routine. She sniffed in the cool morning air, wrinkling her nose at the smells of hay and manure.

"Can I help you?" said a gruff voice from the rear.

Marla spun to view an older guy wearing a brown cowboy hat, a tweed sport coat over a tan dress shirt, jeans, and ankle-high boots. He had a goatee that matched his silver hair. Her gaze dropped to the black leather satchel in his hand.

"We're looking for the vet," she said, forgetting her husband's goal for the moment. "Would that be you, by any chance?"

"You guessed right, young lady. I'm Doc Harrigan, as they call me around here."

"We're Marla and Dalton Vail from Florida. Dalton is Wayne's cousin. We're on our honeymoon and are staying at the ranch, thanks to Wayne's invitation."

"I recall hearing mention of relatives from the east coast."

Marla glanced over his shoulder. No one was on the path behind him. "Don't you normally work with your son?"

"He's busy with a mare about to birth on another ranch."

"Do you have a minute to talk to us? I understand you've known the family for a long time, and we're interested in the history."

He frowned at them. "I suppose I could spare a few minutes before they call me inside. Shall we get more comfortable?" Without waiting for an answer, he twisted the door knob leading into the Riders Entrance and entered. Fortunately, no one else was present.

After she and Dalton took seats on the

leather sofa, Marla spoke. Dalton appeared to be comfortable letting her lead the conversation. Maybe he didn't care to be seen as spying on his uncle.

"Did you know Raymond and Kate when they grew up here?"

A distant look came into the vet's eyes. "Oh, yes. They were an active pair of kids. Feisty as ever, they kept their mom busy. A ranch is a good place to raise children. They learn to be closer to the earth and to appreciate nature. There's none of them fancy trappings you get in cities."

"I imagine they learned to ride very early." Marla's gaze flitted to the artifacts decorating the room. She liked the feathery dream catcher on the wall.

"Those kids knew how to fit a saddle before they could read. They were taught the dangers of the desert as well. Raymond, being the eldest, should have known better."

Marla nudged Dalton so he would remain silent. She played along, pretending she knew what Doc Harrigan meant.

"You're absolutely right. Were you around when it happened, then?"

"Yep. My daddy ran the practice then. We're a generational family. Always loved horses along with farm animals. They've been helping mankind long before we white folks settled these hills."

"Can you tell us your version of what went down? Raymond isn't very forthcoming, and we'd like to know the truth. Carol is the one who suggested we see you for more information."

"Is she?" His fingers tapped the handle of the satchel in his lap. He sat in an armchair opposite them. "I imagine that son of hers is getting near their age."

"Brian is nine years old. Both of her kids are adorable."

"It wasn't so with Hannah and Sean's brood. Raymond had a touch of the devil in him. Or maybe it was Hugh's influence like they said. Either way, Raymond had it in for his younger sibling. It didn't help that the kid was smart as all get out and topped his grades in school."

"So Kate had been a top student?"

He stared at her. "I'm not talking about Kate. Harold, or Harry as they called him, never took to the ranch like they did. He was into books and math. It was almost freakish how he could do calculations in his head."

"So you're saying that my mother and Uncle Ray had a younger brother?" Dalton enunciated each word as though he couldn't believe what he'd heard.

The vet grinned at him. "I gather you have a bit of him inside yourself. Must have passed down from Hannah's side of the family. You like calculating who committed a crime, don't you, detective? Oh yes, I've heard a few things here and there."

"So Harry was a math whiz," Marla gathered. "What of it?"

"His siblings teased him unmercifully. Raymond couldn't understand why Harry didn't love ranching as much as him, and Kate was every bit the cowgirl in those early days. She hopped on a horse like she was a natural. I'll bet you wouldn't know it now. How is your mother doing, son? We miss her around here."

"She's great. My parents are looking for a condo to move to Florida so they can be closer to us. Dad has retired, so there's nothing keeping them in Maine. Most of their friends have moved away."

"Did Kate ever mention her childhood here?"

"Mom said she'd been raised on a ranch, but she and her mother had moved east to Boston to be near my great-grandmother. I assumed my grandfather must have died, and she never indicated otherwise. It wasn't until Marla and I were planning our wedding that I asked about that side of the family. I hadn't even known Mom had a brother."

"So Kate lived her life as though Raymond didn't exist?"

"Yep. We were astonished to learn about him. He had married and had grandkids. An entire branch of our family lived out west. We sent wedding invitations to all of them and were happy when Wayne and Carol accepted. Raymond didn't bother to send back a reply."

"That doesn't surprise me. Raymond can't face the ghosts of his past, and seeing his sister again would remind him of events he'd rather forget. He pushes his workers hard, like he's punishing them instead of himself. For everyone's sake, he needs to shed his guilt and move on."

"We're not clear on the details. Can you tell us more?" Marla asked, hoping to finally get some answers. "It would help us understand Raymond better."

The vet scratched his head. "I reckon you have a right to know. Here's what happened."

CHAPTER SEVEN

Doc Harrigan stared into the distance as he related the story. "Raymond, Kate, and Harry often played together along with their friend and neighbor, Hugh Donovan. Harry was the butt of their pranks, being bookish and not an outdoorsman like the rest of the gang. Plus, they were all jealous of his being smarter."

"So they teased him," Marla said. Or worse, they'd bullied him, but she didn't express her theory aloud in case it was wrong.

"One day the foursome was playing cowboys and Indians up on the hill, and they came across an open mine shaft."

Marla's gut clenched. She could guess what happened next.

"The sheriff warned us about the area," Dalton inserted. "Craggy Peak used to be an active copper mining camp."

"The shafts should have been sealed,"

Doc Harrigan continued in a somber tone. "Most of them are covered over with brush now, so you can't even tell they were there. But the spot which the boys and Kate discovered must have eroded because the opening was exposed."

"Surely they'd been told to steer clear?"

"No doubt. Those old abandoned mines have hazards aplenty — spiders, bats, scorpions, even mountain lions if they can get inside. Lower levels might be flooded from groundwater seeping in, and rotten timbers could collapse at any time. They're dangerous to explore."

"Plus explosives might have been left behind." Dalton related the latest accident at the ghost town.

Doc Harrigan's face paled. "How did Raymond take it?"

"I'm sure he felt bad for the workmen who'd been injured and for the families of the guys who died, but he appeared more concerned with the construction delay."

"The accident must have hit him harder than he let on. The man didn't tell you?"

"Tell us what?"

"That's how his brother died. Raymond taunted Harry that he was a coward. He could prove his mettle by going inside the mine and bringing out a tool. It was common knowledge that when the mines closed, the miners walked off and left their equipment behind. With copper prices hitting an all-time low, most of them didn't have other jobs waiting for them."

Marla wished she could shut out the rest, but she had to hear it. "So Harry took the bait?"

"Poor kid always wanted his brother's approval. From what they said later, Kate protested, but the boys ignored her."

"And Hugh Donovan was a party to this? What did Harry care about his opinion?"

"You know how children want to fit in. Raymond and Hugh were tight as a rider to a horse. Harry was always the third man out when the three kids were together. Raymond paid more attention to Hugh than to his own brother, but that was natural since their ages were closer. Still, Harry must have felt he had to earn their respect. So he entered the mine."

"And Kate stood by, knowing something bad could happen?"

"Heck, no. She'd remembered the warnings and was afraid the mine might cave in and trap Harry inside. Pretty little Kate ran for help. But by the time her dad got there, it was too late. Harry had found his tool all right, but he didn't realize what he held in his hand."

"And that was?" Marla prompted, dreading the response.

"A pack of dynamite. As he neared the exit, waving the item gleefully in the air, it exploded. Likely, he was killed instantly, and then the roof of the mine collapsed on top of him. It was nasty when they dug out his remains."

Marla clapped a hand to her mouth. "How horrible."

Doc Harrigan's eyes glazed over. "It was an awful time. Hannah and Sean ended up separating. She took Kate with her and moved back east to be near her mother. Hannah blamed Sean for pushing the boys to follow in his footsteps and for not valuing Harry's quieter talents. Kate blamed Raymond and pretended thereafter as though he didn't exist. And Raymond blamed Hugh for egging him on. Everyone had regrets that haunt them to this day."

Marla swallowed in commiseration. She'd experienced a tragedy in her past, and it had taken years to forgive herself. Its influence still held sway in her decision not to have children of her own. As a nineteen-year-old babysitter, she'd answered a phone call the parents had told her to expect, but in that instant, the unthinkable had happened. The child under her care drowned in the backyard pool.

Losing a child could easily cause discord between the parents. Little Tammy's mother and father had argued, but they'd cast blame on Marla. She'd had to hire an attorney to fend off a lawsuit. How she'd paid the law firm had led to another blot on her past, but she hadn't wanted to burden her family.

Her throat tightened at the memories. Her mistakes didn't end there. She'd made another bad choice and married the attorney in charge of her case. At the time, Stan had seemed like a lifesaver. She didn't realize until later how much he enjoyed controlling people.

She hung her head in shame. No matter what Raymond did, it wasn't her place to judge him, not with the sins hanging over her own head. At least she'd turned her misdeeds into good, working for the Child Drowning Prevention Coalition. And Dalton had helped her find forgiveness and acceptance of her own worth. It sounded as though Raymond needed the same. He wasn't only tormenting himself. His behavior affected the people around him.

Was history repeating itself in how Raymond belittled Annie's decision to become a dietitian? She'd taken the intellectual route just like Harry and had no desire to get involved in ranch operations.

Dalton must have sensed her distress, because he took her hand and squeezed it. "Is that why Raymond and Hugh are at odds with each other?" he asked the veterinarian. "Raymond blames Hugh for the accident that killed his brother?"

Marla heard his terse tone and felt bad for him. No one wanted to hear about the black deeds of their relatives.

The vet snorted. "Those two might have forgiven each other and made amends, considering how tight they'd been as kids. But then Raymond did another bad thing. That guy has made plenty of mistakes in his life. Maybe what they say about the ghosts at Craggy Peak is true. The spirits of the dead seek justice by haunting him."

"What else did he do?" Dalton said in a resigned tone.

"Sorry, but that's not my story to tell. You'll have to ask your uncle."

The door banged open, and a wrangler stuck his head inside. "Have any of you seen Carol?"

Doc Harrigan shook his head. "No, why?"

"She went for her usual ride this morning. Her horse has returned with a limp.

She wasn't on it."

"Dear God. Has Wayne been informed?"

"He's gathering a search party as we speak. Do you want to join the posse, Doc? Carol might be hurt if the horse tossed her."

"I should tend to the beast, but maybe I can be of some use." Dr. Harrigan jerked his thumb at Marla and Dalton. "You guys wanna come along?"

"I'll join you." Dalton stood, and Marla followed suit. "Can you get a horse ready for me?" he asked the wrangler.

"Yes, sir. Won't take me but a minute. Meet me in the corral out back."

"I can't go," Marla said in a disappointed tone. "I'd slow everyone down. I'll wait for news in the main lobby."

Wayne might return to his office eventually, or at least he'd notify one of the other managers when they'd found Carol. Her heart thumped as conjecture flashed ugly images in her mind of possible scenarios. Carol was a seasoned rider who wouldn't fall from her saddle without reason.

Outside, the men rode off in a cloud of dust toward the trail Carol normally took each morning. Their group got smaller and turned into specks against the mountainside. Marla recalled a time in the recent past when she'd been warned to vary her morning routine by a killer who'd taken advantage of her habits. With a possible saboteur on the ranch, Marla should have given Carol the same advice.

Oh, gosh. Standing rooted to the spot, Marla clutched her stomach. What could be the goal of hurting Carol? Was this an indirect way of getting at Raymond?

The search had brought ranch operations to a halt. From the looks of it, most of the wranglers had ridden away with the posse. Guests were even now congregating in front of the building and wondering why no one was there to greet them.

She wandered toward the lobby, a fog of dread encasing her. Maybe she should look inside Carol's office. What if Wayne's wife had received a note from somebody to meet her at another location? That would throw off the search party when they couldn't find her.

Someone seemed to have it in for the whole family. Marla couldn't discard the notion that it might be Hugh Donovan. What had Raymond done to distance himself further from the man?

Shrugging away those concerns, she focused on Carol. Maybe her horse had simply stepped on a nail in its path. That could cause a limp. Or its shoe had become loose, not that Marla knew much about horse care. The animal's sudden stop could have unseated Carol. That was a more logical explanation than paranoia. Or maybe someone hoped to spread the seeds of distrust by causing this incident.

She only prayed Carol was lying stunned and not seriously hurt.

Marla entered the brightly lit lobby that smelled like fresh lemon oil and leather polish. A middle-aged couple was checking out, so she waited until Janice was free. The redhead signaled for her to come over.

"Hi there, hon. Any news on Carol yet?"

"I was meaning to ask you the same. Will Wayne call in when he's found her?"

"I'd hope so. We're all worried. This is totally unlike her to be missing. I can't imagine what might have happened."

"Well, I can, and none of it is good." Marla paced back and forth, hands clasped behind her back. "I'll check her office to see if anyone left her a note. She might have gone to meet somebody, in which case they won't find her on the usual trail where she rides."

"Good point, although I'd expect she would have told one of us if she was deviating from her routine. She's careful that way."

"Do you mind if I take a look? We

shouldn't discount any possibilities."

"Sure, go ahead." Janice gestured toward the staff door.

It didn't take Marla long to riffle through the papers on Carol's desk. She saw nothing that might be a summons or urgent note. As the financial officer for the resort, Carol had printouts of spreadsheets as well as handwritten ledgers scattered about every available surface. She must follow her own system of organization.

Opening drawers, Marla searched for anything unusual but came up empty. Other than the clutter, it appeared to be a typical office. No doubt Carol could find exactly what she needed amid the piles of papers. Marla liked that Carol's home might be neat and tidy, but here she had few reservations about cutting loose.

"I got nothing," she told Janice a few minutes later.

"Do you want some coffee? We have a break room in the back."

"No, thanks. I'm wired enough already." Marla waited until Janice checked out a family of four, who were so enthused about the place that they reserved a date for next year. "Has Carol been behaving any differently lately? Do you think she had something on her mind that might have bothered her?"

"No, she seemed perfectly chipper yesterday. You stopped by in the afternoon to talk to her. How did she appear to you?"

"I didn't detect any problems." Marla sank into an empty seat beside Janice, the lone receptionist on duty. If one of the managers normally worked alongside her, likely he had joined the search party. This moment of privacy might not be repeated.

"How much do you know about the relationship between Raymond's family and the Donovans?"

Janice's astonished gaze met hers. "The Donovans? Surely you don't think Hugh had something to do with Carol's disappearance?"

"Why not? I've heard there is bad blood between him and Raymond."

Perhaps Carol had taken it upon herself to visit Hugh Donovan and ask if he'd been responsible for the explosion at the ghost town and the incidents on the ranch. She might be more rational about it than Wayne, whose father had been personally involved with the Donovan clan. But then what? Hugh had done something to Carol?

Or maybe she'd run across the saboteur during her ride. Could the same person be causing trouble in both locations, or was there more than one mole involved, assuming these weren't random incidents? And if so, whose payroll was backing them?

Janice studied her pink-painted fingernails. "Look, hon, I've been working here for a long time, and I don't stick my nose into the family's personal affairs."

"It's not so personal when guests at the ranch could get hurt or when the bottom line at the resort gets affected, as might happen in the near future. What do you know about Raymond and Hugh?"

A mobile radio on the front desk crackled with static. Were they missing important transmissions from the search team? Marla wanted to hear what the redhead had to say, but it was more important to learn if Carol had been found. Nobody appeared to be using cell phones. The trails must not be within service range.

"Mind you, I don't know if this is true or not," Janice said, lowering her voice, "but Raymond knew Hugh's wife from high school. Word on the street has it that the two of them got reacquainted after Hugh's son left home."

"What?" Having expected Janice to mention Raymond's sad history with his dead brother, the woman's proclamation startled her. Hugh's wife and son? What did they have to do with anything?

"I've got her," Wayne's voice burst from the radio. "She's just off the trail, half-hidden under some bushes." He rattled off the location.

Marla sat upright, instantly alert.

"Looks like she hit her head on a rock when she fell," Wayne said in a grim tone. "We'll need a stretcher."

"The sheriff is on his way," someone else replied. "He had to deal with a car accident on the other side of town. I'll call for an ambulance."

"Don't move her," Dalton's voice sounded in the background. "They'll need to assess the extent of her injury. Doc Harrigan, are you there? Can you take a look until the paramedics get here?"

Although Dalton had been trained in emergency procedures, he probably figured the vet knew how to treat injuries better, even on a human. Marla clenched her hands in her lap, breathless to hear more.

"She's not coming around." Panic laced Wayne's tone. "Carol! Can you hear me?"

"Wayne, you'd better come see this," said another guy. "There's a wire tied to this tree."

"I can't leave my wife."

"If it's evidence, don't touch anything," Dalton cautioned. "The sheriff will need to investigate. Wayne, the doc and I are heading your way."

Static cracked the air and the radio cut off, leaving a heavy silence.

Marla stood, too agitated to sit. How bad was Carol's injury? Had she truly hit her head on a rock when she'd tumbled from her horse? What did the guy mean by a wire?

She fought an urge to run outside. It wouldn't help, as she couldn't see the posse in the distance. Best remain here until one of the managers returned.

Then again, some of the wranglers might ride back first. They had duties to their guests. Wayne could handle things along with Dalton and Doc Harrigan, plus the sheriff was due to arrive. She should go wait over by the corral for news.

Or not. She mashed her lips in frustration. What could she do from this end to help? Man the front desk along with Janice? Answer phones?

If Carol was going to be indisposed for a while, she could offer to manage the books. She owned a salon and possessed business skills. But the job might occupy her for several days, depending on Carol's condition, and that wouldn't be fair to Dalton on their honeymoon.

Well, guess what? He was already involved in an investigation of sorts. It wasn't in their natures to sit idly by while things happened around them.

"What do you suppose they meant by a wire?" Janice asked with a wide-eyed gaze like an elk in headlights.

"It appears Carol's accident wasn't random."

Janice gave a furtive glance toward the front door. "But why target Carol? She's a sweetheart. Everyone loves her and Wayne."

"So I gather." Marla voiced her thoughts aloud. "Maybe the intent had been to hurt Raymond through her."

Janice gasped. "You mean, to threaten the ones he loves the most?"

"That's what I'm thinking."

"You're saying someone laid a trap to trip her horse? And then she hit her head on a rock when she fell? That part must have been an accident."

"It sounds like that's what happened." *Or else somebody beaned her and made it look that way.* "Look, can I help you with anything? I feel so useless just waiting around until the men get back."

"Sure, if you wouldn't mind. You can answer the phone if I'm busy with a guest."

As she spoke, a party of eight entered the lobby to sign up for various activities.

Janice got occupied with them and then with a foursome wanting to check out, while Marla fielded a call about a leaky bathroom faucet and a closet door that got stuck. Janice told her how to notify maintenance, and she took care of the problems.

Once free, Janice grabbed the radio. "I can't stand this silence. I have to find out what's going on." She pushed a button. "Can anyone hear me? This is Jan at the front desk."

"Dalton," Marla called in the background. "Are you there?" She could try his cell phone, but this seemed quicker.

More static sounded, and then a voice answered. "Kevin Franks here."

"Who's that?" she whispered to Carol.

"Kevin Franks is one of the wranglers. He must have ridden out with the boys," Janice explained in a hushed tone. "Kevin, what's going on? Is Carol responsive yet?"

"Yes, ma'am. She's awake but a bit confused. They're taking her to the hospital. We're riding back now. Wayne is bringing his horse in, and then he'll follow her there in his car."

Marla snatched her purse and rose. "I'll go outside to wait for them." She hesitated a moment before patting Janice on the shoulder. "Everything will be okay, you'll see. We'll help out if Wayne needs us. Will you be all right by yourself?"

Janice gave a wan smile. "I'll be fine. Thanks for keeping me company."

Marla rushed out the door and hurried down the winding path toward the corrals.

A cloud of dust mushroomed from the direction of the hills where the men had gone. That must be their posse returning. From far away, a siren pierced the crisp morning air. Marla shivered under her sweater. Somehow a beautiful morning had turned ugly. Poor Wayne. At least she and Dalton were there to offer support.

Wayne dismounted along with the rest of the guys, including Dalton. The wrangler, Jesse, was present, too. He must have ridden in from one of the distant paddocks.

After handing their horses over to the employees, Wayne and Dalton stood aside in deep conversation. Dalton's brow creased in that way he had when displeased. What were they discussing? His face brightened when he spotted Marla, and he waved her over.

"How's Carol?" she asked first thing.

Wayne replied, his tone somber. "The paramedics say she might have to stay overnight at the hospital for observation. I'm heading over there to be with her."

"You said something on the radio about a wire?"

"The sheriff is handling that aspect. We found one end of a trip wire tied to a tree. It must have been strung across the trail. Her horse wouldn't have seen it. That would account for his limp. The Doc can tend to him now."

"If they were going fast, Carol would have been thrown when the horse stopped abruptly," Marla guessed.

"She might have held her seat unless someone tampered with her saddle."

Marla exchanged a knowing glance with Dalton. Whoever had done it knew Carol's daily habits. That implicated someone close enough to observe her.

Guests stepped forward as wranglers called their names and apologized for the delay. Horses snorted in the background, while birds twittered against a clear blue sky. It would have been a perfect morning except for this happenstance.

"Hey, Jesse," Wayne hollered.

The wrangler stood conferring with a couple of the other guys. He glanced up at Wayne's summons, said something in parting, and sauntered over.

"Yeah, boss?"

"I want you to supervise a full inspection of our equipment. A wedding party is due to arrive in two weeks, and we don't want anything bad happening to them. Understand?"

"I've got it covered, don't worry."

"I'll help you," offered another fellow who aimed their way. He had a lean frame, a mustache and beard with dark brown sideburns, and a loping gait.

Dalton introduced Marla to Kevin Franks, the wrangler she'd heard on the radio.

"Jesse's in charge," Wayne said in an insistent tone. "He'll let you know if he needs a hand. I'll check in with you later," he told the younger man.

Doc Harrigan strode by after settling his horse. His face haggard, he carried his satchel and nodded a greeting on his way past. This morning's disruption must have set him off schedule, but thankfully he had been around to offer his expertise. She wondered what he'd find upon his examination of Carol's mount.

Marla and Dalton accompanied their cousin to the parking lot where he kept his car.

"You're making a mistake," Dalton said to him. "Jesse could be involved, and you're letting him conduct the inspection?"

"Despite what you think, I believe in Jesse. He's been outstanding at his job from the start. I can't see him risking it for a family feud between us and Hugh Donovan."

"You still blame the man, even for this?"

"My father is right. Who else would want to cause us grief? If you ask me, he's after our land. We've had offers on both this resort property and the ghost town."

"It could be someone else who has you and Raymond in their sights."

"I don't think so. Carol had better pull through this, or Donovan will get his due."

Dalton placed a hand on his arm. "Wayne, don't be rash. You have no evidence to prove your theories."

"We'll have it soon, if the sheriff does his job properly." He shook off Dalton's hand and stormed away. A moment later, his car careened from the parking lot and headed into town.

Marla hooked her arm into Dalton's and led him toward their room. "What now? You've had your morning ride. Let's do something relaxing to get our minds off these problems."

"I'm not in the mood. Carol could have been killed. She might still have complications."

"I know." Marla worried about her, too, but she wouldn't let it bring them down. "It's not right for Wayne or Raymond to blame this Donovan guy without proof. He's doing the same thing to them, claiming they're responsible for spoiling his grazing land."

"We should talk to the guy."

"No, we shouldn't. It's our honeymoon."

Dalton's jaw clenched, and his eyes took on a determined glare. "Wayne asked for my help. We have more questions than we have answers. That doesn't sit well with me."

Marla realized she wouldn't be able to raise his spirits until they talked this out. Once he was in investigative mode, he became focused on one goal, like her poodle when he stalked a squirrel. She needed to act as his sounding board to calm him.

"Let's go sit on that patio behind the conference center. No one should be there this early. We can compare notes."

"All right. You know what's really on my mind?" He gave her a troubled glare. "We're related to Raymond, too. That means *we* could be next."

CHAPTER EIGHT

Seated on the terrace overlooking the mountains, Marla wished for a state of tranquility. "It should be peaceful here. How could anything bad happen when we're surrounded by such natural beauty?"

"Ask the forest ranger who's dead or Carol who's lying in a hospital bed. This territory has been rife with battles between Indians and settlers, prospectors and thieves, gunmen and the law. It hasn't progressed much in that regard."

"I wish Doc Harrigan had finished his story. We might have learned more from him. Janice hinted at something that might have occurred between Raymond and Hugh's wife at one time. Is she still living?"

Dalton's shoulders rose and fell. "I have no idea, and I doubt my uncle would tell us."

"We need to find someone who will talk. Let's review what we know so far." She ticked off the points on her fingers. "Garrett Long, a forest ranger, is dead under mysterious circumstances. A worker is missing from the ghost town project. Accidents are being staged at Craggy Peak as well as here."

"It does seem as though there might be a connection between all these events."

"Plus Hugh Donovan is complaining that his water supply has dried up, and his livestock is suffering. He blames your uncle's project for contaminating the environment. Yet I saw white smoke pouring from the water bottling plant up on the mountain. Is it really steam or something more toxic? Maybe we should accept Otto Lovelace's offer to tour his facility."

"It's a long shot if you think he's involved. The man has no personal relationship to either family. What would he stand to gain?"

"Who knows? Maybe he caught Garrett snooping near his operation," Marla said. "The shopkeeper in town mentioned armed guards patrolling the place."

"Lovelace could be afraid of eco-terrorists in the area. Besides, the sheriff said he's looking closer to home toward Garrett's friends and family."

"That would include your Uncle Ray. We need to pay him another visit, unless he shows up for dinner tonight. Carol won't be able to cook. Maybe we should offer to bring in some food. And who will pick up her kids from school?" Marla whipped out her cell phone. "I'll call Annie. I can't just sit around when people need our help."

"That's my girl. You're never happy being idle."

"Believe me, I'd rather get a massage or lounge by the pool."

He tickled his fingers along her thigh. "You know what I'd prefer to do?"

"Save it for later. We should help Carol's family. Let's see what needs to be done." A few minutes later, Marla packed her phone away. "Annie has it covered. She'll pick up her niece and nephew from school and will fix them something to eat for dinner."

"Has she heard anything new about Carol?"

"Carol is awake and coherent. She had a mild concussion from her nasty whack on the head. The doctors will keep her under observation until tomorrow. Wayne is still there with her, and Raymond came over to keep him company."

"So we're free for the rest of the day?"

"We could visit the sheriff again," Marla suggested. "If someone did mess with Carol's saddle or string a wire across her path, Sheriff Beresby might consider it a case of attempted murder in view of her injuries."

"I wonder if she actually hit her head on a rock or if someone bashed her while she lay stunned on the ground. Carol might not remember."

Marla pursed her lips. "The sheriff would be able to determine that possibility from the angle of her fall and the type of bruising, wouldn't he?"

"Most likely." Dalton checked his watch. "Let's wait until after lunch to decide what to do. I'd rather not bother Luke Beresby again. He hasn't asked for our help, whereas my cousin has. Our obligation is to him."

Dalton called Wayne to be certain they weren't needed elsewhere for the afternoon. He put the call on speaker phone so Marla could hear.

"Thanks, but Carol is stable, and I'm okay. The safety of our guests is paramount. Whoever has it in for our family might decide to broaden their reach. It would be a way to stab at us financially if reservations started to drop off."

"They're already hurting Uncle Ray's wallet by delaying construction at his project. Did we tell you about the latest incidents there?"

"Nope, but I'll ask him. Hey, I *would* appreciate it if you could review the background info on my employees. Before this stuff started, I'd trust any one of them with my life. But now, I'm not so sure my judgment is clear. I'll tell HR to make the personnel files available to you."

"No problem. We'll stay on the ranch for dinner tonight. Let me know if you need our help for anything."

"Oh, joy," Marla said when he signed off. "We get to spend the rest of the day doing paperwork."

"A lot of my job as detective is tracing paper trails. You don't have to bother. Go get a body treatment at the spa."

"Good idea. I can always sound out the staff there. We haven't met any of them yet." She gathered her purse and rose. "It's too early for lunch. What do you say we go back to our room to recoup our energy?"

He gave her a lazy smile. "Is that what you're calling it now? I'm all for that idea."

They descended the steps to ground level and started along the meandering path to their hacienda. Already the day was heating up. By noon, Marla could discard her sweater.

A biker passed by, wheeling his vehicle back to the bike shop. She observed him with raised eyebrows. "We could rent bikes one day. Biking on these hills would be good exercise."

"I wouldn't mind doing the nature hike one morning and learning more about the plant life. That's more appealing to me than riding a bike. We'll get enough of a workout each morning on a horse."

Dalton's mention of a nature hike gave Marla a brilliant idea. After she ate a delicious buffet lunch in the guest dining room, she headed to the nature center instead of the spa. The naturalist might be a better source of information than the spa staff, especially if he'd been around a while.

Inside the museum, a man with white hair and a beard stood to greet her. She smiled as though she'd struck gold, although in these parts, it was more likely to be a lode of copper. "Hi, I'm Marla Vail," she said, extending her hand. "My husband and I are cousins of Wayne and Carol. We're here on our honeymoon at Wayne's invitation."

The older guy gave her hand a vigorous shake as though thrilled to have a visitor. He wore a button-down plaid shirt and a pair of jeans tucked into scuffed boots. His name tag said he was Bob Washburn. "Thanks for coming in, ma'am. We're proud of our display here."

172

Marla stepped back to scan the interior of the adobe structure. Natural materials were used in its construction as evident from the flagstone floor to the ceiling made of wood beams and saguaro spines like in the dining room. This place, too, had copper light fixtures decorated with cutouts of Indian figures.

Glass cases lined the perimeter. They displayed mineral rocks, live snakes, and animal skulls. A rare red bat, labeled as such, sat next to a stuffed black bird that might be a raven. A stone wall divider had a fake bobcat peeking out from behind, a bird's nest, and an owl sitting on top gazing down at her. Behind it was the naturalist's alcove and a shop with outdoor gear.

Photos of mammals and insects decorated the walls, along with a framed display of dead butterflies, a poster of Gila monsters, and various stuffed animal heads. A tall bookshelf stood next to a stone fireplace in one corner, while a boulder in another nook featured a winged bird.

"This place is a hidden treasure. How long have you been working here, Mr. Washburn?" she said to start the conversation.

"Call me Bob. I've worked here for years. I'm a former park service ranger, and I also worked for the forest service later on. The other guy who rotates here with me is a history teacher. He covers Saturdays and Sundays."

"You used to be a ranger? Did you know Garrett Long?"

"Sure, he was a good man. I was sorry to hear of his death."

"I'm not really sure what a forest ranger does, other than conduct tours and enforce the rules. Is it a dangerous job? Do you, like, fight fires and arrest criminals?"

Bob chuckled. "Have a seat, and I'll explain." He motioned to a wood bench in front of the wall divider. As she complied, he folded his arms across his chest. "Garrett worked for the forest service, but you're probably more familiar with park service rangers. Those are the uniformed personnel who conduct tours, give nature talks, and run visitor centers. The park service also has law enforcement officers whose duty is to enforce park regulations. To confuse the issue, other people with the park service may be scientists, scholars, geologists, or historians."

"So which one was Garrett?" Marla studied a stained glass window depicting a rabbit. Other windows showed a lizard, a bobcat, a mountain lion, and a rattlesnake.

"He worked for the forest service. His job

involved preventing forest fires, managing campgrounds, preserving natural resources, and protecting the environment. As a law enforcement officer, his duty also included things like chasing away poachers. It's confusing because there's a cross-over of roles between the two agencies."

"Wait, did you say poachers? You mean people illegally hunt animals on national land?" Maybe that accounted for the stuffed heads decorating the walls at the resort. But who had shot the creatures? She couldn't see Raymond as the hunter, even though he condoned putting the heads on display. He must have bought them somewhere.

"I mean fellows stealing saguaro. There's a thriving black market for the cacti in Arizona. Harming a saguaro in any way is illegal in our state."

"Really? I had no idea."

"That's not even half of it. Garrett may have had to deal with fugitives on the run, smugglers, pot farmers, domestic terrorists, and target shooters who start fires, among other things."

"How can I find out more about his involvement in this stuff?" Possibly one of these miscreants had held a grudge against him.

"You could talk to his patrol captain."

Had Sheriff Beresby already interviewed Garrett's superior? Maybe the ranger had discovered something among his own colleagues rather than outsiders. If policemen and politicians could become corrupt, so might a co-worker on the take or one who had a vulnerability to be exploited.

"Where would I find this guy?"

Bob stroked his white beard. "There's a district office in Wendall, beyond Sedona. That's likely to be the place where Officer Long reported for duty."

"Officer Long? Why not Ranger?"

"Technically, the LEOs for the park service are called ranger. The forest service law enforcement personnel are officers."

So besides natural hazards like fires erupting from dry weather conditions, flash floods, and lethal wildlife, forest service rangers had to deal with smugglers from Mexico possibly dealing in human trafficking or drugs, poachers of valuable saguaro plants, pot growers, squatters, and the occasional wacko cultist or environmental activist who went to extremes to make his views known.

It would be helpful if Marla could talk to his colleagues. Did Garrett work alone or with a team? She understood so little about the forest service, and this discussion had

176

left her even more confused. Marla hadn't realized a distinction existed between the National Park Service and the U.S. Forest Service.

It wasn't her place to follow through on this information, however. Sheriff Beresby was conducting the investigation into Garrett's death. He should be the one to track all the possible leads. But was he doing so?

And why should she care?

Marla shifted in her seat, her doubts surfacing. Maybe Raymond was involved in more ways than they realized. That could be why his family was being targeted.

She laced her fingers together and steered the conversation in another direction. "I don't want to take up too much of your time, but I've been curious about Raymond's relationship to Garrett Long."

Bob shrugged. "They often went riding together. Their families never socialized with each other, though. I don't think Ray could abide Garrett's wife."

"Why not?"

"Beats me. Never met the lady myself."

"What about the woman Raymond married? Did you know her?"

He nodded, his gaze distant. "Now she was a gem. Susan came out here for a stay at the ranch with her family one winter, and

Ray was smitten as soon as he laid eyes on her."

"That sounds romantic."

"Ray can be persistent when he sets his mind to something. Susan agreed to marry him not six months later. They had a good life together until she died."

"I've heard about his problems with Hugh Donovan. I imagine Raymond's wife knew about the tragedy with his younger brother. It's too bad she couldn't convince Raymond to let go of the past."

"Huh, Raymond can be a fool sometimes. He wouldn't let go of the past in more ways than one."

"Can you elaborate? You know we've been having unexplained accidents on the ranch. Any information you share may be helpful in finding the person responsible. Wayne believes these aren't random acts."

"Didn't Raymond tell you? He'd known Hugh's wife since high school. They'd been sweethearts until Hugh came between them. Flora chose him to marry. She was a devoted wife to Hugh, at least until their son left."

She sat up straight. "What happened?"

"Their younger son, Jake, stormed out of the house one day and never came back."

"So Hugh blamed Raymond? I don't get it."

"No, Ray wasn't at fault for the kid leaving. But he was around to comfort Flora."

"Oh, I see." Her forehead wrinkled. No, she didn't, at least not clearly. She needed to discuss all this with Dalton.

Rising, she brushed off her pants. "You've been very kind to speak to me. I'd better go check on my husband." She wandered to a display case and pointed admiringly to a deep blue mineral rock labeled as azurite. "That's beautiful."

"Azurite is one of two copper carbonate minerals, the other one being green malachite." The naturalist moseyed over to join her. "When found, they're often indicators of copper ore deposits. Although she's pretty, she isn't worth nearly as much as that crystalline structure next to her that contains a rare earth element, or that gemstone-quality chrysocolla."

"What's a rare earth element?" Marla understood chemical hair solutions better than geology.

"It's a substance used in electronics such as cell phones, televisions, and even weapons systems. Most of our supply comes from China, but they limit their exports. Our old mines might prove to be a valuable resource. Like, there's talk of reopening the old Lavender Pit down by Bisbee. You should take

179

a tour of the Queen Mine if you're in the area."

Marla poised to ask another question when her phone trilled with a text from Dalton. *Where are you?* She answered him, then turned to the older gent.

"I appreciate your taking the time to talk to me, Bob."

"Sure, it's been a pleasure. If you need to outfit yourselves for any of the hikes offered, our shop is in the back. Let me show you."

Marla ended up buying a couple of backpacks, flashlights, extra batteries, and nutrient bars. She left with a parting wave to go meet Dalton back in their room.

They stretched out on comfy lounge chairs on their covered patio facing the trees and mountains. A tangle of branches and shrubbery, interspersed with tall saguaro, led to the foothills.

"Did anything unusual about the resort employees stand out during your paper search?" Marla said.

"I flagged a couple of items. They didn't do a proper background check in regards to criminal records or drug testing. Jesse has been here five years and has a recommendation from Ben Donovan."

"Ben? Who's he?"

"Hugh Donovan's son."

"Is that so? I learned Hugh had a younger boy, Jake, who left home in a huff."

"So this Ben must be the older son. How does he know Jesse?" Dalton's brow furrowed. "Maybe they went to school together. I'd have to know their ages."

"As I texted you back earlier, I stopped by the nature center. Bob, the naturalist, indicated your Uncle Ray was around to comfort Hugh's wife after Jake ran away from home. She and Raymond had been high school sweethearts."

"Had Wayne's mother still been alive then?"

Marla spread her hands. "How should I know? Do you think this Jake kid could have it in for his father? We don't know what led to his leaving home. Maybe he wants revenge on Hugh, and he's the one at the heart of your uncle's problems."

Dalton examined her as though she had a loose screw. "Where are you going with this?"

"Hugh's estranged son could have sent Jesse to your ranch with orders to cause trouble. He could have forged his brother's signature on the job recommendation. Considering how Raymond and Hugh hate each other, they'd be quick to cast blame for any disturbances on their properties.

Jake would know how to exploit their weaknesses."

"To what end? What could he hope to gain?"

Marla gave a heavy sigh. "You've got me there. It wouldn't explain the sabotage at the ghost town."

"I learned something else that's interesting. Kevin Franks had a recommendation from Garrett Long."

Marla's scalp prickled at the mention of the dead ranger's name. "How did they know each other?" She supposed the wrangler might have saddled Garrett's horse on occasion.

"I'm hoping to find out. I've signed us up for a breakfast ride in the morning." He noted her skeptical glance. "Don't worry, you'll do fine. It's an easy walk to a campsite where they make blueberry flapjacks and scrambled eggs. It'll be fun."

"I'm glad I bought these boots. Let's hope Jesse or Kevin will be along for the ride."

Neither wrangler made an appearance Thursday morning, disappointing both Marla and Dalton. She wasn't disappointed in the ride, however. It turned out to be more pleasurable than she'd expected. Her rump and thighs sore from the exercise, she returned to their room after the excursion to change. Her stomach felt satisfied from a filling breakfast that seemed to taste better than usual out in the open, fresh air.

Dalton glanced at her dressed in her underwear after a shower. "I should massage your legs. You must be feeling the effects of the saddle."

His sexy gaze stirred her longings. "Maybe you should."

That activity diverted them for a while. When they were both dressed once again, Dalton phoned his cousin to check on Carol's condition.

"She's left the hospital and is back home with orders to rest for today," Dalton told Marla. "Wayne doesn't need us for anything right now."

"Good. What shall we do for the rest of the day?" She consulted the resort schedule. "I'm not interested in Birding for Beginners or Navajo Basketry. There's mountain biking, a fishing expedition to some lake, team penning, or a yoga class."

"I'd like to talk to Uncle Ray about some of these developments. Are you up for another trip to Craggy Peak?"

"Okay, but when do you want to go to Wendall? Bob suggested we speak to Garrett's superior there."

"The sheriff should have covered that ground."

"True, but Wendall is just beyond Sedona. The scenery there is supposed to be spectacular. And truth be told, a change of pace would be welcome."

He tickled her under the chin. "It's our honeymoon, remember? We're supposed to be relaxing here and enjoying the amenities. Let's plan on Sedona and Wendall for another day. I'd like to snag Uncle Ray again first."

She glanced at her watch and groaned. "It's almost time for lunch. I feel like we just finished breakfast. Let me fix my makeup, and then we can stroll around. We might run into Juanita again. The maid knows something about Jesse, if we could convince her to talk."

"Okay." Dalton rummaged through one of the built-in drawers. "Have you seen my blue shirt? I thought I'd put it in here."

She pointed to a set of cabinet doors. "Check the closet. I might have hung it up."

"Nope, not there either. Maybe it's still in my bag. I didn't unpack everything." He'd stashed his suitcase under the bed. Crouching, he tugged his luggage into view and unzipped it.

Marla heard the rattle at the same time as

Dalton's muttered expletive.

She spun around, her jaw dropping. A snake sat atop his clothes coiled and ready to strike.

CHAPTER NINE

"Omigod, don't move!" Marla cried. "What should we do?"

Dalton froze in place, staring at the snake tensed in his suitcase. "Look for a stick. Is there a broom around? Or you could get my .38 and shoot it." He'd brought his weapon and locked it in the room safe.

"Are you crazy? I'm likely to shoot you instead."

"Will you stand still? You're liable to spook the thing."

Marla shifted feet, too nervous to remain immobile. "He's probably scared and angry after being trapped in there. I'm surprised it didn't strike right away. Can you back off very slowly?"

Revulsion clogged her throat as she surveyed the snake's brown body, the diamond pattern along its back, and the triangular-shaped head raised and ready to attack. Its forked tongue darted out, tasting the air for its prey.

"He'd get me first. What if you sneak around and shut the lid?"

She swallowed past her fear. "I can try."

Keeping her eye on the snake, she sidestepped to her right. When nothing scary happened, she took another step and then another.

The rattling sound halted her in her tracks.

Dalton dove to his side as the snake leapt forward. Marla screamed as he hit the ground. The snake slithered across the floor toward the foyer.

"Did it bite you? Are you hurt?"

He examined his boot. "It got the leather, but I'm okay." He stuck his hand inside to make sure his skin hadn't been pierced. "I was lucky." Scrambling to his feet, he pointed to her cell phone lying on the nightstand. "We have to call for someone to get that thing out of here."

"Wait, I want to take pictures first. We need proof that this happened. Then we should see if Wayne is in his office. He'll know who can handle the snake."

Marla retrieved her cell phone and zoomed in on the creature to take a couple of shots. Then she and Dalton left the room through the glass patio doors.

"Someone deliberately put that snake in

your luggage," she said on their way down the winding path toward the lobby building.

"I agree. However, I don't think they necessarily meant to kill me. Snake bites can be fatal, but we're close to help. Unless that species is particularly toxic, likely I'd have pulled through from a strike."

"Maybe. Or you'd have died instantly. I don't know enough about snakes to identify this one. Either way, you'd have been out of commission for a while, if not for good."

Still shaky, she watched her footing. A line of ants trailed across a crack in their path toward a tall ocotillo. Its slender branches brought to mind grasping fingers. A shudder racked her. What next? A scorpion under their bed sheets?

She scanned the shaded walkway, thinking how appearances could be deceiving. The dude ranch appeared to be a tranquil resort where you could chase your worries away with a horseback ride or a campfire cookout. But beneath the surface, tensions seethed and bubbled.

They reported the incident to Wayne, at work inside his private office. Wayne's face registered surprise mixed with anger as Dalton related his tale.

"Damn, we have to catch the person responsible for these incidents. I'll send

188

Zeke from Maintenance over along with Bob Washburn. They'll know how to capture the snake and release it in the wild." He narrowed his eyes. "Are you sure the bite didn't penetrate your skin?"

Dalton showed him the indentations in his boot. "It didn't go through, thank heaven."

"How's Carol?" Marla asked while Wayne waited for a response from his staff members. Her knees wobbly, she sank into a chair. Images of the snake invaded her mind, and a shiver of horror shook her. She wouldn't feel safe in their room again until she'd checked every corner.

"Carol is much better, thanks. I dropped the kids off at school this morning before bringing her home from the hospital. Annie will get the children later this afternoon. I told my impatient wife she has to rest today. She can come back to work tomorrow if she's up to it."

"I could have kept her company to make sure she doesn't overexert herself."

"That's kind of you, but it's not necessary. She has a neighbor on call if needed."

"Carol is fortunate she wasn't hurt worse. So is Dalton. Why target us?"

Wayne closed his office door before responding. "You guys belong to our family.

189

Indirectly, a hit at you is an attack on my father. I know of one person who would be so underhanded as to strike at us that way."

"Don't tell me you're obsessing about Hugh Donovan?" Dalton scoffed. "You're sounding more like your father every day. You won't concede the culprit might be someone close by whom you've trusted."

"Why do you think I asked you to examine our employee records? I'm not so stubborn that I won't consider all the possibilities."

Good point, Marla thought. But then again, Donovan could have hired people to do his dirty work. Or his younger son might have done the same, aiming to get back at Hugh for a past grievance. He'd know about the angst between the two families.

"I'm doubtful the Donovans are guilty," Dalton said. "It's too easy to cast blame their way. Somebody else knows about this family feud. We should have a talk with Hugh Donovan in person to clear the air."

Wayne gave an adamant shake of his head. "You steer clear of him. You'll only incite the man further."

"When is the last time you spoke to the guy?"

"We don't speak. Dad forbade us when we were growing up."

"What about Ben, his older son?"

Wayne's lips compressed. "Ben seems all right. We knew each other in school. But generally, we kept out of each other's path."

"This can't be left alone. The incidents are escalating. Some of Uncle Ray's workers were killed in that explosion at Craggy Peak. Things are getting out of hand, and aside from what's happened to me and Carol, they seem less related to a personal feud between two men than to something more. I can't shake the feeling that we're missing the bigger picture."

"Nonetheless, I'm worried about you." Wayne's brow furrowed as he regarded his cousin. "I didn't mean to put your lives on the line when I asked you to investigate for me."

Dalton walked over and clapped his hand on Wayne's shoulder. "As long as I'm here, I won't let you face things alone. Meanwhile, Marla and I will pay another visit to Uncle Ray at his ghost town. I'd like to learn where the funding originated for his project."

Wayne's complexion darkened. "Good luck getting him to share his secrets."

"He might be persuaded to talk, considering how much we know at this stage."

Wayne's radio crackled, cutting their conversation short.

"We've got the snake," Bob's gravelly voice said on the other end. "It's a western diamondback. Their species isn't as deadly as some other snakes, but its venom can cause considerable damage."

"Would it have killed Dalton if he'd been bitten?" Marla raised her voice to be heard.

"Not necessarily. This type of snake is known for not backing off from a confrontation, but it will rattle to warn its victim. It bites hundreds of people a year, more than any other venomous snake in the country."

"Wonderful," Marla muttered.

"The diamondback is a pit viper, meaning it has heat-sensing facial pits to track its prey. Pit vipers differ from coral snakes, whose neurotoxic venom paralyzes the diaphragm so you can't breathe. Instead, a pit viper's venom is hemotoxic, meaning it affects blood vessels. The venom works as an anticoagulant so you bleed to death."

Marla's heart thudded in her chest at her husband's near-fatal miss. "How fast can that happen?"

"It depends. A rapid heart rate will spread the toxin faster."

Oh, like I could be calm if I'm bitten by a poisonous snake.

"So getting help right away is the crucial factor?"

"Absolutely. Bites by western diamond-backs can be fatal. The victim needs immediate medical treatment, including anti-venom."

"If I'd been bitten but got to the hospital right away, what would happen?" Dalton said. From his somber expression, Marla surmised he was imagining the dire prospects.

"You'd receive IV fluids to combat low blood pressure. After twenty-four hours, the main concern would be tissue death, plus infection from bacteria in the rattlesnake's mouth. Besides the anti-venom, you'd get antibiotics, a Tetanus shot, and antihistamines."

"How long might I have been out of commission?"

"Up to two weeks, if you responded well."

Dalton's jaw clenched, while Marla glanced at him in alarm. Two weeks? That would have been their whole vacation! She supposed it was better than dying, though.

After Wayne said a few more words and hung up, Dalton addressed him. "Marla and I will get lunch, and then we plan to visit Uncle Ray. Is he even at Craggy Peak?"

"Yes, the sheriff allowed him to resume operations. Watch your back, cuz." Wayne walked them to the door. "I'm not sure who to trust anymore."

"And you watch yours. Regardless of who's ultimately responsible, you have a mole on this ranch."

"Who do you suspect?" Marla asked her husband later on their way up the mountain.

Magnificent vistas opened on either side of them as they veered around curves and climbed at a steady pace. Clamping her hands together in her lap, Marla tried to relax but recent events kept her tense. So did the steep drops on either side of the road. While the scenery was breathtaking, she preferred the flatness of Florida. You couldn't drive off a cliff there, only into a canal.

"It couldn't be another guest," Dalton replied. "It has to be someone who's been around a while. Many of these folks have worked on the ranch for years, and they'd know Carol's riding habits. Any one of them could have been compromised."

"Like, they're being blackmailed into working for the person behind these threats, rather than seeking revenge directly on their own? Raymond believes Donovan is after his land."

"The prospective buyer could be someone else entirely."

"It that's true, then who's paying the saboteur?"

Dalton detoured around a dead animal in the road. "If the offers to buy Uncle Ray's property came through a real estate agent, his assumption that Hugh is behind them might be incorrect. We should speak to the agent."

Marla folded her brow. "I'd still like to interview Jesse. That man has something to hide. Remember how he reacted when he heard about Garrett's death?"

"I'm not discounting him, but he might have secrets for other reasons. Anyway, let's see what Uncle Ray says about his funding. He has to fess up. For all we know, he borrowed the money from a loan shark and lapsed on his payments."

Unfortunately, Raymond wasn't available when they checked in with his foreman.

"Sorry, *señor,* but the boss went into town for a meeting," the fellow said, raising a hand to shade his face from the sun. They'd found him supervising a crew set to demolish a concrete wall, the only evidence left of a former building.

"Do you know when he'll return?" Marla asked, unwilling to depart without gaining an iota of new information.

"Not really. You can wait around but not

here. It's too dangerous."

"Any word on the guy who went missing?" Dalton put a foot forward to brace himself on the sloped sidewalk.

"Eduardo is long gone. He was not lured by a ghost like these ignorant peasants believe. Maybe he got a better job else-where."

"So you think he ran away of his own voli-tion?"

Gomez glanced between them. "What I think does not matter. It is these *hombres* who need to focus on their work and not on their superstitions."

"I imagine the same could be said of the miners who used to live here," Marla said. "They must have had plenty of accidents and disappearances."

"The risk was part of their job." Gomez waved to a laborer who'd signaled him. "I have to go. If you intend to stay, keep to the side streets, out of the way of harm."

Standing among the weathered structures, Marla let a sense of history pervade her. Years of hard labor, passion, drinking, and gunfights weighted the crisp morning air. She admired Raymond, if not for his mate-rialistic expectations, then for his preserva-tionist fervor. It wasn't hard to picture the street restored to its former glory. Filled with cafés and boutiques, Craggy Peak would be a picturesque tourist attraction as well as a tribute to the mining camp.

Hmm, hadn't someone else been mentioned as a history buff? The person's name floated beyond her consciousness, but this might be an important clue if she could remember.

"Gomez wasn't much help," she remarked as they trudged up the hill toward the mountain at the far end. She stopped to catch her breath, recalling the altitude. At least she'd worn sturdy boots this time.

"His work is hazardous enough without having to worry about sabotage. I can't help wondering why someone might want Uncle Ray's project to fail, if it's not Hugh Donovan seeking revenge for past wrongs."

"They could desire the land for other reasons."

"Like what? If this person doesn't intend to restore the town, what value does it hold for them?"

"There has to be something more at stake here."

"That's what I've been saying." Dalton's face eased into a teasing grin. "Are we starting to read each other's minds? I hear that happens to married couples."

"What a scary idea." Her smile belied her words.

"Let's climb onto that ridge again. Maybe we'll see something we missed last time." He pointed to the spot overlooking the ghost town.

They moved off road further along. Marla grunted as she hefted herself over a pile of red rocks. This climb hadn't been easy the first time around, and it had not improved.

The views were worth the effort, though. Once atop the hill, she got a spectacular vista from any direction. It made her feel very small and part of an infinite universe.

"It's a good thing we ate a big lunch," she said as they continued on. Dalton seemed to handle the exertion with ease, while she had to pause every few feet.

Her vision wavered. Was she getting dizzy from lack of air, or had she seen something shimmer up ahead?

Dalton stopped to regard her with a frown of concern. "Are you okay?"

She pointed to a spot dense with shrubbery. "I thought I saw a sparkle there. It's in the vicinity where I felt a chill the first time we passed this way. Let's go and take a look. Maybe I'm imagining things."

Skirting boulders and treading cautiously over rocks, she made her way toward a dense tangle of shrubs. Gaining ground, she came to the area and halted abruptly.

"Be careful, there's a fissure."

Dalton peered over her shoulder at a wide crack in the earth. "I thought Carol said they don't have earthquakes in this territory."

"It could be a cave-in, perhaps from an old mine shaft. Craggy Peak must have miles of tunnels underlying these hills. Did you bring a flashlight?"

He gazed at her in dismay. "It's in the car. I should go back and get our supplies."

"I'll wait here so we don't lose this spot again. The sunlight must have struck a mineral in the rocks and made them sparkle. I wonder if that missing fellow, Eduardo, noticed the same thing."

"You'd better back away from there in case the area is unstable."

"I'll be fine. Go get our stuff."

She found a flat-topped boulder and sat while wishing she'd tied her hair back. She had grown it to shoulder length, which Dalton preferred, but it made her neck hot under the sun.

Her thoughts wandered to Annie and how she'd promised to cut the girl's hair. She should make a date to do the job when Annie had some free time. Her fingers itched to lift a comb and a pair of shears.

She silenced her thoughts to enjoy the peace. Wind whistled in her ears.

Wait a minute. There weren't any tall trees here with branches to rustle in a breeze. The sound was higher-pitched, like air zinging through a narrowed space.

She stood and edged closer to the gap in the ground. It was a pretty large hole. If you walked past without looking, you might stumble down into who knew where.

Her heart thudded in her chest. Could this be where Eduardo had vanished?

He might have seen something glittery and believed he'd seen an apparition. Gomez had said the workers were a superstitious lot. Or did the foreman suspect more than he let on? Maybe he thought something like this might have happened, but he didn't make more of an effort to investigate in order to keep his labor force on the job.

Marla wouldn't know anything definite until they had a better look. She hoped their flashlight would be powerful enough.

"Here's your sack," Dalton said upon his return. He tossed her a bulging backpack.

She unzipped her bag and rummaged among the packaged snacks, bottled water, and other supplies. "Where's the flashlight?"

"Right here." He lifted it to show her.

"What are you waiting for? Shine the light down there. Be careful not to fall in."

They touched shoulder-to-shoulder as they lay flat and stretched toward the fissure.

"My guess is this had been a ventilation shaft." Dalton aimed his beam downward. "It wouldn't have been the main entrance to the mine."

"And where is that exactly?"

"Uncle Ray said it's around the other side of the mountain. We'll have to research the area's history to see if any maps exist to the mine system." A strangled sound came from his throat.

"What is it?" She followed the path of light. Her gaze fell upon a man's body sprawled below. "Oh, no. Could that be —"

"Yes, I'm afraid so. I'll notify Luke Beresby."

"Can you get a cell signal up here?"

"Good question." He pulled out his phone. "Nope, we'll have to climb down a bit."

"Is he, you know, dead?" Her voice rasped in the dry air.

"He's not moving, and it's been several days now. You'd think he would have tried to get out, but maybe the fall broke his neck. Looks to be pretty far down there."

"What should we do?" Marla couldn't believe they'd found the missing worker.

"Call for help. Even if we had a rope, I wouldn't go down that hole."

Marla wouldn't either, but now she had an insatiable curiosity to learn more about the copper mines underlying the mountain.

That wasn't a concern for now. They had to summon the authorities and verify this man's identity. If he truly was the worker who'd gone missing, Raymond would have to be informed. He'd tell Gomez, who would share the news with his workmen. But first things first.

She trailed Dalton down the mountain with a heavy heart. They'd hoped for answers but not this somber ending.

Hold on. What if Eduardo had been lured there on purpose? Someone might have pushed him to make his demise appear accidental.

Acid burned her gut. They needed details on Garrett Long's death. Had the man been pushed off a ledge in a similar manner?

Wondering if they had a murderer on the loose gave her the willies. She stumbled in her anxiety and caught herself on a waist-high rock. A creature's tail slithered out of sight, and she leapt back with a cry. Rocks

202

could hide all sorts of critters. The sooner they reached civilization, the better. These hills were hazardous in more ways than one.

When the sheriff arrived, he brought with him a contingent of emergency personnel. They made quick time of accessing the site that Marla and Dalton had marked off with a trail of white wildflowers she'd picked along the way back.

Luke Beresby stroked his mustache. "I agree this might have been a ventilation shaft that caved in. The mountains in these parts are laced with tunnels. It's a good thing you weren't so foolish as to climb down there. What brought you to this specific location?"

Marla waved a hand. "I saw a sparkle. It may have been the sun hitting a mineral on one of those rocks."

"At least you're not claiming to have seen a ghost."

No, but if that guy is dead, there is one more haunting this hill.

It took a team effort along with a helicopter to lift the victim from the crevice. After confirming Eduardo's identity, Beresby strode over to Marla and Dalton who waited nearby.

"I'll call Raymond. He'll have info on the guy's family."

"What else did your team find down below?" Marla pointed to the crack in the earth.

"It opens into a mine shaft. We'll seal this entrance, but be careful if you're exploring." His eyes narrowed. "What were you two doing here anyway?"

Marla shifted her feet. "We were attempting to determine what might have happened to the missing worker. Raymond should have filed a missing person's report. It wasn't right to assume the guy had deserted his post."

She glanced at Dalton, who'd gone to examine the broken-off branches of the shrubbery overhanging the pit. Was she correct in thinking this might not have been an accident?

"Anything new on Garrett Long's death that you can share with us?" Dalton said, returning their way. Sweat glistened on his forehead.

"I'm concerned about this one at the moment," the sheriff replied.

The sun blazed down upon them in a clear blue sky, making Marla regret leaving her hat in the car. Just because the air was drier here didn't mean she should neglect the same precautions she took against the strong sun in Florida.

She regarded her husband through her sunglasses, wondering what he'd want to do next. They should probably leave to allow the sheriff to get on with business.

"If you don't require us for anything else, we'll move along," Dalton told Beresby. "I'd like to see if Uncle Ray needs our help. He'll have to deal with the fallout."

Raymond had returned to the ghost town by the time they approached. He stood conferring with his foreman, who stepped aside so they could have a private moment with Dalton's uncle.

"Luke told me the news," Raymond said without preamble. "The boys took it pretty hard. Alberto gave them the rest of the week off since it's already Thursday. Hopefully, we can get back to normal after the memorial service."

"The body might not be released for days," Dalton warned his uncle.

"I know, but these fellows are going to be high strung for a while. They still believe he saw a ghost that summoned him to his death. Did you two see anything up there that might indicate foul play?"

"Not necessarily. Eduardo might have spotted a glimmer, as did Marla, and gone to investigate. He could have stepped right into that hole without seeing it."

205

"Didn't you say the main entrance to the mine was elsewhere?" Marla asked. "Have you ever looked to see if it's still sealed?" Had Raymond consulted a survey of the tunnels to see how far they extended? Wouldn't that have been necessary before he began construction?

Raymond's hand fluttered in the air. "The main staging area for the mine is on Otto Lovelace's property now, and no one can get through his perimeter without an invitation."

"Otto invited me to tour his water bottling plant," Marla said, propping a hand on her hip. "I should take him up on his offer."

"You'd be one of the only people to see it, other than that engineer who performs the inspections." Raymond's sardonic tone revealed what he thought about Matthew Brigham.

"I met Mr. Brigham at his office in town. He seemed friendly enough."

Raymond glowered at her. "I don't care for either one of them. Take my advice, and be wary of Lovelace. That man isn't all there." He tapped his temple for emphasis.

"In what way?"

"The guy has an obsession with being on time. He's constantly looking at his watch, and gossip says he has a clock in every room of his estate."

"Why, Uncle Ray, I didn't realize you listened to gossip," Dalton teased.

The white-haired man harrumphed. "You can be sure there will be plenty of tales going around after this afternoon's activities."

"Not to belittle the dead man, but he's one more ghost to add to your ghost town."

"Yes, but I don't want those stories to scare people off."

"Where can we learn more about copper mining?" Marla said in a breezy tone to change the subject. "Didn't you say you were planning to open a museum here?"

Raymond lifted his brows. "Have you heard of the library? It may actually prove more useful than the Internet."

"Who are you planning to hire to run your museum? Do you have some old miner in mind?" She chuckled at her phrasing.

"I'll deal with that when the time comes." Raymond's curt tone was like a splash of water to her face. Had she said something to offend him?

"Is there anything we can do to help?" Dalton indicated the construction crew who lingered. Some stood chatting in clusters while others stayed to secure their equipment.

"No, thanks. I'm used to handling things on my own."

Maybe that's your problem. You don't know how to confide in family or give them your trust. It's a lonely path to follow.

"Come on, Dalton, we should go back to the ranch and rest."

CHAPTER TEN

It wasn't until they'd driven down the mountain that Marla recalled the reason why she and Dalton had visited the ghost town in the first place.

"We forgot to ask Raymond about his funding."

Dalton grimaced, his hands on the steering wheel. "That's right. I got distracted by our discovery. We should go into Rustler Ridge. I'd like to research town records to trace the ownership of the mine. Maybe I can find some blueprints to the tunnel system."

"Good idea. Drop me off at the library. I'll look up the mining industry and see what I can learn."

They split up after setting a rendezvous. Hours had elapsed since they'd set out to explore the hillside, and it would be dinner time soon.

Inside the library, she found an entire shelf

of books on the copper mining industry. Eager to read about the region's history, she picked an easy text and read the basics about the job. It wasn't an easy life for the men who chose it. Danger accompanied them deep into the shafts where accidents happened more often than not.

"The men lit their way by candles," she told Dalton when they met up in front of the post office at their allotted time. "Since they worked twelve-hour shifts, they brought their lunch pails with them and even had toilets in the mines. When mules were brought in later to haul the ore cars, the animals lived down there."

"That seems cruel."

"Nonetheless, mining was a prosperous occupation. Boomtowns sprang up around the mines, and support personnel flooded the area. The mines closed when copper prices dropped or the ore supply got depleted."

"In today's market, copper is highly valued. Some of those old mines might still have viable ore deposits." Dalton led her toward their car, which he'd parked at city hall. They traversed some of the narrow back streets as a shortcut. Electric wires were strung overhead, an anomaly against the stark blue sky.

"These days, the open pit technique is preferred over hard-rock mining. It's more cost efficient even though it ruins the land. And yet the underground mines produce better quality copper, according to what I've read. Some of those mines are being re-opened. Other minerals that are found along with copper could prove more valuable."

"I suppose those other elements are separated out during the refinement process?"

Marla nodded, feeling the warmth of the sun penetrate her back through her short-sleeved top. "Copper was processed at stamp mills. First the ore went through crushing machines and then powerful stamps broke it into smaller chunks. From there it went to the refinery, where chemicals melted the ore into a paste. This mixture was put into steam-heated pans where the precious minerals separated from the rocks. Coal-burning boilers produced the steam and provided power."

"So the stamp mill was separate from the refinery?"

"It could be, or they might be in the same place but in different buildings."

"Didn't we hear the mill for these mines had been located on Lovelace's property?"

"He probably tore it down before building his bottling plant." She gave a startled glance ahead. "Speak of the devil, there he is."

Two men stood speaking on a street corner in front of a house with a sign out front. Marla recognized Otto Lovelace's pudgy frame. The other guy appeared younger, with jet black hair and an angry stance. As she and Dalton neared, Marla read the business sign. It belonged to an accountant. Had the two of them come from there?

Otto recognized her with the precision of a man who memorized the features of each person he met. A flicker of displeasure crossed his face but it was quickly replaced by an expansive smile. "Mrs. Vail, how delightful."

"Hello, Mr. Lovelace. This is my husband, Dalton. I was just telling him we should take you up on the offer to tour your plant."

Otto indicated the other man, scowling at them as though annoyed they'd interrupted an important discussion. "This is Tate Reardon, our general manager. Tate, I understand Mrs. Vail is writing a blog article. She had some questions about plant operations, so I invited her to come see the facility for herself."

"I'd be happy to show you around," Reardon said in a stiff tone. He wore a navy sport coat with a blue and silver striped tie and midnight blue pants.

In contrast to his formality, Otto wore an open-neck shirt and belted trousers that appeared European in style. He pulled out a pocket watch and checked the time.

"It's nearly cocktail hour, Tate. I have to get home."

"Is your wife waiting for you?" Marla asked, wanting to learn more about him.

"I'm not married. Solitude is preferable, since most people don't appreciate the value of time. Every minute in our lives is precious. We must be precise in following our daily routines, or life slips away."

"That's true. How about you, Mr. Reardon?"

"I live with my wife, Eleanor, and our daughter."

Marla didn't mention her encounter with Christine at the nutrition clinic, but she wondered if Annie had made an appointment to speak to the girl's mother as planned.

"Why are you concerned about us?" Lovelace swept his hand in a broad gesture. "You two are on your honeymoon. What brings you into town this time?"

"I went to the library to read up on the

213

mining process," she said, glancing at Dalton.

His lips pressed together in his agreed-upon signal for her to continue. He let her lead the conversation while he looked for tells, or indications the men were lying. They worked well as a team that way.

"It's a fascinating history lesson, is it not? Life back then was a hardship." Lovelace shook his head in pretended sympathy. "No electricity. Miners had to work by candlelight and hammer their drills into the rock. Things are much easier today, except for the long hours."

"I read that the open pit technique is the preferred method these days."

"In most cases, but certain minerals are only obtainable below ground."

"I looked up real estate titles at city hall," Dalton said in a casual tone.

Lovelace gave him a sharp glance. "Is that right? And what did you learn?"

"That when you buy a piece of property here, the rights extend underground to a certain degree. That is, if nobody else steps in to stake a mining claim."

Lovelace's face darkened, and Reardon jabbed an elbow in his side. "You'll be late for your gin and tonic, Otto. You'd better go. I'll expect that information I requested on my desk by tomorrow morning."

"I told you what you wanted to know."

"That's not enough. I want documentation."

"I said it'll take more time."

Reardon snickered. "Time is one commodity you can't control, despite your attempts to do so. It's tomorrow or else."

Marla's scalp prickled at his words. How dare he bark orders at his boss? What hold did he have over the man to threaten him?

"Man, I could use a drink after our discovery on the mountain," she said to defuse the situation, fanning herself as though hot and weary. Dalton didn't move a muscle, doubtless eager to see what would happen next.

"You went hiking?" Reardon glanced at their boots, dusty from their efforts. "It can be dangerous on these hills if you're not familiar with the territory."

Garrett Long's familiarity with the area didn't help him. "We explored the hillside above the ghost town and discovered the worker who'd disappeared. Didn't you see the helicopter?"

"What?" the other two men said in unison, staring at her.

"Eduardo fell down a hole, evidently a collapsed ventilation shaft left from the min-

215

ing days. The poor man is dead. He must have broken his neck upon impact."

"That's horrible." Reardon's face paled.

"I imagine the surface caved in. It makes you wonder what's beneath the town my uncle is renovating," Dalton said, raising his eyebrows.

"People should steer clear of the mountains around these parts." Lovelace's mouth curved downward. "They're full of hazards."

"Rescue personnel lifted the body out with the helicopter. I wonder what else they saw below. It appears the shaft connected to the old tunnel system," Marla added.

"Whatever existed of historical value would have been removed when the mines were closed, so I doubt anything worthwhile remains. The entrance was sealed off for a reason. Don't think of going down there," Lovelace warned in a blustery tone.

"I understand the old stamp mill sat on what's now your property. Did you tear it down before building your bottling facility?"

"Naturally. What would I want with a dilapidated place like that?"

"It must have been an immense, dirty old structure with lots of rusty machinery." She stared into the distance at the barely visible white plume in the sky. "I wonder what color smoke it produced."

Lovelace glowered at her. "I wouldn't know, Mrs. Vail. I haven't studied the ore separation process."

"Oh, but I have. The miners would have had a changing room near the main staging area. Did you come across that place when you bought your property? Would you believe they only washed their work clothes once a week? Ugh, it must have stunk in there."

"I'm glad you find the region's history so compelling. What did you say your blog was titled?"

"That's not the only reason we're interested," Dalton said, catching on. "My Uncle Ray has run into a few snags with his ghost town project, and he's asked us to help straighten things out while we're here."

"You're related to Ray Campbell? Good luck to him. If he's hired immigrants to do the work, he'll have his hands full."

That's a biased statement. Marla wanted to call him on it but didn't.

Lovelace gave a slight bow. "Now if you'll excuse me, it's nearly time for my nightly restorative. One mustn't break with routine, or havoc will ensue."

"Of course." Marla smiled at the men. "Nice to meet you, Mr. Reardon. I'll look

217

forward to a guided tour at the bottling plant. I imagine it's close to the source? I heard you pay the city for a certain amount of natural spring water each month."

"That is so." The guy hadn't once cracked a smile. "I hope you folks have a good visit while you're in town." His scornful glance indicated he took Dalton for a harmless tourist, but then Dalton's casual attire and silly grin would reinforce that belief. Her husband could play act when necessary.

She loved that about him. Hooking her arm into his as they strolled along later, she told him so. "You were great. What did you gather from that meeting?"

Her gaze lit on the landscape as they headed toward their car. She still couldn't get used to the lack of grass, and yet that made for a quieter neighborhood. No lawn mowers, weed trimmers, or leaf blowers making a racket.

"Those two are at odds about something. We should go tour that plant. It might be enlightening. I should have asked Lovelace why armed guards patrol his perimeter."

"He could be afraid of eco-terrorists as the sheriff suggested."

"Perhaps. Or he has something to hide. By the way, I'm not the only one interested in town records. Jesse Parker has been to city hall recently. I saw his name on the visitor list."

"Really? I wonder what he was researching?"

"Me, too. Why would a wrangler be involved in these affairs?"

Dalton's phone rang. He glanced at the caller I.D. before answering. "Hey, how's it going, cuz?" A pause. "Sure, we'd be delighted." Covering the mouthpiece, he addressed Marla. "Is it okay if we go to dinner at Wayne's house? He says Uncle Ray and Annie will be there. She's cooking dinner to give Carol a rest. We can drive over directly from here."

Her musings about Jesse Parker evaporated. "That would be nice, if they won't mind the way we're dressed. We don't have time to change."

"I wouldn't worry about it." Dalton confirmed their invite and then hung up. "I got the impression Wayne wants us there for support. Uncle Ray is disheartened by today's events."

"I don't blame him. Another death in the area? It makes you want to believe the ghost stories. Maybe his project is cursed."

"Or maybe somebody wants it to seem that way to scare off his work force."

"The laborers might not have heard about

the forest ranger."

"My experience is that news travels fast in these small communities. It *is* strange that both men experienced a fatal fall, though."

"No one else could have known a ventilation shaft was there. Eduardo's death seems more likely to have been an accident."

"You could be right." He took her hand in his large palm. "At any rate, let's try to relax and enjoy the evening."

Raymond was in a sour mood when he greeted them inside Carol's kitchen. "Come and join me for a beer. My project has another delay, so I might as well take advantage."

"By drinking yourself into a stupor?" Annie, bringing over a plate of cheese and crackers, clucked her tongue. "You've had two bottles already. What's eating you, Dad? You're not responsible for the guy's death."

"Huh, that's easy for you to say. As his employer, I could be held liable."

"So? You have insurance."

"I know what's bothering you. It's those mining tunnels, isn't it?" Dalton leaned against a counter. "They bring back bad memories."

Raymond popped open a bottle top and took a long gulp. "The sheriff said they'd

220

probably release the fellow's body by Sunday. I notified his next of kin."

"That's never an easy job. It's one I've often had to do myself. But you didn't answer my question. Tell us about your brother Harold and how he died in a mine."

A dish clattered, and Carol's gasp echoed throughout the room.

"Wayne, get in here," Dalton called. "You'll want to hear this. Carol, are you okay?"

"Yes, I'm fine," she said as Wayne joined them.

Marla was glad Carol didn't seem any worse from her tumble off the horse. She looked a bit pale and moved more slowly but otherwise appeared well enough.

Raymond's gaze radiated pain as he regarded them all, standing and staring at him. Fortunately, the kids were playing in a back room so the adults had time alone. Marla agreed they had to clear the air. It was the only way to mend their broken fences.

"We learned what happened to your younger brother," she said in a kind tone. "It was an accident."

"Dad, what's she talking about?" Wayne said, his voice rising. "I had an uncle? Is this why we don't have any of your early family pictures, because you didn't want me to know?"

"I imagine the memories are too painful for him," Dalton said in a wry tone. "Do you want to tell him, Uncle Ray, or should I?"

"Come, let's sit down." Raymond's shoulders slumped as he deflated like a balloon. "It's a long story and not a happy one."

Annie turned off the oven and followed them into the family room, where they took seats on the couch and the barstools. Raymond hung his head and twisted his hands together as he repeated the story Dr. Harrigan had told Marla and Dalton.

"You can't blame Hugh Donovan, Dad." Wayne put a hand on his father's knee. "You were both kids at the time. Things like that are bound to happen."

Raymond's eyes glistened. "I should have listened to Kate. She ran to get help, but by the time she returned, it was too late. I'd favored Hugh over my own brother. It's my fault he died."

"You weren't responsible then, and you are not responsible now for that workman's death or the explosion at Craggy Peak."

"Kate still doesn't talk about me, does she?"

"No, but then you've never made any attempt to reconcile with her," Dalton said. "Maybe after all this time, she'd offer forgiveness. But you need to forgive yourself first."

Silence fell heavily over them. Marla sought words of comfort. She'd been through a similar guilt trip but had survived and used the experience to better herself.

"Why did Grandma leave and take Kate with her?" Wayne said in a choked tone.

"She blamed her husband because he pushed Harry to be more like me. We couldn't accept his quieter nature and love for books. Pop wanted him out among the horses, loving the outdoors and land same as I do." Raymond gazed into the distance, his face crisscrossed with lines like the cracked, dry earth. "So Ma took Kate and moved back east to be near her parents. Being close to me reminded her of Harry's death."

"You must have felt abandoned."

"I considered it my just punishment for what I'd done. I couldn't be near Hugh after that. He'd told my folks he was sorry, but my father forbade me to associate with him anymore. Said he was a bad influence."

"So it was easy for you to project your guilt onto him."

"Man was a bastard when he grew up, too.

223

After he chased his younger son away, I ran into Flora one day in town."

"Wait a minute," Annie's voice squeaked. "Who's Flora?"

"His late wife. They had two kids, Ben and Jake. Flora and I had known each other in high school." His skin flushed beet red. "Heck, we'd been sweethearts in those days. But she chose Hugh over me. I guess after the accident, nobody saw me in a good light. I'd let my younger brother die."

"Dad, stop beating yourself up over it," Annie said in a pleading tone. "You have to let go and put Harry to rest."

Marla exchanged a glance with Carol, feeling like an outsider during an intimate family moment. Maybe they should leave their men alone for privacy. But then, the guys needed support. This skeleton had hidden in their closet for too long.

"You mentioned Hugh's younger son," she ventured, to get the older man talking again. "Why did he run away from home?"

"Poor kid was like our Harry. Jake grew up on a ranch, but he loved computers and wanted to go to City College. Hugh wouldn't hear of it. I don't know what happened to break them apart. Jake hasn't been heard from since then."

"He didn't stay in contact with his

mother?"

"Flora died a year later from cancer, although I think heartbreak brought it on. Stress can do that to people, you know. I tried to comfort her, and we . . . well, the old flame rekindled."

"Oh, no, Dad. You didn't!" Annie jumped up to pace the room.

"Well, your mom was gone, and a man has needs. It's a kindness that Flora died not so long after, or Hugh might have done the deed himself. He was furious when he found out."

Wayne shot his father a derisive glance. "No wonder he hates you."

"Look, I wish I could go back in time and undo all the bad things I did, but I can't. I have to live with these memories, and that's my retribution."

"It's more than retribution if Hugh is trying to destroy you," Wayne said. "You both have reasons to resent each other. He egged you on with your brother, and you seduced his wife. So now you're left without a sister, and his son is gone."

"Maybe you two have more in common than you dare to admit," Marla remarked. "You'd been best friends once. Have you ever thought about apologizing to Hugh?"

"Who, me? If he hadn't been so mean-hearted, Flora wouldn't have needed comforting."

"But you took advantage of the situation. Maybe your subconscious saw it as a way to get back at Hugh and cause him the same pain he'd brought you."

"It doesn't matter now, does it? He's out to get me one way or another."

Marla lifted her exasperated gaze to meet her husband's. This wasn't like any kind of honeymoon they might have imagined. *Oy, vey.* Family issues could be so complicated.

"It does matter to my mother," Dalton said to his uncle. "She was very happy to meet Wayne and Carol at our wedding. I'd bet she would love to hear from you."

"Time can soothe a lot of injuries," Marla said in a gentle tone. "She was only a child then, too. Maybe part of her silence is guilt mixed with regret."

"Or maybe she heard about me and Flora through the grapevine, and that compounded my sins in her mind."

"Speaking of sins, what other secrets are you keeping from us, Dad?" Wayne's brows lifted in sharp angles like two pointed arrows. "Such as, where did you get the cash to buy Craggy Peak?"

"That's nobody's business but mine."

"What affects you touches the rest of us.

226

If you're saddled with debts, we should know about it now. Carol is a financial wizard. She could help you."

"You needn't worry. I don't owe any money."

"You didn't borrow from anyone? Or take out a loan?"

"Nope." Raymond shot to his feet. "Isn't dinner ready? That roast must be over-cooked by now." Indeed, a fragrant aroma scented the air, but it had a tinge of burnt meat to it.

Everyone scrambled to their posts to get the meal ready, while Dalton took Marla aside.

"You know what I think? Uncle Ray has an investor, and he doesn't want to give away the guy's name."

"Like a silent partner?"

He nodded, his face grim. "And I'm afraid this might be another bad choice my uncle made."

CHAPTER ELEVEN

"I have a proposition for you," Annie said to Marla after they'd cleared the dinner dishes.

"That's great, because I have one for you, too." Marla had remembered that she'd stuck her shears in her purse before they'd set out that day. Maybe Annie would have time for a haircut now. "You go first."

"I have an appointment tomorrow at two o'clock with Eleanor Reardon to discuss her daughter's progress. Would you like to take a drive with me? She lives in the Big Rocks section, and it's a beautiful area. Tourists drive through just to see the homes wedged among the rocks."

"I wouldn't want to intrude on your conversation."

"You could sit outside and admire the view. We'll go to lunch first — my treat — and then ride over."

"Okay, that sounds great." She felt a

twinge of guilt for making plans that didn't include Dalton, but he could manage alone for a few hours.

"What did you want to ask me?" Annie picked up a couple of dessert plates to bring to the dining room table.

"Do you still want me to style your hair? If so, I have my shears with me."

"Yes, I'd love it!" She put the plates down on the table and clapped her hands. "I am *so* ready for a makeover. Will you need to shampoo me first?"

"I can wet your hair with a spray bottle if you have one handy."

Marla couldn't wait to get started on Annie's hair. Once they'd finished dessert, she set up shop inside one of the bathrooms. They left the men right as Dalton began telling Wayne and Raymond about their encounter with Lovelace and Tate Reardon. She'd miss what his relatives said about the pair, but he could fill her in later.

She told Annie instead while snipping her damp strands of hair.

"We ran into your client's father in town today. Mr. Reardon was speaking to the owner of the bottling plant in front of an accountant's office."

"Is that so?" Annie watched her movements in the mirror. She sat on a desk chair they'd appropriated from Carol's home office. "That wouldn't be anything unusual. Mr. Reardon works for Lovelace."

"They seemed to be arguing."

"That would go along with my theory about Christine's father having problems at work."

"Have you heard anything else to make you suspect otherwise?" Marla's fingers paused, but then she carried on, trimming Annie's hair and adding layers.

"Not really. I'm hoping to learn more at my interview tomorrow. What's Lovelace like? I've never met him."

"He's a big guy who speaks with a cultured accent and always acts pressed for time. At least he dresses decently." She couldn't imagine Lovelace in a cowboy's plaid shirt or jeans.

"I did hear he comes from Europe and likes expensive clothes."

"What about his water product? Is it popular?"

"Heck, yes, you must have seen Arizona Mountain High in all the stores."

Marla gripped her shears tighter. "I wonder why he picked that particular location for his plant? I'd looked up water bottling facilities in Arizona on the Internet. Most of them appear to be located in big cities."

"They probably use purified municipal water. Lovelace may have wanted to be near the source of a natural spring. Imagine the competitive edge he'd have in his advertising campaign."

"I suppose you're right. I'd rather buy bottled water that comes from a fresh mountain stream than from a city system." She wrinkled her nose, thinking of processed sewer water. The cities must obtain drinking water from their underground aquifers which the processing plants ran through filtration systems. Still, she liked the idea better of a gurgling mountain stream as a source.

"His brand is doing well." Annie crossed her legs, making Marla halt a moment.

"Is it publicly or privately owned? I mean, could I buy stock in the company?"

"No, it's private. I know that much." Marla unclipped a top section of hair and cut it at an angle. The snipped pieces fell to the tile floor. She'd get a broom and sweep it up afterwards.

"I'm wondering about the ranger who died. Could Lovelace's compound be located anywhere near forestry land?

"Lovelace built his facility on the foundation of the old stamp mill. I suppose it's possible the location might be near federal-owned territory. You'd have to talk to the forest service people to see how far their boundaries extend."

"That might be a good idea. I'm curious about where Garett fell to his death and how that site relates to Lovelace's facility."

Marla had a lot more questions about the industrial complex on the mountain, but she put them aside for now. She'd take Lovelace up on his offer for a tour and sound him out then.

Annie loved her new haircut and told Marla so again on Friday when they met for lunch, followed by their excursion to the Big Rocks section of town.

"I hope Mrs. Reardon remembers our appointment. We confirmed yesterday so it should be all right." Her hands on the wheel, Annie concentrated on the winding road that curved up yet another mountain.

Marla's jaw dropped at the enormous boulders that made up these hills. How had these rocks evolved? And how could they be stable over the years? She'd be afraid to live in a place that might be crushed in an instant. The boulders could be a giant's creation, tossed there during child's play like so many pebbles. Piled onto each other, they formed a towering mountain whose harsh landscape was broken by an occasional green shrub. Against a brilliant blue sky, the enormous rocks were an awesome sight.

One spectacular view after another revealed itself as they wound around each curve. In between one craggy piling and another gentler slope sat a flat-roofed house, its wide glass windows on a second-story balcony overlooking the valley. A singular stalk of saguaro cactus stood its ground like a defiant finger aimed at the sky gods.

The next dwelling was a three-story house supported by concrete pilings. Good thing this region doesn't have earthquakes, Marla thought with a shiver. *You couldn't pay me to live in one of these homes, no matter how beautiful.* She liked her feet to be on solid — or make that flat — ground. She did admire the next multi-level, Spanish-style home painted peach with white trim.

If the Reardons lived in this area, they must have a good income. Imagine what you had to pay workmen to haul materials to these heights.

Annie pulled into the driveway of a French country-style residence. The two-story structure sat on a relatively flat area amongst a compilation of boulders. The house had a stone exterior, brick chimneys, and a sloped shingle roof. As they emerged from the car,

233

Marla noted the careful placement of cacti and plants on a yard made up mostly of granite chips. A few graceful trees provided shade and a splash of color against the relentless rocks.

They approached a columned front porch that held wicker furniture and a magnificent view of the valley. A warm breeze whistled through the hills, stirring her hair. Otherwise, the eerie stillness unnerved her, especially when no one answered the door bell.

"Maybe Mrs. Reardon is indisposed," she suggested. "Give her a minute."

When the lack of response persisted, Marla prowled around to the side of the house along a flagstone path. She noted two rear entrances and a bicycle leaning against a wall. Beyond was a detached three-door garage. Not hearing any summons from Annie, Marla strode forward and peeked inside the garage window. A sleek black vehicle was parked inside.

She hurried back to the porch where Annie pounded on the door to no avail.

"I've never had a client stand me up before. Do you think she forgot?"

"You said you'd confirmed the date, and there's a car parked in the garage."

"That doesn't mean anything. It could be

a spare."

"Maybe Mrs. Reardon had to pick up Christine at school and forgot to notify you."

"I guess that's possible. I'll give her a call." Annie's brow creased with worry as she withdrew her cell phone from her bag.

Does she feel the same sense of unease as I do?

"I'll try knocking on the rear door," Marla said. "Mrs. Reardon might be inside the laundry room or somewhere she can't hear us."

She glanced into each window as she swept past. A living room had contemporary furnishings, cream-colored walls hung with paintings, a grated fireplace, wood floors partially covered with an Oriental rug, and expensive-looking accent tables.

The dining room must be on the opposite side as both faced front. At the rear corner, she spied a study. As that appeared empty, she moved on to what must be either the master suite or a guest bedroom. It had a king-sized bed, a cherry wood dresser and mirror, and other furnishings. One door led to the rear terrace from this room. She knocked there and waited a few heartbeats, but no one responded. The next window must belong to a bathroom.

As Marla moved on, she called Annie on her cell phone. The line was clear, and Annie picked up after the second ring.

"Has anyone come to the door yet or answered your call?"

"No, where are you?"

"I'm in the back. I haven't seen anyone so far. Wait, here's the kitchen. There's another door. I'll try this one." The door's glass inlay allowed her to survey the modern granite countertops, stainless steel appliances, white cabinetry, and tiled backsplash.

The kitchen opened into a dining nook at the far end with a mountain view. Her gaze slid toward the commercial-style gas range and then beyond.

Her heart somersaulted in her chest.

"Wait, I see something on the floor. Good God. I think it's a pair of men's shoes."

"So what?" Annie's voice sounded in her ear.

"You don't get it. Someone is lying on the floor. Call for help." Marla rattled the door knob, but it was locked.

She rushed to rejoin Annie on the front porch, where both waited impatiently until the sheriff arrived.

Sheriff Beresby greeted them with a stern expression. "What's this about, ladies? Has there been an accident?" He singled out

Marla. "Don't tell me you found another body."

She bristled at his condescending tone. "Annie had a business appointment with Mrs. Reardon, but when no one appeared to be home, I went around to the back door in case she didn't hear us knocking. That's when I saw him."

"Who?"

"A man lying on the kitchen floor."

The sheriff's eyes narrowed, and his lips thinned. "Stay here while I take a look."

He disappeared around the side of the house. Returning less than ten minutes later, Beresby spoke rapidly into his radio. "That's right, get a unit up here. And send out a call for Dr. Shapiro. The M.E. is out of town today."

"Did you go inside?" Marla asked as soon as he'd hung up.

"No, the door is locked. I called for a hazardous materials unit in case there's a gas leak. If so, nobody goes in until the air is clear. You'd better wait at the bottom of the driveway."

Annie drove them downhill and parked on the side of the road. It would be a hike to climb back to the house, Marla thought with a grimace as they exited the vehicle.

"What will happen if that place explodes?"

Annie said with a fearful glance at the rocks piled behind the house.

"It might loosen some of those boulders. Or not. The house appears to sit on a fairly solid piece of ground. At least they don't have to worry about evacuating any neighbors. But how could there be a gas leak? Does that happen here often? And where is Mrs. Reardon?"

Annie's face turned the color of bleached hair. "She could be inside in a bedroom."

"Let's hope Christine is still at school." But who would tell the girl if something bad had happened to her parents? Marla prayed that wouldn't be the case.

Firefighter trucks arrived along with the special hazard unit, another sheriff's department car, and a silver Lexus SUV. That car must belong to the doctor they'd called. It wasn't the medical examiner's vehicle.

A flurry of activity ensued, while Marla paced in her anxiety. She texted Dalton that she'd gotten tied up and would be delayed in returning. She'd tell him the details later. No sense in worrying him now since things were under control.

An hour or more passed while she and Annie sat on a flat-topped boulder and waited for an all clear signal. When someone finally opened the front door, Marla gathered it was safe to return.

Voices came from inside the foyer as she and Annie stepped across the threshold.

"I assume the risk of explosion has ended?" she said upon spying the sheriff. He stood consulting a tall, dark-haired fellow she didn't recognize. "I don't smell anything."

An umbrella stand stood incongruously next to a radiator in the hallway. *Umbrellas, in the desert?* Her quick scan took in an oval mirror on one wall, a curio cabinet, and a large potted plant.

"You wouldn't detect an odor," the stranger said, glancing at her and Annie with raised eyebrows. "Carbon monoxide is odorless but deadly. We aired the place out before coming inside."

"You mean, there really was a gas leak?"

"It appears so, but we're still investigating."

"We had an appointment with Mrs. Reardon," Annie said in a breathless tone. "Did anyone check to see if —"

"There's no one else in the house, miss . . . ?"

"I'm Annie Campbell, and this is Marla Vail."

"Dr. Steve Shapiro. I have a medical practice in town. Sometimes the cops call me if the M.E. isn't available." When he smiled at them both, his cheeks dimpled and his dark brown eyes radiated warmth.

From the way he was eyeing Annie, Marla wondered if he was single. He looked to be in his thirties. What had brought him to this small town? Maybe he liked the great outdoors. From his athletic build, either he worked out to keep in shape or he was into riding and hiking. Or perhaps he enjoyed mountain biking. She remembered the bicycle propped outside the Reardons' house.

That brought a lump to her throat. She'd almost forgotten their reason for being here.

"Ladies, I appreciate your hanging around." The sheriff stroked his droopy mustache. "I have a few quick questions for you now, but I'd appreciate it if you'd stop by my office later to give a formal statement."

"What about the man in the kitchen?" Marla asked with a sense of dread.

"I'm afraid we were too late for Tate Reardon."

Annie clapped a hand to her mouth, while Marla's mental gears zipped back to the heated discussion between Reardon and Otto Lovelace. Had that happened only yesterday? She couldn't wrap her mind around the ensuing conclusions.

Annie suddenly teetered on her feet. The sheriff shot out an arm to steady her.

"Whoa, are you all right? Do you want to sit? We could go into the living room."

Annie shook her head. "I'll be okay, thanks."

"You say you'd had an appointment with Mrs. Reardon?"

"Yes, and I've been unable to reach her or their daughter. I called Christine's school and told them I was her nutritional advisor. They said Christine didn't show up for class today. Her mother had phoned and said the girl was sick. That can't be true, or they'd have been home."

How did Tate happen to be off from work, anyway? Marla's heart skipped a beat as another alarming thought surfaced. Reardon's wife hadn't fled the scene because she'd instigated it, had she?

"Did you speak to Eleanor on the phone when you confirmed your engagement?" she asked Annie.

"Well, no. We texted each other. Here, I can show you." She retrieved the messages and flashed them at Marla and the men.

"Tate was alive yesterday. Dalton and I ran into him talking to Otto Lovelace in front of an accountant's office," Marla

241

informed the lawman. "They appeared to be arguing."

Beresby's gaze hardened. "I'll have a talk with Lovelace."

The doctor interrupted. "Sheriff, if you're finished with me, I'd like to get back to work. I have patients waiting."

The men shook hands. "I owe you another one, Steve."

"I hope the family is found unharmed." Dr. Shapiro extended his hand to the women. His grip held Annie's for longer than usual. "Ladies, I wish we'd met under different circumstances. Do you live around here, or are you visiting?"

Annie gave him a shy smile. "I own a nutrition clinic in town. In fact, I'd love to get together with you to discuss my services. You might want to refer some of your patients my way."

"That would be great." They exchanged business cards. "If you don't hear from me, give me a call. And you?" he asked Marla in a polite tone.

"My husband and I are on our honeymoon. We're staying at Last Trail Dude Ranch. Annie and I are cousins by marriage."

"Well, I hope you enjoy your visit. I'm sorry this tragedy had to happen."

As soon as he left, Marla spun to face the sheriff. "So was this accident a terrible tragedy, or did someone have a hand in it?"

He scrutinized her. "Why would you say that?"

"I'm wondering about your investigation into Garrett Long's death."

"What does that have to do with this incident?"

She shifted feet, feeling overly weary and wishing she could sink into a chair. "The two cases might be connected."

"We haven't made any determinations yet." He glanced past her as a crime scene unit pulled into the driveway in the space vacated by the doctor's vehicle. "Our forensics team is here. They're called routinely for unattended deaths. As a detective's wife, you should know these things."

She didn't care for his disapproving tone. Her glance extended down the hallway. "I know a lot more, Sheriff. Here's a question for you. How come the smoke detectors didn't go off? Don't they have sensors for carbon monoxide?"

"Hmph, you're right. That's a valid point. I'll have the boys check them." He took out a notebook and pen. "Now if you can give me Mrs. Reardon and Christine's contact info, I'll be grateful. I would also like for you to repeat exactly what happened when you arrived here. And let me see that text message from yesterday again."

He took notes while they spoke. When he appeared satisfied that they'd told him everything, he dismissed them with the reminder to visit his office and sign a formal statement.

As Annie drove downhill, Marla studied her pursed lips and worried eyes.

"Are you okay? It's been a tough day."

At least you didn't see the body. I've been through that experience a number of times, and it never gets easier. I don't know how Dalton appears so calm at crime scenes.

He wasn't immune, not really. The man looked to her for comfort and normalcy when he came home. Her heart swelled, and she yearned for his presence. She'd drive straight to the ranch after Annie dropped her off.

"I'm concerned about Christine and her mother. Where could they have gone? It's lucky they weren't at home when this happened, but who's going to tell them?"

"That would be Sheriff Beresby's job." Was it luck on the wife's part, or was her absence deliberate? Was Eleanor missing because she had perpetrated a crime? And was it a crime or merely a sad accident?

244

Another possibility reared its ugly head. Maybe Eleanor and Christine had been abducted.

Heaviness weighed on her soul. It wasn't her task to investigate, thank heavens.

"I wish I could help, but it's not my case," Dalton said, after she met him back at their hacienda and related her story.

He'd gone for one of the guided rides into the hills and had already showered and changed by the time she'd returned. Now she faced him, marveling at the handsome figure he made in his sport shirt and jeans.

"But the sheriff might be glad for your input. He seems to be in charge of every investigation. Why don't you offer him your assistance?"

It's not as though she wanted her husband to leave her side, but the sooner they solved these mysteries, the sooner peace would reign on the ranch.

"We came here to help Wayne, remember? That's our first priority, and I feel bad enough that we lack any solid answers."

Marla conceded his point and sought to comfort him. "We've learned a lot so far. Don't discount the various pieces of information we have gathered. It all ties together. We'll figure it out. Meanwhile, we should return to the mountain where we found

Eduardo."

"What for?" Dalton gave her a quizzical glance.

"Maybe there's another opening to the mines below," Marla suggested.

"You're insane. Why would you want to go there when we've been warned a hundred times about the risks?"

"We could hire a guide, someone who knows these mountains. I'd like to determine where Otto Lovelace's property is in relation to the ghost town and the crevice where we found Eduardo. We could also check out the ledge where Garrett fell to his death. If we find something significant, it might resolve the issues with Hugh Donovan."

"It's becoming more remote that he's involved in these incidents. My uncle is wrong to blame him and disregard other possibilities."

"I agree." She yanked off her boots and flopped onto the bed. "What did you think of Raymond's confession? Your uncle has a lot of black marks on his soul."

"He's a character, all right. The man has paid the price for his brother's death. You can see it in his eyes."

"It would be a nice gesture on Kate's part

to make the first move toward reconciliation."

"At least my mother left the ranch when she was young, so she wouldn't have known about Uncle Ray's philandering. That's another strike against him."

"Who doesn't make mistakes, Dalton? I've done my share." Marla stretched out and scanned the ceiling for spiders. Oops, she'd forgotten to check under the pillow before laying her head down. "You can also tell how guilty he feels by his reluctance to talk about these events. He knows he's done wrong. It could be that his fervor about the ghost town is his way of atoning for his sins. He's giving back to the community by preserving the region's history."

"Yes, by using somebody else's money. If we knew who was funding him, we might learn who is causing the accidents. Maybe the silent partner wants Raymond to fail so he can take over. I'll talk to the sheriff about it. He's probably looking into my uncle's affairs and might know something we don't."

"What can we do to uncover the mole among Wayne's staff? Have you tracked down Jesse to interview him?"

"He was on the ride this morning, but I didn't learn much except that he knows the territory. He's a natural sitting on his horse, like he was born there. He asked me about my work and the technology we use. I thought it was odd."

"How so?"

"His face lit up when we talked about computers. He seems more enamored of those machines than horses. When I brought up the problems at the ranch, he scowled and said Uncle Ray was too quick to jump to conclusions."

"What does that mean?"

"He wouldn't say. As for Garrett Long, Jesse got defensive when I mentioned Long's name. It's clear Jesse had some sort of relationship with the man that went beyond his duties as a wrangler." Dalton sat next to her and tickled her arm, giving her a sexy smile. "What do we know about Long's family?"

"Not a whole lot. We should inquire about the memorial service. The funeral might have taken place already."

"If so, I'm sure the sheriff attended."

"Now he'll be busy investigating Tate Reardon's death," Marla said, disconcerted by her husband's roving fingers.

"We could pay a visit to the forest supervisor's office as you'd suggested."

"Or not. You just told me we should stick to Wayne's affairs."

248

"All right, so I can't help myself. Where there's a crime, my nose follows." He grinned at her before bending down to nuzzle her as though to demonstrate his words.

"Not now. It's dinner time, and you're already dressed."

"Then let's head out. What's tonight's lecture?"

She scrambled up and went to check the schedule. "*Cactus Up Close.* I think we can skip that one. Let's relax for a change and plan our excursion for tomorrow. Where can we hire a hiking guide?"

"I'll ask Uncle Ray in the morning. He'll know who's experienced around here. Besides, we'll want to park at Craggy Peak and set off from there."

Raymond must have been on the same wavelength, because he called Dalton right after they finished breakfast on Saturday morning. While Dalton listened, his face registered surprise followed by dismay.

"What do you mean, you found a bomb inside one of your buildings?"

CHAPTER TWELVE

After a quick interchange with his uncle, Dalton pushed the End button. The dour look he gave Marla didn't bode well.

"Get your things. We're heading over to Craggy Peak."

"Raymond found a bomb there? For real?"

"He's already called the sheriff, but he wants us to come. He's got something to show us. Don't worry, we'll stay at a safe distance from the incendiary device."

She strode alongside him at a brisk pace away from the dining hall. The morning air was cool and delightfully dry, and she didn't miss the droplets of moisture you could almost see suspended in the air at home in South Florida. In the distance, the hills rose with majestic beauty, colored beige in the rising sunlight with splashes of greenery.

The message spray-painted on a wall at the ghost town was done in green as well. The words "E.F.A." didn't mean anything to Marla. She glanced down the hilly street, deserted except for emergency personnel.

"Where is everyone?" she asked Raymond, who'd met them upon their arrival. The older man looked haggard this morning, as though recent events had taken their toll.

"We gave the guys this weekend off, remember? I've arranged a memorial service for Eduardo. He doesn't have any relatives here, so his body will be shipped home. We'll resume work on Monday. Gomez came over to inspect the site, and that's when he discovered the device. We're lucky it failed to detonate. Don't look so worried, it's been secured."

Dalton waved to the sheriff who'd spotted them. Beresby stood consulting with a couple of men from the bomb squad. "What does E.F.A. stand for, Uncle Ray?"

"Environmental Freedom Alliance. They're a known activist group in the region."

"So now they're targeting your project?"

"Not necessarily. Anyone could have sprayed those letters to point the blame their way."

It occurred to Marla that Raymond could have planted the bomb. But to what purpose? To throw suspicion off himself? To divert the sheriff from his investigation into

Tate Reardon's death? And what about Garrett Long? Their relative had something to do with the forest ranger that they had yet to determine. How far would Raymond go to keep his secrets?

Dalton's brow furrowed. "Do you believe someone meant to mislead you?"

The older man glowered at his nephew. "These environmental groups have been known to sabotage construction projects, but I can't believe they're at fault on this occasion. We're acting to preserve a historical site. So why attack us? And would the E.F.A. really do something subversive like drop a chandelier on our heads? I smell a rat, but it isn't them."

Marla didn't know what to believe. His rationale made sense.

"And the dude ranch problems?" Dalton said. "There wouldn't be any reason for the E.F.A. to be involved at the resort. I agree with you on that point."

"I still think it's the work of one man. Hugh Donovan hates me. He wants to ruin me financially."

"I'm not convinced Donovan is the guilty party."

"No? Then tell me what you've learned so far. You're supposed to be a top-notch investigator, and yet I haven't heard a word from you about any suspects."

Maybe because he knows you're withholding information. Marla didn't voice her thoughts aloud, but she sensed her husband's tension as he replied.

"I'm still working on it. Marla and I want to take another look up on the mountain. Can you recommend a guide who knows this area well? We don't care to fall down a hole like your unfortunate employee."

Raymond regarded them from behind his sunglasses. "Is that wise? These hills are treacherous, as you've been warned numerous times. I wouldn't want anything to happen to you."

"We'll be careful," Dalton reassured him.

"Then you'll want to see Quinn O'Malley. He runs the Harmony Café in Rustler Ridge. The fellow used to work in the mines until they shut down."

"So how old is he today?" Dalton's tone held a hint of skepticism.

"He's pushing seventy, but he stays in shape. Sometimes he'll run hiking tours on Sundays when the outfitters in town get an influx of tourists. People come from the city for day trips. I'm hoping to tap into that crowd when we open Craggy Peak."

"Anything else you need us for, then?"

"Nope, you can be on your way. I just

wanted you to see this graffiti with your own eyes, in case you noticed something the sheriff might have missed."

Marla stared at him. Despite his earlier snide comment, he sounded as though he respected Dalton's deductive abilities. It only reiterated how little she knew about the man.

"Can you show us the site where the bomb was found?" Dalton asked.

Raymond signaled for them to follow him into one of the dilapidated structures. "We haven't decided if this building should be torn down or rebuilt. The second story is a mess, but she stands clear of the other two buildings on either side and might make a decent small hotel. Look at the ironwork up there."

The railings added an attractive decorative touch, but Marla could see where part of the roof had caved in and some of the inner walls were gone, too.

"The foundation is still solid and so is much of the framework," Raymond said. "You should put on hardhats if you're planning to stick around."

"I'll wait outside." Marla stood on the sidewalk and took out her cell phone to look up the Harmony Café. It was located on an offshoot of the highway that led into town.

She checked her watch. They could do some shopping and have lunch there. She'd check in with Annie, too. Maybe her newfound friend had heard from Tate Reardon's family.

Heck, why wait? The sheriff was right here. She could ask him directly.

With a guilty glance over her shoulder, she proceeded to the beehive of activity by the bomb squad truck.

"Hello, Sheriff." She grinned at him, a hat shading her face from the glare. "I guess this was a false alarm, huh?"

He raised his bushy eyebrows. "By God's graces, yes. That thing might have gone off. We're fortunate the yahoos who built it didn't know what they were doing."

"Do you believe the Environmental Freedom Alliance is responsible?"

"That's what the message on the wall says."

"I know about the graffiti. What do you think?"

"I'll reserve judgment until I have more information."

"Have you heard from Eleanor or Christine Tate yet? I'm worried about them."

"So am I. We've got it under control."

Marla supposed that meant he was answering in the negative. "What's next? Too many bad things are happening to be mere coincidence. Did Dalton tell you a rattlesnake nearly bit him? Somebody put one inside his suitcase."

The sheriff's eyes widened. "No way. Did he dust the valise for prints?"

"Did he . . . we didn't even think about it!" All they had been concerned about was escaping from the room. But the lawman made a valid point. Too late now.

"Whoever is behind these accidents is dangerous, Mrs. Vail. I'd suggest you let the proper officials handle the details."

"Of course, you're right. Sorry to bother you."

"No problem. I'm only trying to do my job and keep folks safe."

"I know. Dalton used to brush me off in the early days, too. He knows better now."

With a smug smile, she turned on her heels and left as her husband emerged onto the street. They drove into Rustler Ridge while discussing their finds and possible conclusions.

By the time they made a few shopping stops and reached the café, lunch hour was in full swing. The place was small but cozy with decorations in a Native American motif.

"Is Quinn O'Malley around?" Marla

asked the waitress after they'd placed their orders. "We're visitors at the Last Trail Dude Ranch, and we have a proposition for him."

The girl's brows arched. "Sure, I'll let him know. Be just a minute."

She served their drinks before a lean guy with grey hair and a goatee sauntered their way. His blue eyes looked them over as he approached.

"Howdy, what can I do for you folks? Lucy said you had an offer for me." Without waiting for an invitation, he flipped a chair around and straddled it to face them.

"We'd like to explore the mountainside and hear you're the best guide." Dalton folded his hands on the table. "My uncle, Raymond Campbell, recommended you."

"Is that so? I usually do tours on Sundays. You can sign up at the hiking outfitters shop down the street."

"We'll make it worth your while to go today. I understand you used to work the mines? We're interested in locating the original entrance."

"For what purpose?"

"I'll tell you more if you sign on."

"Now you have me curious, buddy. I wouldn't want to be responsible for you going off on your own and getting hurt. I sup-

257

pose I could cut out of here for the afternoon."

"Thanks, we'd appreciate it."

"I'll notify my staff the place is theirs for the rest of the day. What kind of gear do you have?"

"You'd better tell us what we'll need," Dalton said. "We have backpacks with flashlights, water, and snacks, but that's about it."

O'Malley chuckled. "Right. Three sources of light is the rule, if we're going where I think you want to go. And helmets, plus a few other items. Come inside and find me when you're done eating, and we'll get started. I won't take you far if we do find an entrance, mind you. We're not the Bisbee Queen Copper Mine with a fancy public tour."

A couple of hours later found them on top of the mountain near where Eduardo had fallen through the collapsed ventilation shaft.

They had several objectives. The first goal was to locate the original mine entrance. Then Marla hoped to find the spot where Garrett Long fell to his death. Somewhere along the way, maybe they'd run into the boundary of Otto Lovelace's bottling facility.

She stared at the mountains in the distance while the sun blazed in a clear blue sky overhead. Where were the fluffy white clouds that graced Florida's azure skies? This relentless sunshine would get on her nerves if she lived here. She supposed she'd get used to the seasonal changes in Arizona like newcomers did in Florida.

"I'm afraid the main shaft has long since been boarded up," Quinn said in a gravelly tone. "You had to descend from there in a vertical cage, but I remember another entrance with a horizontal tunnel into the mountain. Let's see if we can find that one."

Marla poked Dalton as she accompanied the men. "I wonder if this place would be the one where Raymond's brother died. If so, the entrance caved in when the dynamite went off. That could be when they changed locations and dug a deeper shaft."

"According to what the vet told us, the three boys discovered an opening after it had been boarded shut. The wood had rotted by the time they went exploring. Quinn must be taking us somewhere else."

How many ways into the mine had there been? She hoisted herself over a pile of rocks and skirted a prickly cactus as they climbed higher. Her breath came hard and fast. *Oy,* she wasn't made for mountain climbing. Fortunately, the slopes in this area weren't too steep. The difficult part was avoiding the boulders in their path and watching out for critters.

"Why did you bring along that big knife?" she asked their guide, indicating the blade strapped to his thigh.

"Mine shafts can harbor wild animals like mountain lions," he said with a serious expression. "I hope you're prepared to encounter spiders and bats."

Marla touched her hair, which she'd braided to keep out of her face. "Ugh, I'll be glad I'm wearing a helmet."

"This whole area is a sieve. We're looking for the face to a horizontal drift."

"Could a natural cavern lead into the mining system?"

"Sure, but only through an open fault or a split in the rock."

They'd shown him the site where Eduardo had fallen in, and he'd shaken his head in sorrow. The mines would have many such ventilation shafts, so there could be other pitfalls across the range. He skirted any large areas of tangled vegetation that might hide a crevice. Boulders and smaller rock heaps made their progression increasingly difficult. Marla tried to pick her way between them and stay on the reddish-brown dirt.

She would have missed the shadow in the mountainside if Quinn hadn't stopped them to point it out. Even at their higher elevation, another peak rose before them. Shrubbery occluded the crack along with rotten boards that blended into the landscape.

"This is it!" Quinn trundled forward and began to remove the obstruction. With Dalton's help, he soon had an opening they could all squeeze through.

Inside, rock walls surrounded them. It was eerily quiet but not totally dark since sunlight streamed in. Marla put on her helmet as instructed and activated the light. Quinn operated a handheld lantern that cast a bright glow as they edged forward.

"Stay right behind me," he cautioned her and Dalton. "I'll make sure it's safe."

An earthy smell emanated from the rocky enclosure. Her light bounced off the walls, and her nape prickled as they proceeded into a dark tunnel.

"If this leads into other shafts, we could get lost," she said. "Shouldn't we leave some sort of trail?" Old fairy tales came back to haunt her. They didn't want to lose their sense of direction in a labyrinth.

"I'm already on it." Quinn took out a

piece of chalk and marked an X on the wall. "We could have used a spool of string, but it might not be long enough. Besides, we won't be in here too long. I don't plan on going far." His voice echoed against the rocks.

Dusty ore carts stood on a track to their left. When the passage narrowed, they had to navigate the ties. It wasn't easy, and Marla stumbled more than once. She was glad when the tunnel widened. Now and then, they came across discarded tools or rusty machinery that had long been abandoned. Every few feet, timber supported the walls and roof.

"Why aren't these wood beams more frequent?" she asked, sticking close behind Quinn. Dalton had switched places with her so he brought up the rear. She felt safer wedged between the two guys.

"They reinforce the tunnels as we go along. Normally, a deep shaft is dug in a mine first. At the bottom, a tunnel is started across to where the ore can be found. This ends in an area called a stope. That's where we worked. We constructed square sets out of timber to bolster the roof and walls and added rocks when we finished excavating in that area."

"How did you extract the ore?"

"With blasting, drills, and pickaxes. We sent the broken ore down a chute into a cart. Once mules started hauling the carts, things got easier."

"I understand the animals lived down here."

"That's right. The danger was blindness when a mule finally surfaced. The beasts had to adapt gradually to daylight."

They came to an intersection, where two other tunnels led off into pitch blackness. Quinn drew more X's on the walls along with arrows and the word, "Exit." He chose to remain on the straight path. Further ahead, a series of rickety ladders led up and down to other levels. Cool air made Marla shiver.

"Is it customary for the mines to be chilly like this?"

"No, ma'am. Usually they're hot as Hades. But the Craggy Peak mine is different than most because she has natural cracks to the surface. In other mines, you have to pump air inside, and it gets mighty hot the farther down you go."

Someone tapped her helmet. Marla spun around to face Dalton. "Did you do that?"

"Do what?" He gave her a perplexed glance.

"I felt a tap on my head."

"It wasn't me. You're imagining things."

Oh, no, I'm not. She let it go as dust clogged her nostrils. Should they be wearing filtration masks? For that matter, was lethal gas a danger here? She asked their guide.

"Methane isn't a problem since there is ventilation, but radon is always a possibility. We don't want to be down here for long. Have you had enough of a taste?"

He must have assumed we're crazy tourists. I won't disavow him of that notion.

"It's a fascinating glimpse into a bygone era," Dalton said like a true history buff. "Let's go a little further. Just make sure we can find our way to the surface."

His words reverberated through the tunnel. Had that been his lone voice she'd heard, or more than one? Was her mind playing tricks on her again?

On a whim, she whipped out her camera and snapped some photos as they proceeded into a large chamber. She took pictures at the entrance to another darkened passage and toward a higher level accessed by ladders. How cool was this? She'd want to show her friends back home what they'd experienced. A mining adventure hadn't been on their original itinerary.

"We should return," Quinn said, as they

took a break to rest. "We've descended quite a bit, although it might not feel like that to you since the angle is gentle. But there's always danger down here. Let's head back."

"Wait, do you hear that noise?" A faint clanging sounded in the distance.

The men glanced as her as though she was nuts.

"I don't hear anything." Quinn peered at her. "You don't look so good. We'd better get you out in the fresh air."

Something scratched her back, and she jerked away from the wall. "Who did that? One of you touched me."

"Marla, we're nowhere near you." Dalton's face registered concern. "What's the matter?"

"I'm not imagining things. I heard a banging noise." Mines could be haunted by the ghosts of miners felled in accidents. Quinn was right. They shouldn't linger. But as they turned to go, Dalton halted, a look of rapt intensity on his face.

"I heard something, too. Let's go down this tunnel a bit before we leave."

They came upon another series of ladders leading downward. A faint glow shone from below.

"Someone is down there," she whispered. "Quinn, what's going on?"

265

The man's brows folded together. "I have no idea, but this is damn odd. I'll climb down to take a look. You guys stay here. That ladder might be half rotted by now. I promise to be quick."

Finding nothing to sit on, Marla leaned against a wall after checking it for spiders. Her helmet lamp cast a harsh illumination on the rock face. Quinn had left his lantern behind, so they had that lighting as well. They followed his progress down the ladder until his form disappeared.

Dalton crouched beside her. "It must have been a tough life to be a miner. Who would want such a job?"

"Men who had no other skills? Imagine being down here for twelve hours a day. That's bad enough without the added risks. How many men fell off ladders like that one? Some of them may have drowned if they did. I read that groundwater seeps into these mines. It collected in a pit called a sump at the bottom of the main shaft. They used pumps to keep the water under control."

"And they always had the threat of cave-ins or blasting gone wrong."

"Dust in the air was another concern. That's why they did the blasting at the end of each day, so the debris could settle by the time they returned."

"Speaking of returns, here comes Quinn. He made it fast."

They both stood upright as Quinn scrambled up the last rung. His worried expression set her pulse rate racing.

"We have to get out of here. I may have been spotted." He hurried to their side while tightening his backpack straps.

"Who's down below?" Dalton asked, his expression somber in the lantern light.

"Guys are working the mine. It's an active operation."

"What?" Had she heard him correctly?

"Somebody has resumed ore prospecting." He led them back the way they'd come.

"You're kidding." Marla couldn't believe no one would know about it. "How extensive are these tunnels?"

"They loop around for thousands of miles."

Dalton brought up the tail again as they moved along toward the exit. "According to our research on the subject, mineral rights for local property owners go down a hundred feet or so. What happens when someone wants to dig deeper?"

"If you plan to extract ore from deep underground, you have to register a claim with the federal government. And if you have a smelting plant as well, those require all sorts of permits. I can understand why somebody would keep this operation secret. Possibly the person in charge doesn't own the mining rights."

"But where do they house the workers?" Marla queried, unable to conceive how this activity could be kept under wraps. "And how can the men be prevented from talking? For that matter, how come no one has seen them and raised questions?" Maybe the number of miners was small enough to keep them contained. But they'd still have to live somewhere.

"All valid points, ma'am."

The voices from behind faded as they scurried along. Marla almost tripped over a rail as the passage narrowed. She squeezed past an abandoned ore cart, touching the cool rock wall for balance. At an intersection, they followed the route indicated by the chalk marks. Unfortunately, if anyone pursued them, it gave a clear direction to follow.

"We should take another tunnel to throw them off," she suggested in a low tone.

From her rear, Dalton put a hand on her shoulder. "We could use a map of the tunnel system. Too bad I didn't find one in the town's archives."

"It would have come in handy." Another passage intersected with theirs, winding into the dark. On an impulse, Marla snapped a picture of the inky blackness.

"We don't dare risk getting lost by taking a different route," Quinn said, his eyes bright in the lantern's glow. "Let's hope these guys don't show up at an intersection ahead of us. They might know these passages better than we do."

Marla's throat constricted. What if those men discovered them? This place could easily become their tomb.

"I thought you'd worked down here." *That's why we hired you,* Marla thought. Well, not exactly. Quinn couldn't possibly know every passage.

"This section wasn't near any place where I'd mined the rock. I wonder how they're processing the ore." Quinn's voice sounded hollow in the narrow passage. "It can be a messy business. Stamp mills produce sulfur dioxide emissions and release particulate matter into the air. Plus copper processing requires large amounts of water. They must ship the ore somewhere."

"Surely today's methods are cleaner?" Marla's forehead crinkled. Somehow this information was relevant, but other questions took priority.

Quinn stepped around a rusted drill on the ground. "That's true, but stricter controls raise production costs. I'll bet the person running this mine is ignoring regulations."

Marla fell silent, considering the ramifications. Who would control an operation this large? Moreover, why reopen the mine and go to the trouble unless it was profitable?

"Quick, go down that side tunnel," Quinn urged. "I hear voices ahead."

They dodged into an intersecting passage and squelched their lights just before a gang of four men rushed past, chattering in Spanish. Had they noticed the chalk marks in this section?

"We'll wait it out," Quinn said in a hushed tone. "When those men don't see anybody up ahead, they'll double back down the same tunnel. Then we can head for the exit."

"I wonder if these passages underlie the ghost town Uncle Ray is renovating," Dalton whispered into Marla's ear. "Heavy construction equipment and a lot of surface activity could stress the tunnels and endanger the miners. That might explain why somebody is sabotaging his project."

"You could be right."

This find had the potential to change

everything, but only if they lived to tell their tale.

CHAPTER THIRTEEN

As Quinn had predicted, the mine workers passed them by on their return trip. Nor did they leave anybody behind to see who emerged from the shadows. Marla hoped they dismissed any claims of spotting an intruder as a ghostly apparition. These guys were likely to be as superstitious as Raymond's labor force.

She was starting to wonder if their beliefs were real, though. Had it been a ghost tapping on her helmet inside the mine? She couldn't wait to upload her photos onto their notebook computer to see what showed online.

"I should have taken pictures of those miners as they went past," Marla said, once she and Dalton were safely ensconced back at the dude ranch. They'd paid off Quinn while exacting his promise not to speak about what they'd learned.

"It's best you didn't, or they might have

noticed us," Dalton said, unbuttoning his shirt. "We'll find proof another way. In the meantime, we can tell Sheriff Beresby what we found."

"I'm too tired tonight, and he has enough on his plate anyway. It can wait until the morning. I don't know about you, but I'm starving."

After they showered, changed, and ate dinner, she uploaded her photos to their laptop. She'd captured the tunnels, the square-set constructions, the abandoned machinery, and even the ladders leading away into the dark. But she hadn't counted on the orbs that populated her pictures.

"Look, do you think they're ghosts?" she said in wide-eyed wonder to Dalton.

"I doubt it. Those circles are more likely to be dust molecules caught by the camera."

"I'm not so sure. We should go to Sedona and consult one of their psychics. We can tell the sheriff about the mines later. And if we pay a visit to the forest supervisor while we're in the area, we might have more information to add."

A seat of mysticism and spiritual vortexes, Sedona housed numerous New Age centers that catered to tourists. Late Sunday morning, Marla gazed at the red cliffs that rose around them as they drove into town. Each view unfolded in spectacular majesty. Words failed her to describe the awe-inspiring scenery.

No wonder people felt a heightened spiritual awareness here. Who wouldn't experience this oneness with nature when surrounded by such beauty?

They parked in a public lot and strolled down a main street bustling with tourists, intriguing stores, and outdoor cafés. Stopping at the Pink Jeep tour center, Marla asked the clerk if he knew of any psychics who might have knowledge about the copper mining industry. The guy referred her to a spiritualist center on a side street.

Chimes tinkled on the door as she and Dalton entered. Marla sniffed pine-scented incense as she gazed at display cases showing a dazzling array of crystal rocks. Jewelry, books on New Age topics, and Indian dream catchers were also for sale. In the rear, a curtain divided the front section from the psychic who offered readings.

Marla didn't want a reading. She'd already had one at Cassadaga, a Florida town owned and operated by certified mediums.

"You want to talk about the copper mines? I don't know if I'm the best person for you to consult," Madame Duval said to Marla in her private enclave. She might be well into her seventies, Marla guessed, judging from the deep creases in her face, the wrinkled skin on her hands, and the gray roots on her bleached hair.

"You were recommended to me as someone well versed in the region's history."

The psychic offered her a friendly smile. "Well, then, what would you like to know?"

"I explored an old mine shaft and took photos. Lots of orbs showed up in them."

"That's not surprising. If you're interested in this sort of thing, you should visit the vortexes."

"We haven't had time yet. What are these vortexes supposed to do?"

"They amplify the energy that surrounds us. Two types exist. Upflow vortexes draw energy from the earth. When you stand on a mountain, you are able to view life on a higher plane because of these energies. You'll feel a sense of renewal and spiritual oneness with the universe."

Tell me something I don't know. Anyone standing on a mountain surrounded by the beauty of nature would feel the same thing. "And the other kind?" she asked to be polite.

"Inflow vortexes are where energy flows into the earth, like in a valley."

"How about a cave, or a manmade tunnel

like in a mine?"

The woman's eyes glittered. "You're closer to the electromagnetic grid that circles the globe when you're underground. This cosmic energy field underlies the tectonic plates. The grid lines are called ley lines. Where they intersect, vortexes are located. These resonate and interact with our chakras and meridians. Thus people experience them in different ways."

"Let's talk about ghosts. Why do spiritual beings supposedly appear as orbs?"

"That's the easiest form for them to take. It's not uncommon to find them in the mines. Mining accidents killed more miners than homicides back in the day."

"How so?" Marla asked as though she didn't know. She glanced toward the curtain that partitioned off the psychic's space. Hopefully, Dalton was entertaining himself in the shop. She'd spotted a pen inlaid with turquoise stone that might make a nice gift for him if she could buy it on the sly.

"The miners had to climb ladders, yes? Someone from above might drop a tool. That could hit a miner on the rungs or cause him to lose balance. Rotten rungs could give way, or he could slip and fall. Falling down a shaft was a common hazard. Fires were always a risk, and so were explosions. Often a man would pull out a stick of dynamite from the rock wall where it had been set to go off but didn't. Instead of being a dud, it would blow up in his face."

"What kind of superstitions affected the miners?"

Madame Duval adjusted her patterned skirt. She wore ordinary street clothes enhanced by turquoise stone jewelry. "Crows were a bad sign. If a crow flew across a miner's path on his way to work, he'd turn around and go home for the day. Men carried talismans into work to ward off evil. Some even nailed horseshoes into the timbers where they were drilling. They all feared ghosts, believing the spirits of miners killed on the job still lingered down below."

"My husband's uncle is restoring the town at Craggy Peak. That place has plenty of ghost stories associated with it."

"I'll bet you can find lots of orbs in those old buildings. Arizona is rich with history."

"Some say orbs are merely dust globules or moisture droplets. Camera artifacts do seem more likely than spiritual entities," Marla said, taking Dalton's viewpoint.

Madame Duval hunched forward, shaking her drop earrings. "If you don't believe in the paranormal, why did you come to me?"

"I didn't say I'm a non-believer. In fact, down in the mine, I felt someone tap my helmet more than once. My husband says he didn't do it. And I've had other experiences."

The psychic jerked upright, her eyes widening. "May I hold your hand? Someone wants to communicate with you."

Startled, Marla complied as goose bumps rose on her flesh.

"It's a man who wants you to keep asking questions." Madame Duval closed her eyelids to concentrate. "The entity says you're getting close."

Marla stared at her. Those words reminded her of Jesse's parting sentence when they'd first met him. If this truly was a spiritual connection, who could it be — Garrett Long, the dead forest ranger? Or maybe Eduardo, the man who'd fallen down the hole? Or Tate Reardon, whose wife and daughter were mysteriously missing?

"Close to what?" she said more sharply than intended.

"He warns you to look closer to home. That is all he has to say." The woman's eyes snapped open. "This is why you came here today. You were guided to seek me."

Marla paid the woman and departed feeling more confused than ever. Not spying

278

Dalton inside the shop, she paused to purchase the pen and hide it in her handbag. She'd save it for a special occasion as a memento of their trip together.

Outside, he loitered under a shady tree while storm clouds gathered overhead. Marla glanced at them with concern. Clouds were an anomaly during their visit, and it didn't bode well for the afternoon. She hurried to their car.

"How'd it go?" Dalton said as he pulled out of their space and merged into traffic.

Marla related her conversation with Madame Duval.

"Look closer to home? What's that supposed to mean?"

"Sheriff Beresby said something similar, so we must be on the right track. We just have to fit the pieces together."

They drove to Wendall, fifteen minutes down the highway from Sedona. Unfortunately, the forest supervisor's office was closed for the weekend. Marla cursed their luck. They should have called ahead. Anyway, Beresby had probably interviewed the man by now.

Returning to Sedona, they stopped for lunch. The storm clouds brought rain, but the skies had cleared by the time they finished eating. They explored a few of the area's highlights before leaving town.

As they drove into the ranch, Dalton pointed out a bunch of cars occupying the spaces in the main parking lot. "Wayne had been expecting a wedding party. Was that this week or next?"

"I don't remember. Let's see if he's in his office. We should give him an update."

As they entered the lobby, loud voices emanated from the inner sanctum. Janice gave them a weak smile as they approached the front desk.

"What's going on?" Marla asked the red-head.

"You'd have to ask Wayne. Go on back. He'll be glad to see you."

Dalton led the way past the gate. His boots thudded on the tile floor as he strode toward his cousin's office with an air of purpose.

A semicircle of four men stood facing Wayne who sat behind his desk. The middle-aged individuals wore angry expressions along with the ubiquitous plaid shirts and jeans.

"If you don't do something, we'll call our lawyers in the morning," one guy said. "An injunction should get your daddy to stop his construction."

Wayne spotted the newcomers and stood,

relief flitting across his features. "Allow me to introduce my relatives. This is my cousin, homicide detective Dalton Vail, and his wife, Marla. Come in, please. These folks are blaming my father for the drought on their property. I'm telling them his project has nothing to do with their problems."

"Isn't the desert supposed to be dry?" Marla asked with an innocent expression.

"We used to have a creek running alongside our ranch," said one fellow with a thatch of peppery hair. "The water isn't there anymore because Raymond is stealing it for his project."

"That's nonsense," Wayne said. "He's gotten all the proper permits."

"We know he has the mayor under his thumb."

"What does that mean?"

The man's face reddened. "It means he has plenty of money to spread around. Where does he get his funding? Is your dude ranch doing that well?"

"It's none of your business, Calvin."

"It is when somebody is offering to buy us out."

"That's not my father. You're barking up the wrong tree. We've had the same offers." A vein stood out on Wayne's temple. He looked about to have a stroke.

"Maybe Raymond is poisoning our cattle so we'll have to sell," another man suggested.

Marla leaned against a wall, listening with stunned dismay to the conversation. How dare these men come here to accuse Wayne's father?

"You're way out of line." Wayne hooked his thumbs into his belt, but not before Marla noticed the flicker of doubt cross his face.

With Raymond's dubious history, she wasn't sure they could trust the patriarch. Yet she didn't believe him responsible for climactic conditions on people's land. Plus, he blamed Hugh Donovan for their own problems, although that could be a smokescreen.

Maybe Donovan had put these guys up to this confrontation. The notion made her stand up straight and speak out.

"Someone has been sabotaging Raymond's project as well as causing malicious incidents at Last Trail," she said. "We're in the same boat."

The man named Calvin replied. "Raymond is probably trying to throw you off track by causing trouble himself."

"He wouldn't hurt his own wife or nephew." Marla related the incidents with

282

Carol's horse and the rattlesnake in Dalton's luggage.

"Be that as it may," Calvin said to Wayne, "we're going to sue for injunction if your daddy doesn't remedy the situation."

"And I may countersue for slander if you keep bad-mouthing my father."

"He must have diverted our creek. You get him to fix things properly, or else."

The stand-off ended as the four men stomped from the room.

Wayne sank into his chair and covered his face with his hands. "Will my father never cease to aggravate people?"

"He's not the root of these issues," Dalton said, his tone somber. "But someone else may very well have a motive to induce people to sell. Marla, show him your photos."

She retrieved her digital camera from her purse. "We hired a hiking guide recommended by your father and discovered an entrance to the old copper mine up on the mountain. Guess what? Somebody has reopened it and has an active operation going on down there."

Wayne's face registered surprise as he studied the pictures. The orbs weren't evident on the camera, only on the computer. But ghosts weren't the topic here.

"Those tunnels extend for miles. They might even underlie Craggy Peak. That could explain why someone wants to shut down my father's project."

"You're catching on." Dalton's voice held a note of approval. "But this doesn't account for the problems on Donovan's ranch and elsewhere. Or on our place, for that matter."

Marla's ears perked up. This was the first time Dalton had referred to Last Trail in the possessive.

She put her camera away. "It would help if Raymond would level with us. Why won't he admit where he got the money to buy the ghost town and start construction?"

Wayne plowed his fingers through his hair. His cowboy hat hung on a hook behind the door. "It doesn't make sense. I can't understand why he'd keep something like this from his family. What is he hiding from us?"

"Maybe he took out an equity loan on the ranch," Dalton suggested, his face pensive.

"He said he hadn't taken out any loans," Marla reminded them. "Besides, Carol would have noticed since she does the books."

"I'm fed up with his attitude. This has gone on long enough," Wayne said in a firm tone. "Either Dad reveals his source of funding, or he can hire another general manager."

"Now Wayne, don't let those neighbors or their threats get to you." Dalton settled into a chair opposite his desk.

"I should call the bank to see what I can find out."

"That's a good idea. It's Sunday, though. You'll have to wait until tomorrow. Let tempers cool in the meantime."

"I see Carol isn't here," Marla noted. "Is she feeling all right?"

"She's taking the day off, but she's fine, thanks."

"Then if you guys don't mind, I'm going to rest before dinner. Dalton, I'll meet you back at the room." She'd let the men have some private time to discuss things.

On her way out, Marla stopped at the front desk. "Janice, can you tell me where the housekeepers stash their carts for the day? Is it the same place where they obtain supplies?"

She wanted to encounter Juanita again to see what the maid could tell her.

The redhead glanced up from her computer screen. "I'm so glad you dropped by," she said in a hushed tone. "Wayne would be intolerable after a visit like he had today. Those men are totally off track."

Marla leaned across the counter, keeping her voice low. "Where do *you* think Raymond got his funds to buy the ghost town?"

"He must have had a partner."

"That's what Dalton thinks. Could it be anyone we've met?"

Janice pressed her lips together. "I have my theories. It's pretty obvious if you think about it. Anyway, the maids keep their carts in a storeroom beyond the laundry room entrance. Why do you ask?"

"One of the housekeepers is hot for a wrangler on the ranch. I want to ask her about him."

Janice's brows lifted. "Do you think he's responsible for the mischief that has been happening here?"

"It's possible. I'd like to see what she can tell me."

When Marla finally located Juanita, the raven-haired woman was cleaning her last room for the day. Marla entered through the open door, her arrival prompting the maid to respond with a torrent of words in Spanish.

"Please, calm down. What's wrong?"

"Everything is wrong, *señora*. Jesse does not care for me anymore."

At the bedside, she whipped a top sheet toward the headboard, tucked it in, and then laid out the comforter with jerky motions. She smoothed it with her palms, her face averted from Marla.

"Why would you believe Jesse has lost interest in you?"

"I do not know. I tell him how I feel, and at first he seemed happy. But now he does not come around for days."

"Maybe he's busy." Marla stood back as Juanita sprayed disinfectant into the air. The mist gave the room a fresh smell.

"Not true. He has things on his mind, and they don't include me."

"Oh? And what would that be?" She followed Juanita into the bathroom where the housekeeper lugged a plastic tote holding cleaning supplies.

"You would be surprised. But even though he rejects me, I not give away his secrets."

"Juanita, people have gotten hurt. Carol fell off her horse when it hit a trip wire and smacked her head. My husband almost got bitten by a rattlesnake somebody put in his suitcase. If Jesse knows anything about these incidents, you should tell us."

Juanita paused midway to wiping down the mirror and glared at her. "My Jesse would not do such terrible things."

"According to what you've said, he isn't *your* Jesse anymore. So why be loyal to a guy who's turned his back on you?"

Juanita waved her rag in the air. "I tell you this. He understands you people blame the Donovans. But Jesse believes the fault lies elsewhere."

"Yes, you told me this before. Who does he think is doing these things?" Marla squeezed her fists in frustration.

"Jesse wants proof before he says more. I hope he is not wrong about *Señor* Donovan. It surprises me how he defends the man after . . . well, I must get back to work."

When it didn't appear as though Marla could convince the young housekeeper to say more, she headed back to her hacienda up a sandy path. As she climbed higher, the view stretched to encompass the saguaro forest and the mountains beyond.

A side road branched off, twisting into the distance. Marla did a double take. Had she seen a woman in a white dress and wearing a hat waving at her? But after she blinked, the lady was gone.

Marla dodged past the sign that said Staff Only. This might be a back route to the barbecue pit as it seemed to go in the same direction. She swallowed past a dry throat, realizing she needed to drink more water in this moisture-free climate. Her hair elevated in the static electricity, and her nasal membranes throbbed.

The vegetation grew thicker on either side of her, surprising her with its denseness. Saguaro stalks poked up from among the shrubbery, aiming toward the sky. Ahead, the hills took on a bluish tint in the afternoon sun. Weedy brown grasses grew wild, obscuring the soil and any critters that might live there. In between were large patches of reddish dirt.

Stepping around a rock, she continued along for a short distance before coming to a broken-down wagon that decorated the side of the road. Further along appeared to be a parking area, because a glint of metal hit her eyes. Sure enough, this must be where the staff brought in supplies for the outdoor barbecue dinners. A side road must cut between the areas. Guests could walk from the ranch down the other road.

But who was that up ahead? She paused next to a hedgehog cactus and a branching ocotillo plant. Having to squint to see better through her sunglasses, she wondered if her prescription needed changing. At least she could make out the wiry figure in the cowboy hat talking to another guy. The second fellow handed something to the wrangler she recognized as Kevin Franks. He stuck the item in his pocket.

Wait, was that Matthew Brigham, the engineer from town? What was he doing way out here? Marla hadn't realized the two men were acquainted.

"Hey, fellows," she called, waggling her fingers in the air.

They glanced at her in unison, exchanged a few more words, and then scattered. Brigham jumped into his car, while Franks disappeared into a thicket of vegetation. Moments later, she leapt out of the way as Brigham's car zoomed past.

When she'd recovered her wits and the dust cleared, she spied Franks galloping away on a horse that he must have had tethered nearby. Why had they reacted as though spooked instead of offering her a friendly greeting and asking if she'd gotten lost? And who had that woman been on the trail? Had it been an apparition directing her there? If so, for what reason? To catch these guys meeting together for some clandestine purpose? From the way they'd taken off at her arrival, it certainly appeared as though they'd wished to avoid recognition.

Pondering these issues, she trudged back toward the main road. She'd reached the front stoop of her hacienda when her cell phone rang.

"Annie, is that you? What's up?" she said

upon noting the caller I.D.

"I have news," the younger woman stated in a breathless tone. "Eleanor Reardon contacted me."

"What?" Marla pressed the phone tighter against her ear.

"She's all right, and Christine is with her. Mrs. Reardon wanted to apologize for missing our appointment. Can you imagine? The poor woman said she'd spoken to the police. Somebody had called her the morning of her husband's death and warned her to leave the house along with her daughter."

"Why would she obey without telling anyone? Did she know who it was?"

"No, she didn't recognize the man's voice, and her cell said unknown caller."

"That's odd."

"The person said if she told Tate or anyone else, he'd reveal what he knew about her."

"And what was that?"

"She'd been having an affair with Garrett Long."

CHAPTER FOURTEEN

"Tate Reardon's wife was having an affair with the forest ranger?" Standing in the middle of their hacienda, Dalton stared at her incredulously. He had returned from his consultation with Wayne, and she'd burst out with her news before giving him a chance to speak. "I wonder if the sheriff knows."

"I'd bet he does. Do you think this is what the psychic meant about looking closer to home? Sheriff Beresby did say he was checking into the personal angle regarding Garrett's death. That would include family members and close associates."

"But how did the woman even meet Garrett Long?"

"Tate worked long hours at the water bottling plant. Perhaps his wife was lonely and ran into Garrett in town. Or maybe she visited the nature center and took a fancy to him there."

Dalton scraped stiff fingers through his hair. "This development puts a whole new spin on things."

"Do you believe the same person who killed Garrett also murdered Mr. Reardon?"

"The sheriff ascribes his death to a gas leak."

"Yes, it was a convenient accident, same as Garrett Long falling off a ledge in a place where every rock must have been known to him." They locked gazes. "Garrett was married, wasn't he? We haven't heard much about his wife. Sherry, isn't it? If she'd known about her husband's illicit affair, she would have a motive to get rid of them both."

Dalton's brows knitted together. "That doesn't make sense. I could see her eliminating her wandering spouse, but why kill Tate Reardon instead of Eleanor?"

"Yes, I see your point. And it would have to be a separate issue from the problems at the dude ranch and the ghost town. There's still something we're missing." Her face brightened. "Guess who I just saw together? I spotted Kevin the wrangler talking to Matthew Brigham."

"And who is he again?"

"He's the district engineer responsible for the inspections at the bottling plant. Brigham handed Kevin something, but I couldn't see what it was. The men split when they noticed me. They met on a side road for staff only."

"Interesting, but I'm more concerned about Wayne. He and Uncle Ray are going to pay Donovan a visit to see what the man knows about the copper mine. If you want to come along, get your things. I'm joining them to make sure tempers don't escalate."

"I wouldn't miss this chance to meet the guy, although Jesse says he's not to blame for the incidents here. I caught up to Juanita, the housekeeper. She said Jesse needs proof for his theories before he'll tell anyone about them."

"Theories about what?"

She shrugged. "Who wired the trail where Carol rides every day, perhaps, and the other acts of sabotage around the ranch."

Dalton's lips pressed together. "I wish the sheriff would tell us what he knows. It's so frustrating not being included. I can't help my cousin with only partial knowledge."

Stepping forward, she rubbed his arm. "You're doing your best. We'll get to the bottom of this. Maybe Hugh Donovan will shed light on things."

She ran into the bathroom, fixed her hair and makeup, and hastened outside to join her husband. Raymond had arrived by the time they returned to the lobby. Wayne sat them all inside his four-wheel drive SUV, and they tore off down the road.

A half hour later, Marla studied the view as they approached the Donovan ranch. Shady trees and strategically placed cacti adorned the granite chip landscape in front of the main house. Beyond stretched a series of corrals and occasional outbuildings.

When ringing the doorbell brought no answer, Raymond indicated the fenced enclosures. "Hugh must be out in the field."

Wayne shaded his eyes with a hand. "Somebody's coming. They must have spotted us."

A couple of men trotted over on horseback and dismounted. The younger guy's profile seemed familiar, but the older man attracted Marla's attention. His folded brows and tense mouth didn't bode well for their visit. While the other fellow tended to the horses, this one strode over, a camel-colored cowboy hat on his head and knee-high leather boots on his feet.

"What are you doing here, Raymond?"

"I came to tell you to stop harassing me, Hugh." Raymond's voice rang out loud and clear, piercing the air like a rifle shot on a quiet day.

The two elders sized each other up. Hugh had aged better than Raymond, Marla concluded. His skin didn't show the ravages of time same as Dalton's uncle, although they had to be close in age. Something that looked like regret flared in their eyes as they stared each other down like two gunslingers at an Old West battle. These men had been friends before tragedy tore them apart. Did they yearn for forgiveness? Or were they so accustomed to casting blame on each other that an avalanche couldn't move them?

Hugh jabbed a finger at his visitor. "You have nerve to come here, where my stock is suffering because of your actions, and you tell me to back off?"

"Stop these pranks before someone else gets seriously hurt."

"I have no idea what you mean."

"We have a saboteur on our ranch and at my project. Likely they're working for you to undermine my properties."

"You're insane. I could say the same for you. Did you sneak somebody in here to poison our feed? Is it your intent to kill off my cattle?"

"Hey, guys, let's be rational about this." Wayne raised his hand in a stop sign. He glanced at the younger man whose features puzzled Marla.

Why did she get the feeling she'd seen him before?

"Ben, how have you been?" Wayne said. "This is my cousin and his wife, Marla and Dalton Vail. They're visiting from back east."

Ben tipped his hat at them, his expression wary. "What Pop says is true. We've had offers to sell. They have to be coming from you. You've always coveted our property. Pop claims you and he used to talk about merging the ranches when you were kids."

"Those were pipe dreams, son." Raymond glowered at him. "Any plans we had shattered when Harry died. He should never have gone into that mine."

Marla clutched her handbag under one arm, wishing for some shade. What did Raymond hope to accomplish here?

"The past is over and done, Ray. You can't bring that boy back. God knows I'd want the same thing. Revenge is a petty way of getting even. You kill my livelihood, and you kill me. Is that what you're after?"

"You're the one who's trying to shut down my operations. We've had incidents. Are you telling me your people are not responsible?"

"What sort of incidents are you blaming me for, Ray? Or is this a way to shuffle suspicion off yourself?"

Wayne mentioned the acts of sabotage.

"Somebody is behind them. If not you, then who?"

Dalton stepped forward. "If you'll allow me to intervene, it appears both of you are suffering from a targeted effort." He eyed the opposition. "You've accused my uncle of tainting your feed. Have you had it analyzed?"

Hugh stroked his bearded jaw. "Well, no. We've had a drought in these parts, too. I figured Raymond's project is at fault. He needs water for the construction. He's siphoning from our stream up on the mountain, and I doubt he pays the town for what he takes."

"I have permits for the work, you asshole. The council has seen my surveys and the engineering reports. The more far-sighted among them can see how the ghost town will be a boon to the area. It'll bring in jobs and tourists as well as tax dollars."

"Yes, but at the expense of the environment."

"So are your cattle actually sick?" Dalton persisted. "Have you had them examined by a veterinarian? Or is their grazing ground merely suffering from the dry conditions, and they're feeling the effects?"

Marla grinned at him in approval. He was trying to get them to examine the evidence rather than fling accusations back and forth.

"It's more than lack of water, although that's one problem. The vet has been here. Doc says they aren't right, but he can't pinpoint the cause."

"Why do I care what happens on your ranch, Hugh?" Raymond's mouth pinched. "I wouldn't waste my effort hiring someone to contaminate your feed. There's enough to keep me busy on my own properties."

"Exactly. You don't care what happens elsewhere. That project of yours is an abomination."

"Are you joining the environmentalists now?"

"No, but you should watch out for them. They target places like yours."

"Otto Lovelace up on the mountain seems to fear them more." Marla finally spoke up. These two men seemed too obstinate to look beyond their own noses. "From what I've heard, he has armed guards patrol the perimeter of his water bottling plant."

"Have you considered that his operation might be contaminating your soil?" Dalton asked with a raised eyebrow.

"That's nonsense. Water bottling is a clean industry, and he'd have nothing to gain. Lovelace is right to protect his property. Maybe I should start doing the same."

"I'll bet you know about those caves," Raymond said with a snort of derision, "and you're secretly trying to acquire my property."

"What the hell are you talking about now?"

A black bird soared into the sky, dipped toward them, and then rose toward the hills. Marla's gaze followed it toward a white plume of vapor. Was Lovelace's facility situated directly above the Donovan ranch?

"We've discovered somebody has secretly reopened the copper mine," Raymond added.

Hugh gave a cackle of disbelief. "Tell me another story."

"All right." Raymond hooked his thumbs into his belt and widened his stance. "You've discovered it's profitable again to extract the ore, or else you want the side products. You know the tunnels underlie my renovation project, so you've hired somebody to cause accidents and spook my workers. Well, we found the body of my missing employee. He fell down a ventilation shaft that had been exposed."

"So, what does that prove? You know these mountains are riddled with tunnels. We both understand the dangers."

"Marla and Dalton hired a guide and went

exploring. Someone has an operation going down there."

"It ain't me, Ray. Now I don't know if you're full of hogwash or not, but if this is true, you should tell the sheriff." His expression turned canny. "Or maybe you don't want Luke to snoop around too much."

"Meaning what? Spit it out, Hugh."

Wayne and Ben exchanged an exasperated glance. Marla wondered if they'd ever had the chance to get to know each other. Probably not, considering how their fathers harbored so much resentment. Did the younger Donovan know about his mother's dalliance with Raymond? That would put him solidly on his father's team. Could he have been acting without Hugh's knowledge against a family enemy?

"Garrett Long would have been concerned about the problems on my ranch. He helped folks like us when he was around. And now he's dead, thanks to you."

"I'm sorry for his loss, but I had nothing to do with it."

"Oh no?" Hugh gestured to the bystanders. "You haven't told them, have you?"

"Told us what, Dad?" Wayne asked his father.

"The forest ranger had a love for history." Hugh's eyes sparked with respect when he

301

spoke of the deceased. "He would have backed your restoration project one hundred percent. And he did, didn't he? Garrett Long was your silent partner."

Marla's jaw dropped. "Now that makes sense," she muttered to Dalton. A history buff, the victim might have loved the idea of reconstructing the ghost town.

Raymond kicked at a rock on the ground. "All right, I'll admit it. Garrett invested in my project. He wanted to see it fly as much as I did."

"And now that he's gone, maybe your debt to him is gone as well. What do the legal documents say?" Hugh asked with a sneer. "Do you have right of survivorship, or does his share go to his wife?"

"That isn't your concern. It's true Garrett and I were partners, but I'd never harm him. I have to finish the project to honor his memory."

"His memory ain't so clean. I hear he was fooling around with Tate Reardon's wife."

Raymond raised his fist. "Watch your mouth, you sonovabitch."

Wayne stepped between them. "Dad, calm down. He's provoking you on purpose."

"Whose idea was it to buy the Craggy Peak property in the first place?" said the younger Donovan in a genuinely curious voice.

Ben didn't seem to have the same hard edge as his father, but no doubt in a family feud, he'd stand up for his clan. And yet if he and Wayne could ever meet in private, they might actually get along. They had a lot in common in managing a ranch. But that wouldn't happen as long as their fathers hated each other.

"I had my eye on that town long before Garrett even thought about it," Raymond replied. "He was busy with his job and protecting the forest. But when I broached the subject, he flew with it."

"As a forest ranger, he wouldn't have been paid all that much," Wayne said. "How could he afford a huge investment like that?"

"Garrett came from old money. His family settled here after making a fortune back east. They didn't approve of his occupation, but he was passionate about his beliefs. Conservation was important to him. He ensured we complied with environmental laws."

Hugh snorted. "Maybe Garrett found out you were proceeding without proper permit approvals, and that's why you killed him."

Raymond's shoulders hunched. "I should punch your lights out. You're the one who's trying to kill people."

"I don't think so. Stop trying to divert attention from yourself, Ray."

"You paid someone to fasten a trip wire across the trail where Wayne's wife rides every day, didn't you? Carol is lucky she only suffered a mild concussion from her fall off the horse. And I imagine you suggested putting a rattlesnake in Dalton's suitcase. Did you hope to land him in the hospital, too? You must know he's a homicide detective and would sniff you out."

"I don't know anything about those issues, Ray. Maybe you should look closer to home."

Marla shot him a startled glance. Wasn't that the same advice issued by Madame Duval?

"What do you mean?" Raymond demanded, his posture rigid.

"You must have known about Kevin Franks. That made him the perfect man to hire for your dirty work where Garrett was concerned. That's it, isn't it?"

"Can you be more succinct?" Dalton said in his best interview voice.

Hugh glanced at him as though he'd just crawled out from under a rock. "Franks was Garrett's brother-in-law. If he knew about Garrett's affair, he might have been happy to get back at the guy who betrayed his sister."

"Kevin Franks is Sherry Long's brother?" Wayne's eyes widened. "That's news to me."

"You probably don't know half the things going on under your nose, kid."

"We know what's under our feet," Raymond inserted. "And it's a copper mine that somebody has reopened. The tunnels must run under my town project. That's why you're sabotaging it, so I'll want to sell. You'll never get my property, Donovan."

"It's you who is trying to force me to sell." Hugh's mouth flattened. "That's why you're poisoning my cattle."

Bless my bones, Marla thought, these two will never stop arguing. She shifted her feet, hot and tired of standing. Couldn't they go inside and talk there? She swallowed past a dry throat and yearned for a drink of water.

"I'm telling you, I have nothing to do with the conditions on your ranch. If you weren't so short-sighted, you'd look for real evidence that somebody means you harm. Instead, you're flinging unfounded accusations my way. Is that what you did to your son, Jake? You drove him off with your hard-headedness?"

"Why, you —"

Wayne and Ben had to restrain their

305

fathers and keep them apart. The senior men sputtered and spit at each other, speechless in their fury. Hugh found his voice first.

"Get off my land, or I'll call the sheriff and accuse you of trespassing."

"Fine, we'll leave, but this isn't over. You're trying to mislead me, but I know you're behind the incidents. You've always coveted my ranch to expand your cattle operations."

"You've gone sissy with your fancy resort. I don't need your territory." Hugh wrestled free from his son's grip. "But don't think you can get away with murder. I'll find the means to prove you killed Garrett. Murdering him scored you two points. You don't have to pay him back, and he won't report your environmental violations."

"Let's go." Raymond signaled toward their car. "This man won't listen to reason. No wonder his boy ran away."

Before Hugh could burst a blood vessel, Wayne hustled his father into the SUV. The rest of them piled in after him. Marla sank against the cushion with a sigh of relief. Her temples throbbed, and her muscles tensed. She hadn't realized how much the altercation had upset her. Dalton's hand folded around hers as Wayne drove away.

On the horizon, the mountains were obscured by a haze of dust as wind stirred the dry soil. But the far hills weren't the only objects hidden behind a film. It appeared both Raymond and Hugh Donovan had trouble seeing beyond their enmity. If they would do so, they might realize that someone else entirely was trying to acquire their land.

Possibly, they shared a common enemy, and yet neither one could get beyond their past grief to examine the situation objectively. Was it because they'd shared a deep friendship in their youth? Hate engendered by love could be one of the strongest emotions.

At dinner later in the dining hall, she asked Dalton about his conclusions. She was glad they'd decided to eat here instead of going to Carol's house. After the events today, it would have been a strain to make polite conversation.

"Uncle Ray can be damn stubborn," Dalton said, spearing a piece of lettuce from his salad and lifting the fork to his mouth. "Seeing how pig-headed he is, I understand why Mom stays away."

"I'm sure Kate would respond if her brother made the first gesture. But Raymond has to forgive himself before he can move on. Look at what the past has done to him and Hugh. They used to be friends. Now they're bitter enemies, hurling accusations at each other instead of working together to find a common culprit."

He chewed and swallowed, then gave her the eagle eye. "You believe someone else is behind the incidents here?"

"It makes sense. Both men have had offers to buy their property. So have other homesteaders on the mountain. Who stands to gain if they sell?"

"The person who's operating the illegal mine operation. That's an easy solution, but it overlooks personal motives."

Marla dug into her Caprese salad with juicy sliced tomatoes and mozzarella rounds. The tangy vinaigrette dressing slid down her throat. She could easily get spoiled by being waited on like this for meals. Viewing the guests who laughed and chatted at other tables, she was glad they still had another week left of their vacation. Maybe things would calm down, and she and Dalton could finally enjoy the amenities the resort offered.

In the morning, she should call home to check on Brianna as well as the salon. She'd been so occupied by events at the ranch that she had forgotten about the rest of her life.

"As far as we know, Garrett Long is the initial victim," Dalton said, evidently still mulling over the puzzles eluding them. Having finished his house salad, he pushed the plate away. "Eleanor Reardon and Garrett were having an affair. Next, her husband turns up dead. Think about it."

"What, you think Mrs. Reardon is killing off the men in her life?"

He spread his hands. "I'm just saying . . . she's alive, and they're not."

Marla took a sip of water. "I'd put my bet on Sherry Long. If she found out about her husband's affair, she might have enlisted her brother to murder him."

"But then we're back to the same question as before. Why kill Tate and not Eleanor? That doesn't account for his death. Tell me again where you saw Franks earlier."

"I spied him talking to Matthew Brigham." She remembered the lady in white who'd led her there, and a shiver crawled up her spine. "Brigham gave something to Franks. From the way they vamoosed after I called out a greeting, I'd guess they didn't want to be seen together."

"They could have been meeting about anything."

"I know, but then why didn't they respond to me? Then there's your uncle. Raymond and Garrett were business partners. With Garrett out of the way, Raymond stands to gain his share."

"We don't know the terms of Garrett's will."

"No, but let's assume the debt is erased, and Raymond has right of survivorship."

"Huh. If Garrett was having an affair with Eleanor Reardon, maybe he left her his half of the business instead of Raymond or his wife."

Marla sat up straight, her interest spiked by this new prospect. "Then Eleanor would have a reason to bump him off. Her husband could have found out, and she had to kill him, too."

"Who else might have wanted Reardon dead?"

"He managed the bottling plant owned by Otto Lovelace. It's possible Tate discovered something going on there that's not on the level."

"So someone eliminated him? That doesn't explain Garrett's death."

"This is too confusing. My head is getting muddled."

They waited as the server delivered their next course, then ate in silence, each lost in their own thoughts. Too many loose ends still flapped in the air without connecting.

Marla gave up and focused on her meal.

As they were strolling back to their room, low lights on the path lighting their way, an earlier theory surfaced in Marla's mind.

"It could be someone is intentionally stoking the flames between Raymond and Hugh," she said. "They've both had offers from buyers. So have other ranchers in the area. If these aren't coming from the person operating the mine, then who else might be involved?"

"Normally, I'd look for a property developer, but that doesn't seem to be the case here."

An eerie sensation crossed Marla's nape. Harry couldn't still be alive, could he, seeking revenge on the pair who'd left him for dead?

Nah, Raymond's parents had buried his brother. Then Wayne's grandmother had left town, taking her daughter with her to the east coast. That had nothing to do with recent events.

Or did it?

To distract themselves from their worries, she and Dalton attended a rodeo that night. Marla marveled at the prowess of the wranglers as they demonstrated various techniques. The team roping impressed her, and she could understand how ropers competed for prize money on a bigger scale. The precision of the barrel racers made her admire their riding skills. She cheered along with the rest of the guests in the arena bleachers.

Back in their room, she soothed herself in Dalton's arms and then fell into a deep sleep.

She awoke some time later, coughing as grit entered her lungs.

Her eyes popped open. Why was it so hard to breathe? The air seemed thick, and the nightlight coming from the bathroom appeared blurry.

She sat upright, instantly alert, as she sniffed the distinct aroma of smoke. Did her ears deceive her, or could she hear a crackling noise?

"Dalton, wake up." A coughing fit overwhelmed her as she nudged her husband. Something irritated her throat.

He roused slowly. "What is it?"

"I smell smoke, and it's foggy in here." Her head pounded, and her temples throbbed.

Dalton threw off the covers. He bounded out of bed wearing only his briefs and peeked into the living room. "You're right. The smoke is too dense to see the front door. Let's exit through the patio."

Marla slapped a hand to her mouth and

nose. She wasn't leaving without her purse. After grabbing the wrap lying at the foot of their bed and her handbag from the dinette table, she lurched toward the sliding glass doors. Dalton had opened the drapes and stood fumbling with the lock.

In the next instant, he shoved her outside, and clear, fresh air filled her lungs. When she regained her senses, she realized the awful truth — someone had set fire to their hacienda.

CHAPTER FIFTEEN

Over breakfast on Monday, Marla and Dalton discussed their next move. They'd spent the rest of the night in a standard hotel room, the resort's only vacancy. Dalton's cousin was handling repairs and getting their clothes cleaned. They'd salvaged what they could but needed to make a shopping trip into town. The property's insurance would cover expenses.

"Do you think the sheriff's men will find the arsonist?" Marla asked, taking a bite of her veggie omelet. The bountiful buffet tempted her to overeat, but with all the exercise they were getting, the possibility of gaining weight didn't bother her.

Dalton swallowed a piece of toast. "It depends on what evidence they gather. We need to have a talk with Jesse."

"Why him, and not Kevin Franks?"

"You saw Jesse talking to someone from the Donovan ranch, remember? He could be working for Hugh."

Marla searched her memories and slapped her forehead. How could she have forgotten? "Omigosh, now I realize why Ben looked familiar. He's the guy I saw with Jesse."

"So they're in cahoots together. Ben could be paying Jesse on Hugh's behalf to sabotage Uncle Ray's resort. It makes sense, especially since our place was torched right after we paid a visit to the Donovan ranch."

"But why us? This is the second time we've been targeted, if you include the snake."

"We must be perceived as a threat."

"Why would Jesse get involved? For the money?"

Dalton shrugged. "People have done bad things for less."

"I think Kevin has better reasons. I saw him taking something from Matthew Brigham. Maybe he's getting paid to cause incidents."

"What would Brigham stand to gain?"

"He could be the secret investor interested in buying people's properties. The man is an engineer. He might know about the mines."

"Hmm, you have a point. Let's go talk to

both wranglers if they're around this morning."

"What time shall we go into town? I have to buy new underwear in addition to outfits. Wayne said the cleaners might need a few days to get the smell of smoke out of our clothes."

"The stores don't open until ten. It's early yet." Dalton reached across the table to pat her hand. "This hasn't been much of a honeymoon. I'm sorry for dragging you here."

She smiled back. "Don't be. It's good we're spending time with your family. But next vacation, we head for the beach on a tropical island. Promise me?"

"Done."

His sexy grin gave her other ideas about how to spend the day, but they had things to accomplish. Their stomachs full, they headed to the corrals in the cool morning air.

Jesse was tending the horses in a nearby fenced enclosure as they approached. When Dalton signaled they'd like to speak to him, he let them inside.

"How can I help you folks?" he said with a wary expression.

Dalton offered his best authoritative glower. "Did you hear about the fire that broke out in our place last night?"

"What? Was anybody hurt?"

"Fortunately, we woke up and escaped through the patio doors. The fire started in the hallway closet, blocking our access to the front door. An incendiary device and a pile of old blankets did the trick."

Gossip must be restrained among the staff if news hadn't gotten around. Marla wondered if the small explosive, its sound muffled by the cloth, shared any similarities to the bomb found at Raymond's project. Had theirs failed to explode in the intended manner, or had merely starting a fire been the goal?

"You were lucky. How much damage was done?"

"The hacienda is intact," Dalton replied. "Most of the damage is interior."

"Why are you telling me? Shouldn't you be talking to the sheriff?"

"I'd like your opinion. Who do you think might want to harm us? We're here as guests of the owner. So that begs the question, is my uncle the indirect target? We visited Hugh Donovan yesterday. Is it mere coincidence this act of arson happened so soon afterward?"

Jesse's expression darkened. "Donovan isn't to blame."

"How do you know?"

"I just do, okay? Everybody is quick to point the finger at him, but they're wrong."

"You're awfully defensive about the man. Why is that? Do you believe he's innocent because you know something about Uncle Ray? Could it be he's sabotaging his own place to throw suspicion off himself?"

Marla cut in, surprised he'd voiced aloud her own thoughts. "Raymond would never harm you, Dalton. How could you think such a thing?"

Likely her husband was trying to provoke the wrangler into revealing what he knew. Then again, Raymond had a motive where Garrett Long was concerned. The ranger had been his silent partner at Craggy Peak. Who *did* inherit Garrett's portion? Would the sheriff have that information? Sniffing an unpleasant aroma, she glanced down to make sure she wasn't standing in something she'd regret. Ugh. A horse had let loose a few feet from them.

Jesse patted a black beauty that nudged him. She had soft, dewy eyes and a regal carriage. "You don't get it," he told them. "You're far off the mark about Garrett's death and who's to blame."

"Why don't you fill us in?" Dalton suggested.

"We've already had this conversation. You should relax and enjoy your honeymoon."

"Wayne asked me to help him look into things, and it appears we've disturbed someone with our questions. So tell me again. How well acquainted were you with Garrett? You didn't just saddle his horse when he came here to ride, did you?"

"Garrett was a good man. He could be kind and generous."

"He was generous with his passion. I've heard he was having an affair."

Jesse's mouth tightened. "What he did in his private time was his business."

"Not if it got him killed." Dalton glanced around before lowering his voice. "Is it true Kevin Franks was his brother-in-law?"

"Listen, you guys are messing with bigger issues here. Leave it alone, or you'll pay the price for being too curious. You've already had a taste of what can happen. Now if you'll excuse me, I've got work to do."

Dalton withdrew a business card from his wallet. "Here's my cell number if you feel like sharing." He thrust it at the wrangler, who stuffed it into his pocket and strode away.

"I wonder what kind of proof he's after. You're sure that's what the housekeeper said?" Dalton asked Marla.

"Yes. I'm not mistaken. Why would he withhold information? What can be more important than solving two murders?"

"We never mentioned Tate Reardon. Maybe Jesse doesn't know about him."

They let themselves out of the corral. Marla examined the bottoms of her boots, which she'd salvaged from her bedroom closet. Bits of hay stuck to the leather along with clumps of dry earth, but there was nothing she'd have to scrub off right away.

"So now what?" She swept a hand in a broad gesture. The distant mountains rose bluish in the morning sunlight. It would be nice if they could relax for one day free from worry and soak in the scenery.

"We'll go into town and see what develops from there," Dalton said in a morose tone.

It wasn't like him to lack a plan, Marla thought. He must be feeling frustrated by their lack of access to pertinent data.

She strolled beside him along the path toward the main buildings, passing the arena on their right. Aside from the rodeo, they were missing out on resort activities, not that they weren't getting their money's worth since they hadn't paid. And Wayne *had* requested their help in return for free room and board. Wasn't that termed a busman's holiday?

Before they left for town, Marla called her mother and the salon to check in, after which Dalton phoned his mom from their hotel room. His daughter Brianna had already left for school, but Kate told him things were well, from what Marla could glean by eavesdropping.

"Wayne and Carol have been super hosts," she heard Dalton saying. "His sister Annie has taken a liking to Marla. They seem to have a lot in common. As for Uncle Ray, he's quite a character."

He listened a moment. "He's looking well, Mom, but he has regrets about the past. We've learned about the tragedy with your younger brother. And we met Hugh Donovan. There's still enmity between those two even now. Don't you think it's time for everyone to let go of the ghosts haunting them and forgive each other?"

The conversation concluded shortly thereafter, as Dalton ended the call with an exasperated grunt.

"Mom won't concede an inch where Uncle Ray is concerned. My grandmother must have poisoned her against him and my grandfather."

"Don't give up. At least you've planted the seed of forgiveness in her head."

A couple of hours later, they were loading

their newly made purchases into their loaner SUV downtown when Dalton's phone rang.

"It's the sheriff," he said upon viewing the caller I.D. "Hello?" A pause. "Sure, Luke, we'll stop by. We're nearly around the corner."

"Maybe he wants us to sign statements relating to recent events," Marla mused on their way over. "Or he might have info on the arsonist."

The lawman stood to greet them as a deputy ushered them inside. His hat hanging on a rack, he looked the quintessential western sheriff with his bushy mustache, lined face, and tanned skin. He bid them take a seat with a weary air.

"You haven't had a moment's break lately, have you? It's always that way when there's a case," Dalton said, while Marla noticed the native artifacts on display and the scenic paintings on the wall.

She must have been too absorbed during her initial visit here to notice the décor. Those pictures really depicted the desert well. The artist had an eye for its beauty.

The sheriff observed the direction of her gaze. "It'll be a while before I can sit down with my easel and brush again."

"Don't tell me you painted these?" Marla gaped at him. "They're lovely."

"Thanks. Painting relaxes me. Vail, what do you do in your spare time?"

"Me?" Dalton looked startled. "I grow tomatoes, work crossword puzzles, take walks or go to the gym."

"He watches sports and the history channel on TV," Marla added with a fond smile.

"This hasn't been much of a honeymoon for you two. Have you had any time to relax?"

"Not much," Dalton replied with a wry twist of his lips. "I'm just glad we weren't hurt in that fire last night."

"You were fortunate."

"No kidding. The consequences might have been different if we hadn't woken when we did." Dalton hunched forward. "Wayne said your investigators found an incendiary device in our hallway closet."

"It wasn't meant to explode like a bomb. The thing was set among a pile of blankets that had been doused with a flammable liquid. Starting a fire was the intent."

"We didn't smell anything unusual," Marla said, trying to recall what she'd noticed before turning out the lights.

"It wasn't gasoline, if that's what you're thinking. Household cleaning fluids can be flammable, too."

She stared at him. That opened up possibilities.

"Did your people get any prints?" Dalton asked, his face solemn.

"One set on the front door knob, but it might belong to you. We should get comparison prints to make sure. Was the door locked when you entered the place last night?"

"Yes, it was, and so were the patio doors. That means whoever came inside had a key."

"The managers have master keys, and so do the maintenance crew and housekeeping staff. That doesn't help," Marla added.

"Actually, it does." Sheriff Beresby studied her. "It appears this was an inside job, not the result of a random arsonist. What would make you guys a target?"

Dalton mentioned their visit to the Donovan ranch and their discovery regarding the mine along with their theories.

The sheriff picked up a pen and twirled it in his fingers. "I see you two have been busy. Detective, I could use someone with your knowledge and expertise helping me out. We're stretched thin here, and I have other leads to follow. Would you consider assisting me in an unofficial capacity?"

"How so?" Dalton's face lit up, and his spine straightened.

"Garrett Long made a lot of enemies in his work. Go talk to them. See if anyone has something significant to say."

"Where would I start?"

"Here's a list." Beresby shuffled through the papers on his desk and withdrew a sheet. "I got these names from the forest supervisor. Every one of them has a reason to hold a grudge against Garrett."

"What about other suspects?" Marla interjected. "Like, Garrett's wife may have known her husband betrayed her with another woman and coaxed her brother into exacting revenge. Kevin Franks is a wrangler at Last Trail Dude Ranch."

"The brother is definitely on my list, but not for the reasons you may surmise." The sheriff regarded them with a steely glint. "Franks is a member of the Environmental Freedom Alliance."

"Whoa, how come no one has mentioned this before?" A trace of anger laced Dalton's tone.

Marla put a placating hand on his arm. He needed to curb his impatience.

"The man's activities in this regard have only recently come to light."

"Do you believe he's acting on behalf of this group?"

"Possibly," Beresby said in a noncommittal tone. "Your inquiries with the folks on that list would be mighty helpful."

"All right, we'll do what we can." Dalton's eyes narrowed. "Anything else you'd like to share with us, like how Tate Reardon's death fits into things?"

"We're still working on that angle. I appreciate your assistance, Detective. And you, too, Mrs. Vail. Just please be careful, and watch your backs. Don't do anything foolhardy. If you find a reliable lead, give it to me to follow up on."

Oh, right, Marla thought. Dalton would follow a lead himself until it smacked him in the face or turned into a dead end.

Outside, under a shady awning, they surveyed the typed list. Some of the people lived in the vicinity, but one guy was as far away as Scottsdale.

"That's a two-hour drive!" Marla exclaimed in dismay. It would kill a whole day, and they were running out of time. Their vacation wouldn't last forever.

Dalton checked his watch. "It's one o'clock. We'd better eat lunch. Let's find a place nearby as long as we're in town."

They'd passed a café on a hilltop with an outdoor terrace and a mountain view, so they retrieved their car and headed in that direction.

Marla called Annie on the way to see if she was available to join them, but the nutritionist was busy at her clinic. Annie reassured her that Christine Reardon and her mother had returned home and were involved in making funeral arrangements. It appeared the warning call for them to leave the house the morning of Tate's death could not be traced.

She rang off as they arrived at their destination. The restaurant was every bit as delightful as it looked. Seated outdoors, she sighed in appreciation of the spectacular view. Potted flowers bordered the terrace, and a welcome breeze warmed her skin. They sat under cover from the sun.

After ordering her meal, Marla examined the sheriff's list in more detail.

"Let's see. We have a saguaro poacher, a pot farmer, an anti-government activist, and a cocaine smuggler."

"Don't forget the guy who was angry because Garrett shot his family pet."

"Yeah, a pit bull who attacked him."

"Then there's a squatter family and a target shooter. Seven suspects in total."

"What a lovely bunch of people." The waitress delivered their iced tea.

Dalton gripped his glass. "It's a forest ranger's job to uphold the law and protect the land. I'd expect that can lead to dangerous encounters. Plus, rangers represent the government, so anybody with a beef at the Feds might target them."

"When should we go to Scottsdale? I'd like to see the old town if we go there. It's supposed to be historic with quaint shops, and there's a mystery bookstore. I could buy books for Nicole and Brianna." As fans of crime fiction, they'd both enjoy stories from this locale.

"Let's call the person of interest in Scottsdale first to see if he'll welcome our visit. No sense in wasting a trip."

"Maybe you can interview him over the phone."

Dalton rummaged in the bread basket and withdrew a sourdough roll. "It's better to see him in person. You can learn more."

"That's true." He'd given Marla a lesson on a person's *tells,* or indications of lying.

Dalton made the call and set an appointment for the following afternoon. "This means we're free for today to track down the other six."

"You don't think the sheriff is sidetracking us on purpose, do you? This might be his way of keeping us out of trouble."

"No, he looked relieved when I said we'd do it. I think his department really is overburdened. They have a lot of territory to cover."

Once lunch was over, Marla and Dalton headed off to the first guy on their list and the closest to their location. Raoul Hernandez had been caught poaching saguaro, a serious offense under Arizona law.

He lived in a small town down the highway about twenty minutes from there. His seedy apartment complex made Marla glance over her shoulder as Dalton knocked on the door. The lamp outside mounted on a wall hung loose, its wire exposed.

"Who's there?" came a shout from within.

"Hi, I have an interest in saguaro and was told you might be able to help me," Marla called in a sugary tone.

The door cracked open, and a grizzled face peered out. "Who's he?"

"Dalton is my husband. Please, can we talk to you? We won't take much of your time."

He opened the door wider but didn't invite them in. "So what's this about?"

"I'm researching an article for a blog post," Marla said, offering the same excuse she'd told the engineer in town during their initial encounter. Maybe she should start a blog to be true to her word. "We've heard about the black market for saguaro. How much does one of those plants get on the street?"

"Are you cops? How did you get my name?"

"We're here as tourists, but I'm doing a write-up when we get home. We were referred to you by a friend." She dared not glance at Dalton and hoped he wasn't glowering at the guy in an intimidating manner.

Raoul glanced up and down the walkway. Then he held out his grimy hand.

Dalton rolled his eyes and handed over a couple of twenty dollar bills. Raoul stayed silent, his lips pressed together, until Dalton slapped him another forty.

"I could get two thousand for one plant when I was, you know, in the business."

"Who would buy them?" Marla asked, curious to know.

"Landscapers. A mature saguaro is highly valued."

"Don't those things weigh tons?"

Raoul grinned, exposing metal fillings. "I used to take plants around forty years old, *señora,* because they were only about seven feet in height and easier to transport."

"Did you stop your, uh, activities because of forest ranger Garrett Long?"

Their informant rattled off a string of

Spanish that didn't sound pleasant. "I'd dug up a few saguaros and stashed them alongside the forest's boundary. I had to get my truck to haul the plants away. When I got back, Long was waiting for me."

"So he arrested you? And please be assured your name won't be mentioned in my article."

"Thanks to Long, I got nine months in federal prison and a five-thousand-dollar fine. My girlfriend left me. The ranger ruined my life."

It wasn't Garrett's fault that the man's lady friend deserted him or that he was probably still paying off his debt. Still, he wouldn't view it that way.

"Have you seen Officer Long since your incarceration?" Dalton said, his tone mild but his eyes razor sharp.

Raoul stared at him as though he'd sprouted a cactus branch from his shoulder. "Are you nuts? I hope to never look upon his face again."

"So you've gone legit now?"

"I work for a trucking company."

"You must be happy to hear that Garrett Long is dead, then."

Raoul's eyes popped. "What?"

Marla thought he appeared genuinely surprised. "He fell off a ledge in the forest where he worked. The sheriff believes he might have been pushed."

"Hey, you don't think I had something to do with it, do you? Because while I resented him, I'd never harm the guy."

Right, you only harm valuable plants that are irreplaceable.

"Do you have any idea who else might bear a grudge against him?" Dalton asked.

Raoul snorted. "I'm done talking to you." Kicking Dalton's foot out of the way, he slammed the door shut.

A couple of men lounged outside, admiring the SUV's body parts as she and Dalton approached. Marla didn't like the looks of them. She hastened to the passenger side and dove in, glad when Dalton zoomed away and the doors locked automatically.

Had he stuck his sidearm inside his boot this morning? For that matter, had he retrieved it from the safe when they'd changed rooms last night?

"I believe Garrett's death was news to Raoul," she said, hands clasped in her lap.

"Maybe so, but I don't think he's given up his life of thievery. Did you notice the dirt under his fingernails?"

"Not really, but that doesn't mean he's a murderer. I'll go along with his story in that respect." She took out the list she'd left in their glove compartment. "The pot farmer is next in line."

After giving Dalton directions, she settled back in her seat to muse over their progress. They'd be lucky to find the other people at home.

They got nowhere with their next target, and the smuggler had moved to places unknown. That left the political activist and the dog owner.

"Can you tell us about your encounter with Garrett Long when you went camping with your family?" Marla asked the latter after they'd tracked down his trailer park. Her excuse this time was a blog article on ranger abuse.

The man regarded them with bleary eyes, a protruding belly, and alcohol breath. Barking came from inside his trailer, but he'd closed the door on his pets and gestured his visitors to an outside bench beside a patch of brown dirt.

"We went camping with the kids at our favorite spot, and we'd brought along our mixed pit bulls. They're friendlier than they sound. Anyway, the forest ranger came around to check on permits. Our son Lyle was outside, and Daisy wasn't on a leash. That was one of our dogs at the time. The officer yelled for Lyle to get the animal under control. Daisy rushed forward. She only wanted to be friendly."

"Oh yeah, I know how friendly pit bulls can be," Dalton muttered.

"The next thing we knew, a shot rang out. That ranger had fired at our dog with no provocation."

"He might not have seen it that way. An animal can appear aggressive in a play for attention," Marla suggested in a kindly tone. No matter the reason, it would hurt to lose a beloved pet.

"He claimed Daisy snapped at him, but that's not true. Nor did the ranger give Lyle a chance to get the dog under control."

"Then what happened?"

"Our other pet bolted out of the tent where my daughter had been sleeping. Imagine if that gunshot had gone astray! How could the idiot have been so reckless?"

"And the second dog?" she asked.

"My wife got him on a leash and drove both animals to the vet. Daisy died, but not before the efforts to save her left us with huge medical bills." Towering over them where they sat and he stood, the guy bared his teeth in a snarl. "I don't believe it was any accident."

"What do you mean?"

"Who'd you say you're writing an article

for again?"

Marla mentioned a fictitious name for her online blog. Now she'd really have to start one when she got home. She had enough material from all she'd learned in Arizona.

"Officer Long had it in for us all the time we'd gone camping. He would always sneak up on us to check our permits. I could tell he thought of us as white trash."

"Where is your wife now?" Marla peered past him toward the trailer.

"She passed last year, bless her soul. We'd bought a puppy to take the place of Daisy. At least our dogs were there to comfort her in the end."

The man spoke more fondly of his animals than their children. "How did it affect your son? The dog's death, that is."

"He took a dislike to the police. I tried to explain how this was an isolated incident and the fault of one man, but he doesn't get it. In his eyes, Garrett Long shot and killed his Daisy for no reason other than pure meanness."

"Did you ever see the ranger again?" Dalton asked, taking over the conversation.

"No. We considered suing for damages, but our lawyer said we had no case. The dog was off the leash, which went against regulations, and it would have been Long's word against ours."

"Did you seek revenge another way?"

He gave a mirthless grin. "Not me, but it looks like someone got to him from gossip on the street. Word is that he tumbled off a ledge in a place he knew like the back of his hand. I'm thinking a fellow like him probably had lots of enemies."

"Can you name anyone in particular?"

"Sorry, I can't help you there."

Marla observed the mountains had gone hazy. The wind had picked up, stirring the loose dirt on dry ground. Wary of a dust storm, she tapped Dalton's arm. "We should go. Thank you for sharing," Marla told the pet owner. "Your information will be helpful for my article."

Their visit to the squatter family's last known site was a waste of time since they'd moved to another state. And the target shooter had nothing significant to add. That left the political activist who resided in Scottsdale.

"We could leave now and stay overnight," Marla suggested. "Then we won't waste the whole morning driving there tomorrow. We have our purchases in the car. That should hold us over." They'd have adequate supplies for an overnighter.

"Good idea. I'll notify Wayne so he won't

get worried."

"Okay. I can make a hotel reservation in the meantime."

Several hours later, they chugged through traffic into Scottsdale. The sky was darkening when Dalton suggested they stop by the target's house.

"He might be home from work and willing to talk to us now. It's worth a chance."

"Should I call him?"

"No, let's drop by. We might learn more by catching him off guard. If we come in the morning, he'll have had time to think about what he wants to say."

Marla would never have identified the homeowner as a political protester from the immaculate condition of his single-story house with its shiny barrel-tile roof and brick-paved driveway. But then she'd learned that placid exteriors could hide people's deadly secrets.

The man who opened the door was a lean fellow with bright brown eyes and a hank of wheat-colored hair. Marla's claim of writing a series of blog posts on the environment had interested him, but he didn't invite them inside.

"I thought you were coming by in the morning." His narrowed gaze raked them over as he stood in the doorway.

"We decided to drive into town earlier and hoped you might be home," Dalton replied in a bland tone.

"What is it you want to know?"

"We've studied the forest service and read that rangers are responsible for protecting our natural resources and cultural sites. Do you feel they're doing an adequate job?"

"Hell, no. The Feds are stealing our land and denying access to the people. They're turning our country into a tyranny, and the rangers are merely their puppets. You think those guys are concerned with preserving our resources? Their interest lies in the opposite direction."

He expounded on his theories for several minutes, while Marla tilted her head to hear better as a UPS truck rumbled past.

"What's worse is they're conspiring with the Chinese. You know how foreigners have bought up our country? I've seen them for myself near our national property."

"What's this?" Dalton's eyebrows lifted.

"I spotted them on the mountain above Rustler Ridge by the bottling plant. Do you realize a European owns that abomination? Officer Long was there talking to one of these foreign fellows. I didn't need to hear their conversation to know they're all in it together."

Chapter Sixteen

"Do you really think there's a Chinese connection?" Marla asked Dalton as they zoomed away in their car toward downtown Scottsdale.

The activist had rambled for the next twenty minutes about government conspiracies and how the people needed to be liberated, but he'd claimed to have halted his own involvement. He'd gotten a girlfriend who demanded a steadier lifestyle and one that would keep him out of trouble. Now he worked in computer technology, which alarmed Marla more. Hackers could be just as dangerous as domestic terrorists who set off bombs.

"It's more likely he spotted the miners," Dalton said. "Maybe Long discovered the mining operation and was talking to one of the workers when the activist spied him."

"If Garrett knew about the mines, it could account for why someone wanted to silence him. We should pay a visit to Otto's place to see what he knows."

As they cruised down one of the main streets in Old Scottsdale, she pursed her lips. "Drat, the stores are all closed. We might as well find a place for dinner."

Surveying the Indian Trading Post, Silver Star Jewelry, and Cactus Hut shops, she vowed to return in the morning. The selection of quality souvenirs and jewelry here was much greater than Rustler Ridge, and she could buy gifts for everyone back home.

Old-fashioned lanterns on posts gave the street with its adobe buildings a historic appeal despite the modern diagonal parking. At least that part was free. The town encouraged visitors, unlike downtown Fort Lauderdale where you had to pay for the privilege of shopping and dining.

"The Poisoned Pen Bookstore is still open," she said while searching the Web on her cell phone for a place to eat. "They're having a book signing tonight. I *have* to get Brianna and Nicole some mystery novels. There's a trendy restaurant called Virtu nearby where we can go afterward."

"Okay, give me directions."

Marla stared in awe upon entering the bookshop. Shelves lined the walls and stretched toward the ceiling while other attractive displays lay on tables throughout the store. The author event hadn't started yet, judging by the half-filled circle of chairs further along. Customers milled around or browsed the shelves. Marla snagged a bookseller to recommend mysteries set in Arizona.

"Sure, I can help you," said a tall, handsome guy who wore a button-down blue shirt tucked into belted navy trousers.

By the time Marla left, she carried a canvas tote full of books and a couple of wrapped logo mugs as surprise gifts. Dalton had bought a souvenir mug for himself along with a tee shirt and baseball cap. The store also had a great collection of nonfiction works on the southwest. He'd purchased some history books and field guides to the state's trees and plants, while Marla had gravitated to the travel and cooking section. Besides a regional cookbook, she picked up a few helpful titles on copper mining, life of a miner, and Arizona haunted hotels.

The next day emptied their wallets further. Marla shopped to her heart's content, buying turquoise jewelry and Native American earrings, a western-style blouse, a red sunhat that she could wear in Florida, and various other tchotchkes. She bought an amethyst pendant for Brianna with matching earrings and copper necklaces for them both. It was easier to resist the Mexican woven baskets and pottery.

Dalton shopped the cowboy hats and boots and other leather goods, picking up some new belts in the process. After lunch, he called it a day.

"We should head back to the ranch."

"You're right," Marla said, reluctant to go. She could have spent their whole vacation in this town. Nonetheless, she gamely climbed into the SUV for the drive through the mountains back to Last Trail Dude Ranch. The magnificent scenery drew her attention until their return.

They hadn't missed much in their absence, Dalton determined upon checking in with his cousin from their resort room. Catching up on his phone calls, he called the sheriff next with their report. "I would eliminate the work contacts for Garrett Long. Most of these folks are occupied with their own lives now. They didn't express any regret at Long's death but I didn't detect any real indications of involvement either."

Dalton listened a moment while Marla unpacked their purchases and hung up their new clothing. Heading into the bathroom to sort out their supplies, she couldn't hear the rest of his conversation.

"Beresby discounts the last guy's claim about the Chinese man," Dalton told her when she reappeared. "He probably saw whatever he wanted to see that fit in with his conspiracy theories. But the sheriff says the threat from the E.F.A. is real. They've been known to bomb facilities like Lovelace's place."

"Tate Reardon worked for him. Could the plant's manager have been targeted by this group?"

"The sheriff is looking into it. He says the E.F.A. connection could link Garrett Long's death with Reardon's. He's keeping an eye on Kevin Franks in that regard."

"Oh, joy. That makes me feel safe."

He strode over and massaged her shoulders. "Don't worry. We'll be okay if I have anything to say about it."

She hoped his promise held true as they drove the next morning up the mountain toward Otto Lovelace's palatial residence. She'd called ahead to take him up on his offer for a tour of his facility, and he said to park their car at his house. He would drive them through the gates to his industrial plant. As a precaution, Dalton had notified the sheriff and Wayne where they'd be heading.

The winding road led them to a Mediterranean-style villa nestled among the rocks. Driving up the steep incline of a driveway was an adventure in itself. Marla wouldn't care to drive there at night. A separate cutoff ran to a second garage, but they parked at an upper level near the massive carved front doors.

Otto opened the door after they rang the bell. He wore a buttoned dress shirt and tailored trousers, but it was the worried look in his eyes that drew her attention along with the white stubble peppering his jaw. Those hinted at unrest. Since the new beard growth didn't match his tar black hair, she surmised he dyed the latter. But his vanity wasn't in question here. What had him upset this morning? Could his manager's death have left him shaken?

"Come in while I get my keys. I'm glad you took me up on my offer." His careful enunciation didn't erase the trace of an accent in his voice.

Standing inside a marble-tiled foyer, Marla surveyed the living and dining areas and the terrace beyond. Her gaze fixed on an ornate clock by the fireplace mantle. She'd learned about clock-making back home when investigating a woman's murder. The husband had studied horology, the art and science of timekeeping. He owned a shop to repair and restore chronological works.

As she moved into the living room where a patterned rug covered a polished wood floor, she noted other antique pieces scattered around. A synchronized ticking sounded in her ears.

"I like your clock collection," she said to Otto when he returned, a set of keys jangling in his hand. She wondered if he lived alone. Being unmarried, he might still have companionship. But no other sounds reached her ears except for the incessant tick-tocks.

A furry white cat with slanted eyes slinked from behind a couch and leaped onto the cushion. It settled down with a purr of contentment. Marla glanced at it warily, being more of a dog lover. A pang of affection hit her for Spooks and Lucky, her poodle and golden retriever.

"My father was a watch maker in Germany." Otto's eyes gleamed. "I remember the smell and sounds of his shop as though it were yesterday. He instilled in me a love for fine timepieces. Their precision is unmatched. Young people today don't appreciate the artistry involved. They rely on digital devices to tell time." He glanced at his pocket watch and frowned. "We must move on, or we'll get off-schedule. It's important to structure your time, you know. Otherwise, you waste away your life in meaningless activities. Even if you are late for one minute, this is one moment closer to your death."

My, aren't you cheerful.

"I imagine your work schedule got shot to pieces when Tate Reardon died," Dalton mused as they trailed their host through a hallway toward the garage entrance.

"Poor man. Carbon monoxide can be such a hazard. I don't understand why he didn't replace the batteries in his smoke alarms."

"It's fortunate his wife and daughter weren't home."

"Indeed. I spoke to the police extensively about the fellow. He'd been a good employee, always on time. It'll be hard to find a replacement."

You don't sound too sorry, pal. You're more upset by the disruption to your schedule.

She kept silent as they climbed into his Mercedes. The drive up the mountain took less than fifteen minutes. They approached a barbed fence with a gate and two guards carrying rifles. As soon as they recognized

Otto, they opened the gate and waved him through.

A complex of buildings rose ahead, stark white against the azure sky. From the far building rose the plume visible from the town in the valley below.

"Are you sure that's steam? It looks thicker from here," Marla said from the back seat.

"We run a clean operation, Mrs. Vail. We're dedicated to preserving the environment to the best extent possible. Our facility exceeds government requirements."

"Are all inspections conducted by Matthew Brigham?" Dalton asked in an idle tone.

"Yes, he does a thorough assessment several times a year."

"Who's running the show since Tate Reardon's death?"

"One of our section heads. We have an executive search going on for a new manager." Otto pulled into a reserved space in the employee lot behind the first building. "It's not easy finding a replacement. Our general manager has to understand and agree to follow our exceptional standards."

Noise hit Marla's ears as soon as they entered the structure. Whirling machinery, rattling conveyor belts, and stamping mechanisms made her head spin. So did a thumping vibration that shook her bones.

"Where do you get the water?" she asked, impressed by the speeding rows of plastic bottles and the enormity of the place. "Don't you lease a certain amount from the city?" Disappointed that they hadn't seen the brook gushing down the mountain, Marla couldn't imagine how it ended up here.

"The stream is about three miles from our location. We tap the source through stainless steel underground piping. Our share is less than ten percent of the total flow."

"So you don't use groundwater like the cities?"

Otto glared at her like a teacher to a recalcitrant student. "We have no need to obtain water from an Artesian aquifer when we have a fresh mountain stream."

"Conditions at the Donovan ranch and other properties downstream have gone dry. You wouldn't know anything about that, would you?" Dalton shot him a sideways glance.

Otto tugged on his ear. "Of course not. Drought is always a danger in the west. It can have many causes. At any rate, the town holds senior water rights to the source, and they've granted us a lease. We take our allotted amount and not an ounce more."

He signaled for them to accompany him down a long hallway lined with wide glass windows. Employees gave him deferential greetings along the way. He nodded to them like a beneficent ruler.

"How many people work here?" Marla couldn't begin to guess.

"Two hundred and fifty." Otto made an expansive gesture. "We offer generous benefits. I believe in treating our workers as we would our customers — with courtesy, respect, and outstanding service."

His speech sounded like a commercial. They needed to rock his foundations.

"What's causing that deep vibration and those pounding noises?" Marla asked. It was hard to hear the background thumps over the roar of the machinery.

"That's from our subsidiary operation next door. We make carbonated drinks and flavored waters. We're a diverse company, Mrs. Vail, like many of the better known beverage companies that are household names."

He stopped before one window. "When the water first enters our facility, it goes through several purification processes. Particulate and micron filtration remove any sediment or suspended particles. Our product ends up a lot purer than municipal sources that remove mineral content through reverse osmosis. Then we hit it with ultraviolet light as an extra measure."

"What goes on in there?" Marla pointed to a microbiological laboratory where workers wore white lab coats and paper caps on their heads as they peered into microscopes.

"That's where we test the water. We have ten different production lines, and each one is tested two hundred times per day. That's sixty times more than your municipal water."

He guided them to another window. "See that piece of plastic the size of your thumb? It blows up to become a bottle."

Marla watched in fascination as the newly minted plastic bottles slid overhead to an elevated track where they entered a spinning machine. There looked to be a whole row of gleaming stainless steel carousels whirling throughout the cavernous space.

"Twelve hundred bottles are filled and capped every minute." Otto's chest puffed with pride. "Note those giant spools twirling around. They hold the labels, which are snipped off and slapped on the bottles as they pass by. Then we have lasers check for defects, like crooked caps or bottles that aren't filled all the way."

Marla's gaze followed the rows of bottles moving along a conveyor belt toward wrapper machines, where groups of twenty-four bottles each were packaged by a mechanical arm. It surrounded the cluster with a wrapper that shrank tight. She noticed the labels on the wrapped parcels obscured their bottoms.

Further along, the packages were stacked high onto wooden shipping pallets. The pallets slid down a roller into a gazebo-type structure. There a rotating head wrapped the tower in a plastic wrapper to prepare it for shipping.

"Fifteen hundred bottles fit inside one of those pallets," Otto said, pointing to where men driving forklifts drove back and forth moving the weighty bundles.

"I'm impressed," Dalton acknowledged. "But if things are so environmentally sound, why are you afraid of terrorists? Isn't that why you post armed guards around your perimeter?"

Otto gave him a dark glance. "Follow me into my office. It's quieter inside."

The neat space must have been soundproofed, because Marla could hear much better in there. However, it didn't lessen the teeth-rattling thumps that shook the building. What could be happening in the adjacent structures to be causing that vibration?

Then again, was it coming from next door or from underneath them? Could that be the piping containing the gushing water?

Once they'd been seated, Otto straightened a clock on his desk. "So tell me, what is the real purpose of your visit here today?"

"You invited us," Marla reminded him. "I like to visit places where we can see how things work. It's more interesting than the standard tourist attractions and gives you a flavor for the area. Plus it'll give me a new topic for my blog."

"I sense your husband is after more than a guided tour."

"What do you know about the E.F.A. member Kevin Franks?" Dalton asked, his manner deceptively casual but his eyes eagle sharp.

"I'm not familiar with the man." Otto tugged on his ear lobe. "Is he active in the area? The Environmental Freedom Alliance is a genuine concern. They've attacked places like ours despite assurances that we're doing our best to preserve the environment. They see us in concordance with the government, which puts us on their blacklist. I'd want to know if one of their operatives lived close by."

"Franks works on the dude ranch where

we're staying. We've experienced acts of sabotage there and at the ghost town my uncle is renovating. What's curious to me is how Uncle Ray and other homesteaders on the mountain have had offers to buy their property. I'm wondering if the potential buyer is causing these incidents."

"Is that so?" Otto's eyes narrowed into two tight beams. "I find this interesting, Mr. Vail, but I don't see how it's my concern."

"My wife saw Franks in discussion with Matthew Brigham. Wouldn't you want to know why your plant inspector and a known E.F.A. member were meeting together?"

"It could have nothing to do with my affairs." Otto withdrew his pocket watch and gave an exclamation of dismay. "I'm afraid I shall have to cut our time short." He stood, and they followed suit. "Come along, I'll drive you back to the house. I mustn't get a moment off schedule. That's the only way to get things done, you know. It's all about precision."

Marla mulled over his words once she and Dalton were on their way back to the ranch. "There's something smarmy about that man. You'd think Otto would be more curious about Kevin Franks. I'm sure he didn't tell us the whole *megillah*. And did you notice how many times he tugged on his ear? That's one of your 'tells,' isn't it?"

"Yes, I picked up on that. He's lying about something." Dalton focused forward during the drive down the mountain. "Did you feel that vibration inside his facility? I doubt it's coming from a simple subsidiary operation next door."

"It could originate below ground."

"You may be right. We should return to the mines and investigate further."

"Or not? Maybe we should forget about this stuff and enjoy the last few days on the ranch. I didn't even get to sit by the pool."

"You can do that at home. The threat to Uncle Ray's property won't go away unless we expose whoever is behind it. They're my family, Marla. I can't abandon them."

"Well then, we should all get together again and compare notes. I'll call Carol and ask her when she and Wayne can meet us along with Uncle Ray and Annie. We could offer to treat everyone to dinner at a restaurant in town for a change."

"Sounds like a plan."

They were just turning in to the dude ranch when Dalton's phone rang. Since he was busy driving, Marla answered.

"Luke Beresby here. I have some news. Kevin Franks has been found dead."

"What?" Her heart skipped a beat. "I

don't believe it. How did that happen?"

"Here's the address if you can come by. I'd like Detective Vail to take a look."

"Of course." Marla grabbed a pen and paper from her purse and scribbled down the info. When she'd hung up, she told Dalton the latest development.

"Franks is dead? That's incredible." He made a U-turn and headed in the direction she indicated.

"I know. What do you think this means?"

"We'll have to wait and see. How did he die?"

"The sheriff didn't say."

"Damn, there goes our best lead."

They zoomed through town to a seedier section and an apartment where sheriff department's vehicles were parked amid flashing lights and yellow police tape. People were coming and going from an open door while bystanders gawked.

Beresby greeted them upon arrival. "Here, you'll need these," he said, giving Dalton the standard gear to wear for a crime scene inspection. "Ma'am, you'll have to wait outside."

"That's fine with me." She had no wish to view the gory scene. How had the man been killed? Or had he died from natural causes? Maybe the neighbors would know.

Passing an open apartment that smelled like laundry detergent, Marla wandered toward a woman who'd wrapped her head in old-fashioned curlers. Working at the salon would seem like a balm after this holiday. Her gaze swept past the parking lot to the dry earth beyond and its sporadic plant life. Enough of the desert already. She yearned for the lush tropical landscape of South Florida and her daily routine.

"Hi, can you tell me what's going on?" she said to the middle-aged woman who wore a rumpled top and faded jeans.

"They say Mr. Franks is dead. Nobody heard any shots or other suspicious sounds coming from his place. Maybe his heart gave out, although he was fairly young."

"I think it may have been his allergies," said a young man with a pockmarked face who'd sauntered over. "Whenever we had a block party, he steered clear of foods with peanuts."

"Really?" Marla glanced with interest at the victim's door. Could that be the case? He'd been alone and eaten something tainted? But if he had a known allergy, he'd have kept epinephrine at hand. Maybe he couldn't get to it in time. What an awful way to go.

Dalton stayed inside for an inordinately

long period. Marla chatted up the other neighbors but didn't learn much of value, except Franks didn't appear to have a girlfriend and kept to himself most of the time. He seemed amiable enough when he encountered anyone.

Finally, Dalton emerged and signaled her over, his face grim. "You won't believe what's inside. Franks had a whole wall with photos pinned up."

"Photos? What do you mean?" Clutching her purse under one arm, she accompanied him toward their car.

"It's E.F.A. stuff. He's got pictures of the ghost town and the ranch as well as the bottling plant, maps of the buildings, a journal where he's ranted at length about his beliefs. He had photos of us, too, plus Wayne and Carol and Uncle Ray."

A shudder gripped her. "How did Franks die?"

"The coroner believes he may have gone into anaphylactic shock. He was lying on the bathroom floor, an epi-pen in his hand. We'll know more after the autopsy."

"Why did the sheriff summon you here? To confirm his observations?"

Dalton nodded, his jaw resolute. "His techs seem competent. He said he'll contact me later with more information."

"Do you think Franks was part of a domestic terrorist cell in the area?"

"It's too early to tell. Luke has a paper trail to follow, phone calls to trace."

"How about the offers to buy people's properties? Surely the wrangler wouldn't have had the financial means to be the buyer?"

"His bank accounts will have to be examined. But it's a valid point."

"Who alerted the police to check his apartment?"

Dalton held the car door open for her. "Jesse Parker."

"No kidding? He's another man on our person of interest list."

"Jesse got concerned when Franks didn't report in to work, since the guy rarely missed a day. He notified the sheriff's office."

"Wouldn't it be nice if this wrapped up the case so we could enjoy our last few days here?" She slid into the vehicle, sniffing its leathery scent.

Dalton shut the door and strode around to his side. After they hit the road, he shot her a regretful glance. "We still need more answers. The only option is to pay another visit to the copper mine. Somebody is running a covert operation there, and the sheriff didn't seem impressed when we told him. If we could trace the ore's route, and it surfaces near Lovelace's facility, this might give Luke adequate cause to get a search warrant for the bottling plant."

"It's too dangerous."

His hands tightened on the steering wheel. "One of the stores in town sells historical costumes. It has outfits similar to those worn by the miners. That'll provide a disguise for me to blend in with the workmen, at least on first glance."

"You're not meaning to go alone?"

"I'll call the sheriff to see if he can spare one of his deputies to accompany me. Luke might be busy with his current investigation, but he could send someone else in his place. We need proof about what's going on. It's the only way to identify who's calling the shots behind the scenes."

CHAPTER SEVENTEEN

Downtown in Rustler Ridge, Dalton searched for a parking space while Marla phoned Annie to see if she could join them for lunch.

"Sure, I'd love to meet you. Where shall we go?"

Fifteen minutes later, their cousin arrived and plopped in the seat they'd reserved for her at a popular café. She wore a patterned brick-red top over slim black pants with a colorful scarf around her neck.

"I'm so glad you called. I haven't seen you guys nearly enough."

Dalton cupped his coffee mug. "I know. We'd like to invite the family out to dinner at a restaurant when both you and Uncle Ray are available."

The brackets framing Annie's mouth deepened. "Dad won't leave his project until it gets dark outside every night. He's afraid something bad will happen if he's not there.

And the workers think the town is jinxed by ghosts. It's supposed to be a ghost town, isn't it?"

"He should hire a security force." Marla took a sip of iced tea, while her companions stared at her as though she'd reinvented electricity.

"That's a brilliant idea." Dalton gave her an approving grin.

"Yes, but does he have the money?" If Raymond was hard-pressed to make his payroll each month, he might not have anything left over.

"It shouldn't be a problem now that he owns Garrett Long's share." Annie's gaze averted. "He admitted they'd each signed a right of survivorship clause."

Marla tilted her head. "Didn't we hear Garrett came from a wealthy family, and that's where he got the cash to invest in their business? Who inherits the rest of his estate?"

"I imagine it's his wife, Sherry," Annie said. "Too bad you missed his funeral, or you would have met her then."

"We were in Scottsdale that day. Nobody told us the plans. Did Garrett have any siblings?"

"Not to my knowledge."

"Then he'd be sole heir to his parents'

fortune. They may not have been happy about his career choice. It could be a dangerous occupation. Not everyone he met in his job loved him." Marla told Annie about the interviews she and Dalton had conducted.

"It doesn't sound as though you learned much from those folks."

"If anything, we've eliminated them as suspects. When we were in Sedona, I consulted a psychic. She told me to look closer to home for answers. How well acquainted are you with Sherry Long?"

"We're not really friends. She's involved in fund-raising activities around town."

"Good for her." Marla's stomach growled as the waitress carried a sizzling dish past that smelled like garlic. Too bad the town didn't have a good deli. She missed a nova smoked salmon and bagel sandwich.

"I remember Uncle Ray said Sherry had a son from a previous marriage. Where does he live?" Dalton asked, leaning back in his chair.

Annie picked up her spoon and twirled it. "He's grown and lives in Phoenix."

"What happened to the first husband? They get a divorce?"

"I think he died, but I don't know much about her history."

"Did you realize Kevin Franks, the wrangler on your dad's ranch, was her brother?"

Annie's brow furrowed. "Why do you speak about him in the past tense?"

"He's dead." Dalton explained the circumstances.

"Oh, my." Annie clapped a hand to her mouth. "Poor man."

"Who else might have known about his food allergies if not a family member?" Marla said, seized by an idea.

"What do you mean?" Dalton eyed the waitress as she carried another tray past their table. He must be hungry.

"This reinforces our theory that Sherry Long may have coaxed her brother into killing her husband. Garrett was cheating on her, and he had money. She'd get rid of a cheat and gain his bank balance at the same time."

"So how did Franks end up dead?" Dalton asked in a challenging tone.

"Maybe he threatened to expose his sister if she didn't increase his share of the money. Or else, she just wanted to get rid of a loose end that might lead back to her."

"That's cold-hearted. You'd think she would need her brother as an ally. And how about Tate Reardon? What possible reason would Sherry have to kill off the bottling plant manager?"

"He could be the one who suggested doing away with her husband in the first place." Marla raised a hand at the doubtful look on Dalton's face. "I know this is farfetched, but bear with me. Tate could have had a thing for Sherry. Getting rid of Garrett would clear the path for him."

"You've got it reversed. Sherry's husband was the one having a fling with Eleanor Reardon."

"Wow, do you two do this all the time?" Annie appeared fascinated.

"Yes, unfortunately we often have these conversations at the dinner table," Dalton replied in a wry tone.

Unabashed, Marla continued on. "You're the one who told me to examine all the angles in a murder case. Then again, if Reardon wanted to cover anything up about their operation on the mountain, Garrett would be a target once he'd discovered the miners."

Annie shook her head in puzzlement. "You've lost me again."

"We paid a visit to Otto Lovelace, and he gave us a tour of his facility. Everything appears legitimate, but something isn't right there. We believe it might relate to the copper mine underlying the ghost town."

"What do you mean?"

"Somebody has secretly reopened the mine. We've been down there once already with a guide, but Dalton wants to get proof and see where the ore surfaces."

Annie's face paled. "Are you crazy? Exploring the mines is dangerous. If there's a cave-in, or one of you falls —"

"Marla isn't going," Dalton reassured her. "I'll ask the sheriff if he can send one of his deputies with me. It's the best way for us to get the definitive answers we need."

They fell silent as the server delivered their food. Marla dove into her turkey wrap while Dalton attacked his burger.

After finishing their meal, Dalton gave Quinn O'Malley a call to see if the former copper miner and hiking guide would be available to make a repeat visit to the mine with him. Unfortunately, the fellow was otherwise engaged for the next three days. Dalton called the sheriff next, wherein Beresby tried to persuade him to adopt a different strategy. When Dalton persisted, the lawman reluctantly agreed to send a deputy to join him.

"Can you call Carol to see when we can gather for dinner again?" Dalton said to Annie on their way from the restaurant.

"Sure, I'll take care of it." Annie paused

on the sidewalk. "I'm worried for you. I don't like this plan of yours."

"Marla will have my back. I'll give her a check-in time. If I haven't returned by then, she can call for reinforcements."

"Dalton, I'm thinking that I can't let you go with just the deputy for protection," Marla said. "I should come along."

He shook his head. "Don't even go there."

"Look, you need evidence, right? I'm handy with a camera. Get me into position, and I can snap photos. Or have the deputy take the shots, and I'll act as lookout. Either way, you could use a third person on the team."

"I won't put your life at risk. You are *not* going."

"Oh, and it's okay for you to risk yourself? What if Lovelace *is* the bad guy in charge and his influence extends to the sheriff's office? We might trust Luke Beresby, but we don't know squat about his staff. Lovelace could have some of them in his pocket. I don't like the idea of trusting your life to a total stranger."

"It doesn't matter. You're staying at the ranch where it's safe."

She narrowed her eyes. "But it's not safe there. I'd be alone and vulnerable. I'm safer when I'm with you and we're working together."

Annie, who had been standing by with a look of distress on her face, pitched in. "How about if neither of you go? Let the sheriff handle it."

"He's occupied with a murder investigation," Dalton said. "And our time here is running out. I have to get to the bottom of things, or Wayne will be in the same mess as when we first arrived. I won't leave this job undone."

"He'll understand," Annie said in a pleading tone. "Wayne wouldn't want you to put your lives in danger. Please don't go into the mine."

"I'll follow the arrows we marked on the walls last time. We shouldn't have to go much deeper."

Marla glanced at him. By the *we*, did he mean himself and the deputy, or did he include her?

His cell phone rang. "Maybe it's Luke, and he can join us after all." Dalton withdrew the device and squinted at it. "That's odd. I've received a text message from Jesse Parker. You won't believe this, but he's sent me a schematic of the mining tunnels."

"How is that possible?" It brought up two questions. How did Jesse gain access to that information, and why would he send it to Dalton?

"Wait, there's more. Hmm, Jesse didn't finish the sentence. It says, 'He—.' "

"Text him back."

Dalton did so. "No reply. That's peculiar."

"You know what they say. Don't look a gift horse in the mouth."

"I'll definitely have more questions for him when we return to the ranch."

"Listen, Jesse mentioned he needed proof," Marla said. "Think about it. Why is he so reluctant to come forward? Maybe there's someone else besides Franks on the ranch to cause concern. He could have been about to warn you when his cell cut out. Do you really want me to stay behind when it can be just as dangerous as coming with you?"

"In a way, she's right," Annie said, matching their slow pace along the sidewalk. "There's already been a fire in your hacienda and a rattlesnake in your suitcase. It's easy to assume Franks was to blame, but he might not have been working alone. I hate to admit this, but I'm beginning to agree with Marla. She might be safer in your company."

Dalton's mouth compressed. "Two against one. That's not fair."

"You can give me a check-in time. If I don't hear from either of you by then, I'll call the sheriff. Marla is right about the deputy. You don't know who you can trust."

"Please, Dalton. I won't get in your way." Marla grasped his hand and squeezed it. "You know I can be useful, and we'll watch each other's backs."

"Oh, hell, all right. But at the first sign of trouble, you're getting out of there."

"That works for me." Her spirits lifting, she headed for their car after they arranged a check-in time with Annie and said their goodbyes. She didn't relish the thought of traipsing into danger, but as Dalton said, it was the only way to get the proof they needed. And she didn't like the idea of him going into the mines with a fellow they didn't know.

After a few stops along the way to gather supplies, they headed up the mountain. Clasping her hands in her lap, Marla stared out the window. The road dropped away to her right until they screeched around another hairpin curve. Her ears popped as they climbed. They zoomed through Craggy Peak, aiming higher. The saguaro gave way to pines and other tall trees while huge boulders and cut rock bordered the road.

Dalton parked on a swath of reddish-brown dirt. There they geared up while waiting for the promised deputy to join them. They'd bought a set of equipment for him, too.

The guy wasn't happy about their plan, but he followed his superior's orders. His name was Pete Ralston, and he greeted them with an assessing gaze and a confident manner. He had wheat brown hair, a firm jawline, and an athletic build.

At least Beresby had sent them someone experienced, judging from the way he stowed his gear. He'd brought a heavyweight camera to take photos of the mining operation and stashed it inside the backpack Dalton had provided. They dressed like miners and smeared dirt on their exposed skin and boots. Plus, Marla wore a few layers under her outfit to bulk her up and disguise her form.

"Let's hope the miners didn't discover our entrance," Dalton said, taking the lead to the hidden passage they'd discovered earlier.

"If we're lucky, they figured the intruders were a bunch of kids out exploring." Marla dodged a large rock in their path. "They might not have bothered to follow our chalk marks all the way."

"Well, if the tunnel is blocked, we have a schematic of the system now. It's only showing a portion, but I suspect that's the section we need. We'll find another way inside."

Fortunately, the passage was still available, albeit covered over by a tangle of shrubbery that hadn't been there before. The temperature dropped a few degrees as they stepped inside the passage. The air smelled dank and the illumination narrowed as they went further. Thankfully, they had several sources of light. They each had a lantern, although only Dalton's was turned on to conserve power. Their helmets had lights, plus they had flashlights and candles with matches in their backpacks.

"The chalk marks are gone," Dalton said, his tone laced with disappointment. "Those miners must have erased them."

Marla wasn't fazed by this setback. "We brought more. Take a piece out, and we'll start over again." She shone her flashlight along the rock face when they came to the first intersection. "Look, this section of wall is free of dust compared to the rest. I'll bet this is where we had a mark before, and they scrubbed it clean. The dirt on the ground is disturbed in that direction as well, so it must be the right way to go."

"I knew you came along for a reason." Dalton marked a new arrow on the dust-free portion of rock but lower down rather than at eye level so it would be harder to find if more miners came along. He didn't use the diagram Jesse had sent, preferring to conserve his cell phone power.

They progressed further into the man-made tunnels. The passage soon narrowed, and they ended up skirting a track for the ore carts. It wasn't easy having to hobble forward with one foot on the other side of the rail.

Sweat broke on her brow. Avoiding thoughts of spiders and bats, Marla focused solely on their meager beam of light. She didn't dare look down the side tunnels that extended into blackness or think about being stuck down there. Pete had taken the rear. Wedged between the two men, she felt an iota of reassurance.

Every few feet, they passed under an old square timber construction meant to shore up the walls. That notion didn't bring any comfort. Those beams could have rotted through by now. How often did cave-ins occur?

"Maybe we should have brought gas masks," she said as another fear assailed her. She pressed a hand to her chest, her heart thumping at a rapid pace. The walls felt cool to her touch as she steadied herself in a narrow passage. This trip lacked the sense of adventure she'd had on their earlier visit. Was it because they'd be taking additional risks ahead?

"These shafts have ventilation to the outside, remember?" Dalton told her. "That's why it's cool and not hot down here."

"I'm having second thoughts about our plan. This might not have been such a good idea."

A frown creased his brow. "We knew it would be risky, but Luke knows we're here and so does Annie. If you want to head back to the entrance, though, I'll keep going with Pete. You can wait for us by the car."

"Ma'am, I'll walk you out if you wish," Pete offered.

She shook her head, her hair confined in a ponytail under the helmet. "No, I'm sticking with you guys. I'll be all right." The drop-off to their right didn't help. It descended who knew how many levels? Their lantern light didn't cast that far down.

She moistened her dry lips and gestured for them to move on. An abandoned cart and tools coated with grime lay alongside their path. Spotting them, she had a sudden thought.

"Dalton, do you have your firearm on you?"

"Yes, it's tucked inside my boot. And Pete here is armed. Why?"

She halted and pointed to the collection of implements on the ground. "Those would make good weapons should we need one." Stooping, she lifted a small-sized pickaxe. She'd feel better having a defensive weapon. However, she needed both hands free for exploration. With Dalton's assistance, she tucked the tool into her belt before moving ahead.

The tunnel forked. According to indications, they should take the left descending route.

After another ten minutes during which Marla felt as though the walls were closing in on her, they entered a large chamber with multiple levels. She glanced around in alarm. Now what? Had they gone this far before?

Her breath hitched, and her fingertips turned icy.

Dalton must have heard her gasp because he patted her shoulder. "Marla, stay calm. We'll find the way." His firm tone soothed her.

"Hey, is this one of your arrows?" Pete pointed to a faded mark on one of the columns.

"Yes, I believe so. Those earlier miners

must have taken a different path to intersect with us. Be careful of these rocks." Dalton sidestepped past a pile of boulders. The mark pointed down another black tunnel. Gripping a piece of chalk in his hand, he reinforced that arrow as well as another one aimed toward the exit.

A tap on her helmet made Marla jump.

"What was that?" Her heart raced like a runaway ore train.

Dalton whirled to face her. "What?"

"Something tapped my head. Did either of you touch me?"

"How could I touch you when I'm in front? And Pete is over there. Your imagination must be running wild."

"It's the ghosts. They're warning me. I'm sensitive to these things."

"Come on. We shouldn't linger. It wastes our batteries." Swinging the lantern, he gestured forward.

Shadows followed her as she scurried in his wake. As they proceeded deeper into the tunnel, she noticed a vibration underfoot.

"Do you feel that? We must be getting close to the mining operation." Her voice echoed in the gloom.

The passage curved, and suddenly a faint glow showed in the distance. It couldn't be long now. With a surge of energy, she plunged ahead, following Dalton's broad back. Noise from machinery pierced the stillness as they approached an overlook into a chamber that led several stories down. Dalton dimmed his lantern so they couldn't be spotted.

"Get out your binoculars," she suggested, glad they'd thought to buy an inexpensive pair.

His forehead creased as he peered below. "This must be where we ended last time. That's the operation, all right."

Pete got out his camera, but as he focused, a curse left his lips. "We're too far away. I can't get any pictures from up here. We'll have to move closer."

"I don't see any more chalk marks," Marla said. "What do we do? I'm not climbing down that rickety ladder, plus we'd be spotted too easily that way."

"I'll check our schematic." Dalton gave Pete the binoculars for him to take a look and withdrew his cell phone. "We also want to track the path of the ore. We'll have to go down there and hope we blend in with these outfits."

Marla studied the activity below with apprehension. Where did those workers ascend to the surface? It could be miles from this point. And wouldn't someone notice if three people showed up unexpectedly?

"I think if we head down that tunnel over there, it'll descend to where we want to go," Dalton said. "Don't bet on it, however."

"Great, that's reassuring. Make sure you mark our trail."

While Pete handed him back the binoculars, Marla took a sip of water from the bottle in her backpack. Although her throat was parched, she didn't want to drink too much and have to use the potty.

Another tap came on her helmet. She jerked upright. Were the ghosts of dead miners following her? If so, for what reason? Maybe they resented the intrusion into their earthly tomb. Or were they tapping on her head to warn her not to go any farther?

CHAPTER EIGHTEEN

Marla glanced at her watch. They'd been underground for a couple of hours. At least Dalton's lantern was holding out, although he'd bought extra batteries for all of them.

When they had descended a few more levels and saw the guys drilling not far from their position, she was glad their excursion would soon be over. They could accomplish their task and leave.

Hovering in the gloom with their lighting turned off, they divested themselves of their backpacks after Dalton made another chalk mark on the wall. Marla gave him the pickaxe to carry, while she rummaged in a pile of debris and found a small sledgehammer. She'd donned gloves to hide her delicate hands and painted nails.

She eyed the deputy in his dirt-smeared coveralls. "You won't be able to reach your weapon in that getup, will you?"

He gave her a broad grin as though enjoying their excursion despite his misgivings. "Not to worry, ma'am. I have another one inside my boot."

"Oh, yeah? Your boots look a little too shiny to me, even with that coating of dust. They might give us away. Dirty yourself up some more." She and Dalton did the same. Although she hated to scuff her brand new pair, it was a matter of survival.

"How do we find where they're taking the cage to the surface?" Pete asked Dalton in a hushed tone.

The whites of Dalton's eyes shone in the faint light from the mining site. "We're more interested in the ore carts, but I suppose either way topside will serve our purpose. Can you snap some photos from here?"

"I think so." Pete got out his camera and went to work. After taking numerous shots from their safe vantage point, he stuffed the camera into his backpack. "We'll have to return for these later. This camera is too bulky to hide on my person. I have a smaller one in my pants pocket."

"Marla, you could return the way we came and take our packs out. This part will be dangerous. There's no need for you to risk exposure."

"Oh, and creeping through these tunnels on my own wouldn't be risky? No, thanks.

I've come this far. You're not going to lose me now."

"Well then, pretend as though you know what you're doing," Dalton advised as they moved forward.

Marla slinked into the open beside the men, picking up her pace as they passed through the chamber where workmen were drilling into the rock face.

Keeping her head bent, she entered a tunnel where a group of laborers headed. Some of them carried lunch pails. Others hauled tools or mobile machinery. They jabbered in Spanish, making her heart thud in fear someone would speak to her. Maybe Pete spoke the language. She should have asked him.

Tracking the ore proved to be an impossible task. The chunks of rock got shoved down a chute to carts lined up on a track below. This rail followed a different route to the surface than the workers, and Dalton couldn't find a way to access it. A big sign on a wall saying *To the Exit* pointed them in another direction. At least they could ascend to the surface via the cage.

They slipped into the line of men waiting for their turn, crowding into the steel cage at the last minute and facing forward. A bell sounded, and the cage jerked upward. It rattled and shook, and Marla resisted the urge to clutch Dalton's arm for security. She stood rigid, barely breathing, hoping no one would address them. The other guys joked and laughed, while she counted the minutes as they crept upward at a slow but steady pace.

Finally, they reached the top and gathered outside with the others. The sudden cool air and fresh breeze on her skin came as a shock, as did the darkening sky. Had they been down there that long?

The miners formed a column and headed toward a shack that must serve as their changing shed. According to her research, that's where they switched into street clothes and then handed in the numbered tag given them at the beginning of each shift. In the event of an accident, this piece of metal would identify them like a military dog tag.

Uh-oh. Neither she nor the guys had metal necklaces around their necks.

The man behind them said something in Spanish. A glance over her shoulder told her he was staring at the back of her head. With a jolt of alarm, Marla realized her helmet must be ajar. She straightened it, while others removed their cumbersome headgear. Her ponytail had slipped down, but that shouldn't mean anything. Lots of these guys probably tied their longish hair back.

"People are looking at you," Dalton muttered to her.

"I think it's my ponytail. Why should that matter?"

"Because your hair has highlights. I told you not to change your color."

She'd gotten tired of the plain chestnut and had added subtle tones of bronze. Was that why she was inadvertently drawing attention? Or did they note her smaller build?

"We need to make a break for it," the deputy said in an undertone. "When we get near the shed, duck around the side of that building."

As the ragtag bunch of laborers approached the shed, the three of them hung back. They slipped around the structure's side before the foreman could notice them.

Rolling hills led downhill to their left, while a mountain towered to their right. She spied a ramshackle group of buildings in the near distance. Were those barracks where the workmen lived, housed on the mining company's property?

For the first time since emerging, she studied their bearings. Otto Lovelace's water bottling plant rose directly above them, but they appeared to have come out on the other side by the subsidiary facility. And from this angle, that structure looked downright old. It might have been the original smelting mill.

Dalton followed the direction of her glance. "Am I seeing correctly, or are those ore carts up there?"

Pete got out his smaller camera and peered through the lens. "The ore is being tipped onto a conveyor belt that leads into the facility. I'll need to get closer for some good shots."

"What do you want to bet Lovelace is behind the mining operation, and he's reopened the refinery?" Dalton said. "A water bottling plant would be the perfect cover."

"Now we'll be able to get a warrant to check out the place." Pete gave him an approving grin.

At the instant the last word left his lips, a shot rang out. The deputy toppled over, his camera thumping to the ground. A red stain appeared beneath him, widening in the dirt.

A guard appeared from behind a set of trees, his rifle aimed at them. "Put your hands in the air where I can see them and don't move."

His partner stepped forward and kicked Pete, who lay face down and motionless.

Marla's gut clenched in horror. Had Pete just been killed? No, that wasn't possible.

Her heart racing, she raised her arms. What would happen now?

The first guard radioed ahead. "The boss says to bring these two to his house. He's about to eat dinner, and he doesn't care to have his precious schedule upset. Dumb prick. If he didn't pay so well, I'd tell him where to go. Take off your gear first," he ordered her and Dalton. "We can always use extras."

"What about this guy?" said his partner, indicating Pete's still form.

"Leave him. We can hide his body later."

She and Dalton handed over their helmets and lanterns and stripped off their coveralls. Marla had a moment's foolhardy urge to swing the sledgehammer but gave it up without protest. Under the guard's scrutiny, she felt exposed in her long-sleeved shirt, belted jeans, and boots. At least she was still alive, unlike poor Pete. A sob rose in her throat, but she choked it down.

"Move that way," the first man said, waving his weapon for emphasis.

Marla raised her spirits by telling herself Annie would call for help once they'd failed to check in at the allotted time. Or maybe Luke Beresby would call his deputy for a report, and getting no answer, he'd send backup. But how would either of them know where Marla and Dalton had gone?

They passed a gnarled cholla bush, and she had a fleeting thought to shove the guard into its densely packed spines. But there were two of them, and while Dalton could probably handle the other guy, he had a rifle trained on their backs.

She bit her lower lip, her progress slow around the rocks in their path. They had to pick their footing carefully. What would Otto do to them? Shoot them on the spot? Stake them out in the desert where scorpions could sting them? Or toss them over a mountain ridge like he might have done to Garrett Long, when the ranger discovered his operation?

Otto must have just begun dinner when they were shoved into his presence, because he sat at his long formal dining room table, a napkin tucked under his double chin. His eyes narrowed imperceptibly upon viewing them.

"I've had extra place settings added," he said with a broad gesture. "You may be seated." To the guards, he added, "Leave us and close the door, but stand duty outside."

The balcony doors lay open, letting in the fresh evening air. A breeze cooled the sweat on her brow as she lowered herself into a dining room chair opposite Dalton. Her husband gave her a reassuring nod before smiling pleasantly at their captor.

"Nice to see you again, Lovelace. It's kind of you to invite us for dinner."

"I figured you could join me for your last meal. Enjoy the shrimp with pomegranate." He snapped his fingers, and a man in a white apron bustled in and served their starter course. Four shrimp rested on a bed of lettuce dotted with colorful red fruits. Tempting cheese crisps bordered the dish.

Marla's throat constricted. She couldn't possibly eat a single bite, but her dry mouth begged for relief. She reached for the glass of clear water and gulped down several swallows.

At least they hadn't been searched. Dalton still had a gun tucked inside his boot.

Her glance flicked toward the night-lit balcony. It led to a steep drop off the mountainside. They wouldn't find an escape route that way.

Lovelace made quick work of cleaning his plate except for the lettuce garnish. Putting down his utensil, he gave each of them a penetrating glare. "My guards picked you up outside the changing shed. They said you were dressed like mine workers. Where did you come from? Our perimeter alarms didn't detect you in the forest. And who was that other fellow with you?"

"We entered the mine via another route and met up with your work crew underground." Dalton speared a shrimp into his mouth and chewed. "We're aware of your entire operation. The bottling plant acts as a front for your stamping mill. That other man, who your goons killed without giving him a chance, was a deputy with the sheriff's office. When he fails to report in, backup will arrive. Luke Beresby knows all about your schemes."

Leave it to him to eat despite their perilous circumstances. Too nervous to contribute to the conversation, Marla gripped her fork and pushed the food around on her plate.

Otto gave a sinister chuckle. "No one will think to look for you here. And your friend's body will be long gone by the time the authorities arrive. The good sheriff won't be able to pin anything on me."

Marla forced a calm she didn't feel. "Demand for copper today is high, especially in the electronics industry. But I'll bet the demand for rare earth minerals is more. Is that why you reopened the mine?" she said in an effort to gain some answers.

"I see you've been doing your homework. Those elements are essential to technology. So far, we're the only domestic mine producing them, although other locations around the world are being scouted. The minerals are embedded in the rock along with copper deposits."

"But China is the main supplier, isn't it?" Suddenly recalling what she'd read, she felt her face drain of color. Good heavens, could the Chinese connection be real?

"Indeed. Although they control only thirty-six percent or so of known global reserves, China produces ninety-five percent of the rare earths used worldwide due to their low labor costs, abundant supply, and lax regulations." Otto glanced at his watch while Dalton took his time finishing the appetizer.

Was her husband purposefully trying to throw Lovelace off schedule?

"Speaking of environmental issues, I assume you opened for business without going through the proper hoops." Dalton made it a statement rather than a question.

"Those channels would have taken valuable time that I couldn't afford to lose." Otto's brows drew together, but he refrained from speaking further until the waiter removed their starter plates and delivered the entrée, a juicy filet mignon.

The aroma of roasted beef drifted into Marla's nose, but the food failed to tempt her. Aware of the armed guards beyond the doors, she couldn't touch a morsel.

"Try the meat," Otto said, lifting his fork. "Its sundried tomato butter sauce is divine. The side dishes are creamed Brussels sprouts and wild mushroom bread pudding, just like my grandmother used to make back in Prague."

Marla exchanged glances with Dalton. Could one of them secrete a knife without Otto noticing? She cut her filet into little pieces and then slipped the implement under her napkin.

Dalton distracted him. "Aside from ignoring government regulations, you don't own mineral rights to the mine, I presume?"

"That is correct. But other than you people, nobody has detected my operation. Well, let's not count that pesky ranger. You know what they say." He snickered before stuffing a vegetable into his mouth. "Time is money. I'm saving both by keeping production costs down and doing things my way."

"And who would suspect your water bottling plant of hiding another facility?"

"It's a brilliant deception on my part, is it

not? Ore processing requires generous quantities of water. By leasing my water supply from the town legally, I've covered that base."

"But Garrett Long wasn't fooled, was he?"

"The ranger felt the vibrations from our underground blasting. When he came poking around, I knew it wouldn't be long before he discovered our labor camp. Then he ran into one of our associates from abroad. That proved to be an unfortunate occurrence for him."

"Your miners are illegal immigrants brought in as indentured labor, aren't they?" Marla blurted. "And you house them on your property so no one else ever sees them?"

"You're very astute, Mrs. Vail. Too much for your own good."

More questions sprang to Marla's tongue, but she deferred to Dalton. They needed to eat slowly, so Otto didn't call in his guards to remove them. She stuck a forkful of soft bread pudding into her mouth, afraid if she ate a piece of meat, she'd choke on it.

Otto sipped from a glass of red wine, but he didn't offer them any. The server must have had radar, because he rushed to refill Otto's glass as soon as he'd drained it. Maybe they had surveillance cameras trained on the table that the kitchen staff watched to cue their moves.

"You said the smelting process requires a large amount of water," she ventured. "Are you by any chance taking more than your share? The ranchers downstream have complained about drought and sick cattle."

"Huh. No one has figured out that I diverted the stream."

"We thought it went underground somewhere along the route."

"You and nearly everyone else."

"What about the sick cows? Are those steam emissions from your operation really harmless?"

He peered at her down his nose. "That's not steam, madam. We've gone to great pains to make it look that way. Unfortunately, particular matter from the smelting mill escapes into the atmosphere. If it blows downwind and settles, that could be the cause of the ranchers' problems. However, I'm more concerned about your uncle's renovation project. It's forced the closure of several mine shafts and made some of our tunnels unstable. He has to stop construction."

Marla half-arose from her seat. "You're the buyer who's offered to acquire everyone's property?"

Otto's chest swelled. "I am, yes."

"And I'll bet you are responsible for the accidents that have been plaguing my uncle at Craggy Peak, plus the troubles at the dude ranch," Dalton drawled.

Otto's eyes gleamed with malice. "I knew about the feud between your family and the Donovans. It pleased me to rekindle the flames and rouse the town council against the ghost town project."

"Did you push that workman who'd disappeared from Craggy Peak into the ventilation shaft, or was his fall truly accidental?"

"Oh, he fell of his own accord. Not so for Garrett Long. I arranged for his tragic demise."

"And Tate Reardon? Did your plant manager threaten to blow the whistle?"

Otto slammed down his fork and glared at Dalton. "That idiot didn't believe me when I said the deficit wasn't my fault. He had the gall to accuse me of hoarding copper to sell on my own. When Reardon threatened to tell our Chinese friends I was cheating them, unless I provided proof otherwise, I had to silence him."

So Otto's crew had a rotten apple. Somebody was stealing ore for their own profit?

"Wait a minute." Dalton raised a hand. "You're selling minerals to the Chinese?"

"Actually, my contract is with the E.F.A. They buy the rare earths from me and sell them to the Chinese, who want to keep their monopoly. I get paid. The E.F.A. makes a profit. And the foreigners are happy."

"We'd figured you had armed guards at your site because you were afraid of this activist group, but all along, you've been partners. They act as your middleman in the black market. Tell me about Kevin Franks. Was he your liaison to the Chinese contingent?"

"Franks was valuable until he became a liability. Like you both are to me now."

"Where's our dessert?" Marla squeaked, in an inane attempt to delay the inevitable. "You don't want to disrupt your schedule."

"The apricot tart can wait. Killing you will be just as sweet. On your feet."

Lovelace yanked a gun from under the napkin on his lap and aimed it at her.

CHAPTER NINETEEN

"Let's go outside to the balcony." Otto's gaze danced with anticipation, his weapon hand steady.

They preceded him onto the terrace overlooking a mountain view, now shrouded in darkness. The howl of a coyote sounded, making Marla's gut turn to ice. Where had the kitchen staff gone? Were they watching the scene unfold from within?

"Let me see if I've got this straight," Dalton said, edging toward a shadow between lamp posts. "Someone among your team is stealing ore, but it isn't you."

"Franks was getting greedy. He wanted more money, so I figured he was helping himself to enrich the pot. Nobody betrays me. Poor man had an allergy to peanuts. I got rid of him that way. The dose was so high that even his epi-pen wouldn't work."

"Sheriff Beresby knows this by now. Your time is up, Lovelace. You'd do yourself a favor to surrender before your Chinese or E.F.A. friends blame you for their shortage. At least you'll have the chance to live if you're in jail."

"You're lying. With your deputy friend dead, no one knows where you are. Beresby will assume you three got lost in the mine system or had an accident."

Marla had tucked the dinner knife behind her back when they rose from the table. But she couldn't rush Otto. He'd shoot them first.

Nonetheless, she noted his mouth tightening and his hand raising a notch. If only she could distract him, Dalton would be able to withdraw the weapon from his boot. They'd worry about the guards later.

She turned sideways as though to present a smaller target and gripped the blade in her sweaty palm. With a whirling motion, she tossed it at Otto.

His startled glance was the moment Dalton needed to whip out his .38 and fire.

Otto staggered backwards, a look of shock on his face. His weapon dropped from his limp grasp and clattered onto the tile floor. Blood blossomed on his sleeve.

Dalton charged forward and punched Otto on the jaw. The big man's head snapped back at the blow, but he rallied and surged at Dalton like an enraged bull. As the two men struggled, Marla grabbed Otto's fallen weapon from the ground.

The two guards burst inside the dining room and assessed the scene. As they sprinted her way, Marla aimed and fired through the open patio doors, steadying the weapon as she'd been taught. The kick from the recoil bounced the barrel upward.

She didn't dare look in Dalton's corner. Various grunts and thuds told her he wasn't having an easy time of subduing their host. Her heart pounded in fear for his safety.

One of the guards bent over, moaning at a spreading red stain on his leg. She must have hit him. When the other guy raised his rifle, she held her arm straight, aimed, and fired again with a tighter grip this time. The shot rang in her ears.

"I hear sirens outside, Lovelace. My cousin knows you're involved. She'll have notified the sheriff's office when we didn't check in. Beresby will be headed this way. Your game is finished." Dalton's words were punctuated by his short, labored breaths.

"I won't be safe, even if locked up," Otto said, his voice laced with panic. "My friends have ways of getting to me. They'll say it's my fault for exposing their role. This has to end now. I *will* get rid of you and your tiresome wife if it's the last thing I do."

Marla froze as one guard still came at them. Blood welled from his shoulder, and he'd cast the rifle aside from his weakened hand. But his other palm gripped a steel blade.

As she stood fixated on the knife, Otto dove under Dalton's arm and raced toward her in a change of strategy. He knocked Marla's weapon from her hand before she could blink. Then he aimed a blow at her gut. She ducked to the side.

When he swung at her again, she dodged away at the last minute. She stooped, grabbed his ankles, and yanked them up. He tipped backward.

As she let go, his scream echoed in the night.

She hadn't realized they were so close to the rail. Empty space greeted her horrified gaze.

More thuds from behind told her Dalton had engaged the guard. A loud crash sounded, followed by sudden silence except for the sound of her heavy breathing.

As she whirled around, her mouth gaped in astonishment. Their server had smashed a pottery vase over the guard's head. The fellow lay stunned on the ground.

She and Dalton stared at the young man.

He grinned at them both and spread his hands.

"They are bad people, keep me and my sister imprisoned here. Now we have chance to be free," he said in heavily accented English.

The sirens outside grew louder. Dalton took out his cell phone and called the sheriff. In the meantime, she dialed Annie's number and told her they were safe.

"Luke is on his way here," Dalton told her after they'd both disconnected. "Pete notified him where we'd gone."

"Pete is alive?" Her heart leapt with relief.

"He's just wounded. He played dead until the guards left with us and no one else was around. Then he called for backup."

"Thank goodness. I hope he'll be all right."

Waiting for the authorities on the front stoop, she sagged against a wall. Dalton had dragged the two thugs into the living room with the server's help to truss them. Her body shook in violent tremors. Had Otto really fallen from the terrace? She supposed they'd find out in the daytime.

She wrapped her arms around herself, shivering as their close call took its toll. Her teeth chattered, and her shoulder ached from firing the gun. Summoning her resolve, she clenched her jaw tight. She only had to maintain composure for a little while yet.

Had Dalton collected his weapon from the patio floor? Probably so. He acted cool and confident when securing their assailants as though this were all in a day's work for him.

When he'd completed his task, he hustled to her side, concern etched on his face.

"Are you hurt? Tell me you're okay." He surveyed her body ostensibly for wounds and then glanced at her face.

"Yes. No. I mean, I'm unharmed but I'm not all right."

He drew her into his embrace and patted her hair. Her ponytail had come undone, and her hair streamed down to her shoulders.

"You'll be fine. I'm proud of you, sweet-cakes. You held your own in the fight."

She gave a nervous giggle. "You'd better give me more lessons on the shooting range. You didn't do so bad yourself."

The sirens whooped and stopped as vehicles from the sheriff's department arrived. The cavalry had come. She greeted Luke Beresby with a weak grin.

Bone-deep exhaustion settled over her like a salon drape lined with lead. At Dalton's urging, she sank onto the living room sofa while he conferred with the sheriff and various other authorities who joined them. She became aware of clocks ticking in the background, a steady sonata that played on despite their master's absence. Otto Lovelace's time had run out.

Finally, they were allowed to leave after promising to stop by Beresby's office another time to sign a formal statement. The lawman assured them Pete would be fine. The deputy had sustained a wound to his shoulder but he'd heal quickly.

Back in the resort room, Marla didn't feel like talking. She showered, soaking her sore shoulder under the stream of hot water. It reminded her of the steam issuing from Lovelace's smelting plant that wasn't really steam at all but pollution. Too weary to think straight, she dried herself, donned her nightwear, and collapsed onto the bed where she fell dead asleep.

In her dreams, Otto Lovelace's face appeared before her.

With a snarl, he thrust a knife at her. She dodged the blow, frantic to find Dalton who wasn't in her line of sight. What had Otto done to him? The blade descended again. Marla slipped under his arm and came up at his rear. She pounded her fist on Otto's broad back. A steady throbbing noise pulsed in the background. Machinery from his stamping mill?

The pounding persisted, until the threads of sleep evaporated, and Marla realized somebody was knocking on their resort room door.

Where was Dalton? She gazed with dismay at his empty side of the bed and the rumpled sheet.

"Dalton, are you in the bathroom? Can you see who's at the door?"

When he didn't answer, she rolled upright with a groan. Her wrap lay across the foot of the bed. She spied a piece of ivory hotel stationery there and bent to grab it.

I've gone into town to see the sheriff and take care of a few things. Didn't want to wake you. Talk to you later. Love, Dalton.

Oh, gosh. Now what?

"Who is it?" she called on her way to the door while tying the sash around her robe.

"It's Juanita. Please, I need to speak to you, *señora.*"

Marla surveyed the housekeeper's chalk white face and disheveled uniform. "You can come in, if you don't mind the way I look." She smoothed down her hair, her head still groggy from sleep. "What's wrong?"

"Jesse didn't come to work today, and he's not answering his cell phone. I am worried."

"Maybe he ran into traffic," she said,

wondering if the wrangler could have been in a road accident. Or worse, if he'd tangled with Otto's gang.

"You don't understand. He told me yesterday he almost had the proof he needed to expose whoever was causing problems. I think he found it and got into trouble."

Marla offered the maid some coffee before pouring herself a cup. Dalton had made a pot before he left. She added cream and sugar, then sipped thoughtfully.

"He could have gotten a late start. Do you think he left his cell phone at the ranch yesterday when he went home? Have you looked down by the corrals?"

"*Si*, no one there has seen his phone or can tell me anything. I know in my bones something terrible has happened to him."

"Where does he live?" The scene at Franks's apartment came to mind. She hoped they wouldn't find something similar at Jesse's place.

Her heart skipped a beat. That couldn't be where Dalton had gone, could it?

"Not far from here. Maybe twenty minutes."

"My husband probably took our car, so you'd have to drive if I go with you. Can you leave work for that long?"

Juanita's dark eyes shone in gratitude. "I

call now and give excuse. Sorry, I'll wait outside while you dress."

Marla gulped down the coffee in between putting on a smidgen of makeup and doing her hair in a quick braid. The longer length had its benefits. After donning jeans and a comfortable top, she grabbed her purse and exited.

Juanita already had her keys in hand. Marla dashed off a quick text message to Dalton before joining her.

Could this be a trap? The unbidden thought rose in her mind. What if Jesse, and not Kevin Franks, was behind the dangerous pranks? Juanita could be working with him. But what would they stand to gain by abducting her? She couldn't see how anyone would benefit when she and Dalton had exposed the mining operation and defeated its owner. And the housekeeper seemed genuinely distressed, not that Marla hadn't been fooled before.

Was Otto dead? Is that why Dalton had left early, because the sheriff notified him they'd found the body?

"I've texted my husband that I'm going with you," she told Juanita, who hurried along the path toward the employee parking lot. The cool morning air chilled Marla's skin but it felt good nonetheless. And as soon as the sun rose, the temperature would heat up.

As a further precaution, she added Juanita's license plate number to her text messages to Dalton. Why wasn't he responding?

Her anxiety increased as they sped away. They passed the outskirts of town, veered onto the highway, and got off at the next exit. Juanita drove along an isolated road with nothing on either side except for brown dirt and scraggly shrubbery with an occasional saguaro.

Why would Jesse vanish now? Had Otto's people gotten to him yesterday after work?

Shortly thereafter, they entered a bumpy gravel drive toward a modest single-story house without much of a yard. The place had an isolated location and a forlorn air.

Noting his car was absent from the driveway, Juanita let them inside his home with a key. Marla gaped at the sophisticated computer equipment that took up the entire living room. What did Jesse do in here? And where was he?

A quick search told them the place was empty. Nor were there any signs of a struggle. Marla concluded that Jesse had driven somewhere with a more important errand in mind than going to work. Could it relate to an item he'd found on his computer?

After all, he'd been the one to send Dalton a map of the mining tunnels. What else had he discovered?

She picked up the nearest page on his computer desk and turned to Juanita, who stood by wringing her hands. "These are payroll records from Otto Lovelace's water bottling plant. Did you know Jesse was hacking into their files?"

The housekeeper's face drained of color. "I know nothing, *señora,* except Jesse blew hot and cold for me. I like him, and I did not pry into his affairs."

Too bad you didn't. That would have been helpful.

Marla studied the copies of company checks made out to Matthew Brigham and signed by Tate Reardon. Why had Reardon been paying the engineer? Were those bribes for his passing grades on inspections? Brigham, in turn, had handed something to Kevin Franks the day she'd spotted them together. Had that been a payoff as well?

Her gaze fell upon a familiar diagram poking out from another pile of papers. The hairs on her nape rose. That looked similar to the layout of tunnels Jesse had sent Dalton.

It seemed more and more as though Jesse

had been investigating the same things, but why?

Finding the man became urgent. He could have placed himself in danger. It was becoming more likely that Otto's goons had gotten to him yesterday.

Stymied as to what to do next, she'd put down the papers in her hand when Juanita scooped a printout from the floor with a muttered exclamation.

"Look, it is Jesse's writing on the side."

Marla peeked over her shoulder. "The narrow gauge depot? What's that?"

"I have no idea, but maybe it is where we can find him."

Recollection made Marla wrinkle her brow. Hadn't Raymond mentioned something about a former railroad line?

She sat at one of the active computer stations and turned on the monitor. A search brought up a local branch of the United Verde and Pacific Line. Built in the late eighteen hundreds, the narrow gauge railroad was abandoned years later when the Craggy Peak mine shut down. In the meantime, it hauled in supplies through Bigrock Canyon.

The trip saved time, but expenses remained high due to the necessity of transferring ore products from the narrow gauge depot to the standard grade line at Jerome Junction.

Nonetheless, building the narrow gauge rail had been a lot less expensive than standard grade. The narrower track required less steel, less wood for crossties, and less cutting and filling to go around sharp curves. Most of the stock consisted of smaller locomotives and rail cars. The line reached an elevation of six thousand feet at the summit, where the depot had existed.

Could that building be intact? Moreover, had Jesse gone there?

"Do you have all-wheel drive?" Marla asked Juanita.

"Si, señora." Juanita's eyes filled with worry for her on-again, off-again boyfriend.

What game had Jesse played with her? Why feign interest and then blow cool? Had he befriended her to gain information?

A wave of guilt swept through Marla. Hadn't she done the same thing? Yet, she genuinely cared about the maid's feelings and wanted to help her.

"If your vehicle can manage, this article claims we can drive the old railroad bed up to the depot. It'll be a scary ride, but it's doable."

She tried phoning Dalton on the way, but he still didn't answer. Should she be concerned for him or annoyed that he was too busy to respond?

Maybe she should call Luke Beresby. He'd be occupied in the aftermath of Otto's death, assuming they had found a body. But he could always send backup, and he might know where Dalton had gone.

Disappointment sank in as she dialed his number and got voice mail. She didn't have his business card handy for his office number. Likely the sheriff was out in the field and using his radio for communication. Nonetheless, she left him a message as to her destination.

She supposed it was possible Jesse had experienced an accident along the way and lay injured on the road. Or he might have hurt himself while exploring the dilapidated depot.

They'd find out soon enough.

They bumped and jostled along the hair-raising road that stretched for twenty-five miles with one hundred and fifty curves. She'd printed out the route from the website that described the old narrow gauge line. When the rails were removed, the right-of-way became a forest service road. Had Garrett Long patrolled this section as part of his duty roster?

Spectacular views of red rocks and tree-dotted mountainsides unfolded as they careened around the bends. Marla hardly dared to breathe as they bucked and jolted over the uneven terrain. Dalton would probably enjoy this ride, she thought, gasping as they barely skirted a steep drop at the road's edge. Her ears popped continuously as they continued to climb. Juanita drove like a mad woman, her face fierce and her hands white-knuckled on the wheel.

"Look, that must be the place." Marla pointed to a lone wood structure with a brick chimney on the next hilltop.

As they approached, she noted the paint had long faded and roof shingles were missing, but the building had mostly withstood the ravages of time. A black Jeep Cherokee was parked there. Juanita confirmed it belonged to Jesse.

"He has to be here," Marla said, hoping she hadn't been mistaken to trust Juanita's instincts about the wrangler. He could have been working with Kevin Franks. But then why would Jesse investigate Otto's operation and send Dalton the tunnel map?

"I am scared. Why has no one heard from Jesse since yesterday?" Juanita's lower lip trembled as she and Marla stood outside on the gravel.

A stiff breeze blew hair about her face.

Grit clogging her nostrils, she shivered in the chilly mountaintop air.

"Let's go inside and take a look," Marla suggested. "At least we'll be out of the wind."

Her eyes narrowed as she glanced over her shoulder, a prickle of unease shaking her. Was that a cloud of dust on the road behind them? She sidestepped around a wheelbarrow and headed for the front door.

"Jesse?" The housekeeper's voice echoed in the emptiness that faced them inside. The knob had turned easily, as though recently greased. "Are you in here? It's me, Juanita. I'm worried about you. *Señora* Vail is with me."

No answer. Various sacks lay about the interior, along with some rusty tools and old bits of rails. A blanket covered a mound in one corner. Marla glanced underneath, wrinkling her nose at the pile of rocks.

"I have an idea," she whispered. "Call Jesse's cell phone." She eyed the two closed doors at the far end.

Juanita complied, and an answering ring came from somewhere beyond.

"It's this door." Marla strode over and turned the knob, her heart pulsing in her throat.

Jesse sat slumped against the wall, tied

410

like a chicken prepared for the oven and with tape across his mouth. He gave a muffled cry at their entrance, his gaze filled with hope and concern.

Marla needed a tool to cut his cords. Wait, didn't she have a pair of shears in her purse? She hadn't packed them in her luggage yet after cutting Annie's hair.

Juanita ripped off Jesse's gag while Marla attempted to cut the cord binding him. Damn, her scissors weren't sharp enough. She stuffed them in her bag, put it down, and searched for a sharper tool.

Jesse spoke, his voice raspy. "Get out of here and call for help."

"We will not leave you." Juanita fluttered over him like a mother hen.

Jesse's face looked puffy and discolored, as though he'd been beaten. Who had done this to him? All the suspects who came to mind were dead.

"You don't understand." Jesse's voice turned pleading. "He's been waiting for you to show yourselves."

"What do you mean?" Marla asked, her ears alert for any unusual noises outside.

"I got caught because he keeps cameras along the road. When he realized I had found his stash of ore, he came after me. I knew I'd be dead meat unless I gave him a reason to keep me alive. I said I'd told others about his plans. Despite his attempt to get me to talk, I wouldn't tell him anything."

"So he figured he'd bide his time until someone came looking for you, and then he'd catch us?" Marla said, unsuccessful in her search for a sharp implement. Maybe she'd have better luck in the other room.

"If no one arrived, he threatened to torture the information out of me. His first session didn't get anywhere. Lucky for me, he was interrupted by a phone call and had to leave."

Marla reentered the main room and examined the discarded relics on the floor. "Who is it, Jesse?" she called, anxious to free him and get out of there.

"That would be me."

Marla spun around. Matthew Brigham stood in the door frame, his bearded face a twisted mask of malice. In his hand, he held a firearm.

Oh no, not again.

Her foot rested near a discarded rail on the floor, one of its ends curved up with a broken edge. Without a moment's hesitation, she stomped on the raised portion, caught the tool as it flew into the air and hooked it at the engineer.

She dropped to the ground and rolled

sideways as he fired. The shot went wild.

As the tool hit its mark, he howled with pain. His weapon fell from his fingers and hit the deck, another shot going off into the wall.

Disarmed, he leapt at her, hands outstretched.

A single gunshot roared in the air.

Brigham went down, motionless on the dusty hardwood floor.

Marla glanced up. Juanita stood in the inner doorway, a snub-nosed weapon in her steady grip.

"What?" the housekeeper said upon noting Marla's incredulous glance. "A woman should be ready to defend herself, *señora*. I never said I came unprepared."

CHAPTER TWENTY

"Can you please pass the potatoes?" Marla said to Annie, who sat at the dinner table on Friday night at Carol's house along with the rest of Dalton's family.

It had taken a while to figure things out after events at the depot. The sheriff had arrived and taken Brigham, merely wounded, into custody. His confession, along with Jesse's, had made many items clear. Marla and Dalton shared the news with Wayne and the others at Carol's house where they'd gathered for one more home-cooked meal before their trip home on Sunday.

Raymond harrumphed and glared at her. "So do you mean this housekeeper's boyfriend knew all along what was going on?"

Dalton, his mouth full of food, nodded for her to respond. He chewed and swallowed, while Marla sat proudly by his side. She'd never been more glad to see him than when he had loomed in the doorway at the train depot after getting her text messages. He admitted sheepishly that he had been sharing some newer investigative techniques with the deputies in town.

"Jesse isn't any stranger to the area," Marla said. "I hope you won't fire him, Uncle Ray."

It felt strange calling him that, but Marla felt an integral part of this family now. How different it was from her first dinner here.

"What do you mean? Spit it out, girl."

"Jesse is really Jake Donovan."

"You've got to be kidding me!" Raymond threw his napkin on the table and stood.

"Sit down, Dad." Wayne's commanding tone resounded throughout the dining room. Even the children, playing in the family room after eating separately, hushed into silence.

To Marla's surprise, Raymond complied. His face registered a range of emotions, including resignation. And did she note a flicker of hope there?

"How did Jake end up on our ranch? Did Donovan plant him there to cause trouble?"

"Hugh didn't even know his son had taken a job at the Last Trail." Wayne took up the tale. "Jake took care to grow a beard and dye his hair, but he kept in touch with his elder brother, Ben, after leaving home.

Ben is the one who gave him a recommendation when he applied for the wrangler position. I hadn't seen Jake in years, and so I didn't recognize the man as Donovan's younger son. We had a nice, long talk this morning after the sheriff finished interviewing him."

"So why did he leave home?" Annie asked. She gave Marla a secret smile from across the table.

Marla had been pleased to learn Annie had gone out on a date with the doctor they'd met the other day at Tate Reardon's house. She'd had a feeling the two of them would hit it off.

"Hugh is a Luddite, wanting to keep things the old way, while Jake embraces technology and change," Wayne continued, his broad shoulders hunched forward. He looked every inch the rancher with his granite jaw and tanned face. "Jake's pa refused to acknowledge his son's interest in computers and wouldn't pay for the boy's college education. He said it would be a waste of money, when Jake was needed on the ranch. It never entered his head that one of his sons might not want that life."

"So Jake left to forge his own path," Dalton concluded, chasing down his food with a sip of water.

Carol had made a turkey for the occasion, and it was a true feast with all the dishes on the table. Marla would miss these family gatherings. But more so, she'd miss everyone here and yes, even the tranquility of the desert.

Tomorrow, for their final meal, she and Dalton were treating everyone to the best restaurant in town. It would be a bittersweet end to their vacation.

"What happened that made Jake apply for a job at the dude ranch?" she asked, saddened that the young man hadn't been able to follow his dream.

"He got through one year of college on a scholarship, but then he ran out of money. Deciding to take online courses instead, he returned to what he knew best — horses and ranching. Ben Donovan gave him a recommendation under his fake name. I took him on, glad to have a seasoned ranch hand." Wayne stabbed a piece of asparagus and stuffed it in his mouth. "I suppose we should do better background checks from now on."

"How does Juanita figure into the game?" Carol rose to refill their water glasses.

"He ran across her one day at work and couldn't get her out of his mind since then. They wound up together, and she learned his identity. But he wouldn't share his secrets with her and grew afraid she'd get hurt. So he pretended to lose interest in her."

"Did those secrets pertain to Garrett Long?" Marla guessed.

Wayne gave her a wry smile. "Jake and Garrett shared an interest in technology. Garrett acted as a mentor to him, recognizing his talent and funding his online classes. In return, Jake did Internet searches for Garrett."

"No wonder Jake had so many computers in his house." Marla asked Dalton to pass the cranberry sauce. She needed a dollop to go with the rest of her turkey.

He complied with a sexy grin. Now that the mysteries were solved, they could enjoy their remaining day on the ranch. Eager to be alone with him, she returned her attention to the conversation before her desire shone in her eyes.

"Garrett had shared his suspicions regarding Lovelace's water bottling facility. Upon investigating further, Jake realized someone must have reopened the old copper mine. When Garrett was killed, he remained silent, unsure who to trust."

"Did he know Matthew Brigham must be involved?"

"He suspected Brigham and Tate Reardon, the plant's manager. Jake figured someone at the Last Trail was working for them, but he couldn't pinpoint the mole. So he worked in silence, hoping to uncover enough evidence to tell the sheriff his findings."

"How did Brigham get onto him?"

"He didn't." Dalton answered, having spent a lengthy session with the sheriff. "Brigham confessed to stealing ore and hoarding it at the train depot. He plotted to take over Otto's operation. We played into his hands by getting rid of Lovelace. With the boss, Reardon and Franks out of the way, his path was clear except for Jake. But once Jake discovered the engineer had a passion for trains, he realized the depot was the key."

"So he went up there alone, hoping to collect evidence," Marla said. "Brigham saw him via the video cameras he'd placed along the road."

"When Jesse realized he might not get out of there alive, he sent me a photo he'd taken of the tunnel system. He had come across a schematic of the mine shafts during his research," Dalton added. "Jesse started to type in the word 'help' when Brigham caught him. Beating Jesse didn't gain him any information, so Brigham figured he'd wait and see who came to rescue the guy."

"There's something I don't get." Carol had been occupied with serving the meal and clearing their empty dishes. Now she spoke quietly from her seat, an intense expression on her face. As the ranch's financial manager, she had to be glad things were finally cleared up. "How does the eco-terrorist group fit into this? Was Otto afraid of them or working with them?"

Dalton replied as he understood their connections the best. "Lovelace's armed guards were meant to keep people with prying eyes away from his immigrant labor camp and his illegal mining operation. The E.F.A. was actually buying his refined products. They sold these to the Chinese and used their profits to obtain weapons. The Chinese, in turn, wanted the rare earth elements so as not to lose their global monopoly."

"Kevin Franks, an E.F.A. member and Otto's liaison to the foreign buyers, was the arsonist who set fire to our hacienda and who put the snake in Dalton's luggage. He sabotaged Carol's saddle and put the trip wire across her trail." Marla's tense muscles eased. She hadn't realized her neck had been so rigid. The memory of those incidents still disturbed her.

"How did Sherry Long take the news of her brother's involvement? Was she aware of his activities?" Carol asked with a wide-eyed glance at Marla, as though she had all the answers.

"She'd feared her brother, always a volatile sort, had taken revenge on Garrett for her sake. They both knew about Garrett's affair. But Sherry didn't dare confide her views to anyone, afraid Franks might turn on her next. She'd been unaware of his E.F.A. activities."

"What of Mrs. Reardon?" Carol addressed Annie. "How is she doing?"

A pained expression crossed Annie's face. "Eleanor had no idea her husband was involved in these schemes beyond his work at the bottling plant. She had truly believed the man was overworked. The woman feels guilty about her relationship with Garrett, but at least she realizes their affair had nothing to do with either murder."

"And their daughter?"

Annie shook her head. "Poor Christine. Her parents' problems likely contributed to her eating disorder. Hopefully, with therapy, she'll improve over time. I've started a group for teens, and we'll see how she does."

"That's great, Annie." Raymond, who'd remained silent through their explanations, cleared his throat. "I owe people some apologies. First to you, doll, for doubting your choices. You make a great nutritionist. I'm proud of you for opening your own clinic and managing the business so well."

Annie flushed under his praise. "Apology accepted, Dad. I knew you'd come around eventually. You're not as hardheaded as Hugh Donovan."

"Speaking of the guy, I got an email from him. Hugh gave me his version of an apology, said he was sorry for making assumptions that weren't true."

"What prompted this great change of heart?" Wayne said, glancing at him askance.

"The sheriff notified him and the town council members about the goings-on. The smelting mill's excessive water usage, polluted runoff, and dirty air emissions were the likely causes of the problems on Hugh's ranch and elsewhere. The refinery will be closed along with the bottling plant, and the proper course of the mountain stream will be restored. These actions should solve their issues. Luke told Hugh in no uncertain terms that my renovation project was not at fault."

"Well, that put him in his place," Carol said with an indignant sniff.

The kids wandered into the room.

"When are we going to have dessert, Mom?" the girl asked, her hair in pigtails.

"If you'd like to help me clear the table, I can serve it afterward. Go ahead and take the dishes into the kitchen. I'll be along shortly. I just want to finish hearing what your grandpa has to say."

Raymond resumed after the children left the room. "Hugh's note encouraged me to give him a call. I reckoned it was high time to clear the air, as long as all these other revelations were coming to light. Hugh admitted he'd made some gross errors. So did I."

"You were generous to make the gesture, Uncle Ray." Marla's words of kindness elicited a misty smile from the older gent.

"Did you know your mother-in-law used to sing?" he asked her in a soft tone. "Kate had the loveliest voice that soared like the angels. But she stopped singing the day Harry died. And when Ma left and took Kate with her, part of my heart went with them, too. I could never lift my head in their sight again, after what I'd done. But that was a long time ago, and instead of forgiving myself for my sins, I cast blame on Hugh. He did the same. And I added fuel to the fire by comforting his wife after their son left home. We're both stupid asses, what can I say?"

Wayne gripped his father's arm. "So did he hear you out when you called?"

A tear leaked down Raymond's face. "We both cried like babies. We'd been such good friends. I'm hoping we can mend the rift that's kept us apart for so long."

Marla blinked rapidly, her eyes filling. Oh gosh, in another instant, she'd start bawling.

"Hugh said he wanted his son to come home. He'd make things right and pay for Jake's education if he would return."

"That will make Jake happy. I'll inform him tomorrow morning," Wayne said. "I suppose now he'll be able to court Juanita openly. You did good, Dad." His warm approval brightened Raymond's demeanor, and joy spread around the table.

"Nothing means more than family. I shouldn't have forgotten that principle, but it's going to rule my life from here on." Raymond gripped the hands of those on either side of him, and his gesture moved the rest of them to join hands, too.

"Now let's each offer a prayer of thanks that we're all gathered together." He let go after a few minutes of meaningful silence, except for the kids' chatter in the next room.

"I should serve dessert," Carol said, half-rising.

Raymond waved her back in place. "Hold your horses, I'm not finished. You and Dalton will have to come back next year," the patriarch told Marla with a wink. "With things heating up between Jake and Juanita, I suspect there might be a wedding coming. Did I mention that I'd called your mother, Dalton? You've never heard anyone more shocked in your life than when she answered, and I said hello. I'll do my best to talk her into singing at Jake's reception."

"I'm sure Mom would love to come see you, wedding or not," Dalton replied with a broad grin. "Marla, can I persuade you to return?"

She patted his arm, glad for him that his family issues had been resolved. Her throat clogged with emotion at being part of his clan now.

"I think I could manage another trip out west," she said in a light tone. "The desert has started to grow on me. Besides, I might want to go on one of those advanced trail rides at the dude ranch. I didn't have enough lessons on this visit. After all, what member of this family doesn't know how to ride? I have some catching up to do."

Meanwhile, she'd have to catch up on

salon business and household chores at home. After these recent adventures, she looked forward to her normal routine and seeing friends and loved ones back east. If anything, this trip had given her a greater appreciation for her everyday blessings.

Dorothy in *The Wizard of Oz* had the right idea. There truly was no better place than home.

AUTHOR'S NOTE

I had a fabulous time doing research for this book. With my husband, I took a two-week trip to Arizona and visited most places in the story. Among our adventures, we stayed overnight in a haunted hotel, explored a copper mine, visited a famous cavern, admired the red rocks of Sedona, shopped at Scottsdale, browsed The Poisoned Pen Bookstore, and trod the historic streets of Tombstone. And most critical, we stayed at a dude ranch that served as the model for Last Trail in this story. It was an amazing trip, and I hope you enjoyed following in Marla's footsteps as she visited some of the same places.

If you enjoyed *Peril by Ponytail,* please help spread the word. Here are some suggestions:
Write an online customer review.
Post about this book on your social media

sites and
online forums.
Recommend Nancy's work to reader
groups, mystery fans,
and book clubs.
Gift a copy of this book to a friend.
Consider giving a Bad Hair Day mystery as
a gift to your hairstylist.
Sign up for Nancy's newsletter: http://
nancyjcohen.com/contact-nancy/newsletter
Follow the author on her
social media sites.

ABOUT THE AUTHOR

Nancy J. Cohen writes the humorous Bad Hair Day mystery series featuring hairdresser Marla Vail. Several of these titles have made the Independent Mystery Booksellers Association bestseller list. Nancy is also the author of *Writing the Cozy Mystery,* a valuable instructional guide for writers on how to write a winning whodunit. Nancy's imaginative romances have proven popular with fans as well. Her titles in this genre have won the HOLT Medallion and Best Book in Romantic SciFi/Fantasy at *The Romance Reviews.* A featured speaker at conferences, libraries, and community events, Nancy is listed in *Contemporary Authors, Poets & Writers,* and *Who's Who in U.S. Writers, Editors, & Poets.* When not busy writing, she enjoys reading, fine dining, cruising, and outlet shopping.

Nancy loves to hear from readers. Contact

her at nancy@nancyjcohen.com or via http://nancyjcohen.com.